After the Killings

Bradley Pay

First paperback edition December 2023

ISBN 979-8-9924487-0-2 (paperback)
ISBN 979-8-218-30044-9 (e-book)

For Bis Bradley and Gavin Pay

Other books in the
SPECTRUM SERIES

The Killings Begin

Death in a Dark Alley

A Body Washes Ashore

Dear Readers,

Well, here it is… *After the Killings* is the fourth book in the Spectrum Series. Enjoy! And when you're done, tell us what you think.

We always read your reviews carefully and often considered your comments when planning our books. Thank you for your assistance.

Up until this book, the investigators played a minor role, but as we tightened the noose around our serial killer, it became important for the Raleigh PD and the investigative team to work with the FBI and Interpol. We researched how these organizations work with local police departments and loosely interpreted that for this book. This *is* fiction, after all.

Jody created the company MyDNA and decided to have their headquarters located in Indianapolis, Indiana. Her brief visit to the city in 2000 left a lasting impression on her, and she thought it would be fun to give it a nod.

There are a couple of chapters that take place in a church or on the grounds of a church. Both locations are fictitious, but the look and feel of the structures and the grounds is based on visits Robin has made to churches, convents and monasteries in Europe and the Middle East. And the snippets of the baptism and marriage ceremonies are based on the Episcopal Book of Common Prayer; the blessing of the water for Sarah's baptism is from the service at Christ Church in Columbia, Maryland. The introduction of Baby Sarah to her new family dates back to Robin's teen years.

Once again we collapsed the amount time it takes to paint murals so Gia and Frannie could finish the mural in this book in three days.

We always draw upon our own experiences and those others have shared with us to enrich our storytelling. While writing this book, it was no different…

Dale Burke – you were a Beta Reader, so you have already read our draft of this book. We hope you enjoyed the description of Charlotte's dress. You asked for details, and so we went there.

By the way, Robin wishes she were tall enough to wear a dress like that and had Lydia to design and sew it for her.

Curt Vincent – thank you for sharing with Jody your experiences on temporary memory loss caused by bacterial meningitis. While the cause of your loss of memory was different from Remy's, we drew upon the way you described your situation as we worked her own memory loss, and her reaction to it, into this story.

Sue Watkins – we modeled Penelope's "mistreatment" of her hamburgers after yours. Who else would remove the top half of the bun and the lettuce and tomato? You and our heroine, Penelope! Your charming quirk is so in keeping with Penelope's character. Are you related by any chance?

Peter and Lina Liebhold – the mention of Penelope naturally leads to her friend, Bobby Figg. A huge thank-you to Robin's friends, who name everything. When you gave her tree the moniker "Bobby Fig", we immediately knew we had to use that for our police officer.

PJ Williams – Robin loves reading about your adventures as you summit one 14,000+ foot peak after another. When Tracey did his solo hike on Mt. Etna, you were the inspiration for his friend, Phillip. Thank you, and may you reach the tops of many more tall mountains.

Greg Garcia – Jody really enjoyed your yummy homemade Limoncello. It's because of this gift that our serial killer, Tracey, made it too. While you both picked the lemons from your backyards, his recipe uses Meyer lemons.

The Meyer lemon tree that Tracey and Charlotte often sat beneath on their patio actually was in Robin's backyard in California. It was a favorite place where she and her niece spent many hot summer hours drinking cold, white wine.

Finally, a posthumous thank you to Mary Fernandez for her comments about her struggle with addiction and the fears that accompanied it. It was very helpful for us as we developed Tracey's character.

After living with the many Spectrum Series characters and storylines for seven years, we had a hard time deciding our serial killer's fate. Oh, you wouldn't believe the options we came up with. Some of them were pretty out there. Some we considered seriously. To catch or not to catch our serial killer. If he's caught, what happens? If he's not caught, why not? And what's the outcome? How does that affect everyone in the story – and the series?

Even though the books in this series are a combination of murder mysteries, romances and psychological thrillers, in our previous books, we always strived to end them on a positive note. We felt it was important, especially for this book, to do the same. But how does one make a book about a serial killer both realistic and optimistic? Please let us know what you think. But don't peek and spoil the ending!!

Sending hugs and love to you all,

Robin & Jody

Table of Contents

The Killings Begin

Death in a Dark Alley

A Body Washes Ashore

Acknowledgments

About the Authors

Chapter One

As he cruised into the small market town, keeping one eye open for parking, he saw a fashionably dressed woman with auburn hair wearing a red coat strolling toward the market, her string shopping bags in her hand. He drew a sharp breath as his heart began to race, she vanished from his sight.

Tracey sighed.

His mind drifted back to the hike he'd just finished on Mt. Etna. Winter had been late with no snow to speak of yet on the mountain, and though the volcano had been rumbling for weeks, thankfully, there had been no sign of imminent eruption. While he had hiked to the summit with a guide on several occasions, this time, he'd decided to break the rules and do it solo. As planned, he'd gotten underway in time to see the sunrise from the top, even though it had meant an extraordinarily early start. Fortunately, the sky had been clear, and the nearly full moon had lit his way as he'd begun his climb from the visitor center at Rifugio Sapienza. *Someday, I'd like to follow in the footsteps of Philip and try hiking a series of fourteen-thousand footers like those he hikes in Colorado. Holy cow, last time we talked, he said he's now summitted almost all of them, only three or four to go. And he does some of it in the most dreadful weather.* He shuddered, being more of a fair weather hiker himself.

Tracey had spent a long time in the quiet of the summit that morning, away from everyone and everything, contemplating his future as a father. Though he loved children, he'd never thought of himself in that role until Charlotte had announced earlier that year that she was pregnant. From time to time, he still wondered if they were too old, he was in his early forties, and she was approaching fifty. They'd talked it over for hours, for days, as a matter of fact. At her age, she certainly fell into the high-risk category. *Good Lord, we'll be in our sixties by the time Baby Sarah graduates from high school. Thank goodness we are both vigorous, active people who lead healthy lives.* And now, here they were, a middle-aged couple about to give birth to their first child in just a few weeks. This would be his last hiking trip for a while. He wasn't comfortable leaving Charlotte home alone anymore, up that long, bumpy road on the side of their mountain, not until well after the baby was born and she was back on her feet, especially with only one car between them. A small thrill of anticipation shot through him as he thought about the arrival of Baby Sarah.

Out of the corner of his eye, he spotted a prime parking space along the curb, and flicking on his blinker, he zipped the small car into it. He grinned, recalling his resistance to buying the Mini Cooper that Charlotte had set her heart on when they made the move to Sicily in 2012 to rebuild her one-euro house. With a chuckle, he thought about how insistent she'd been about the sporty little car. *And turquoise to boot!* He'd been sure he'd never fit into such a tiny space, but the interior was surprisingly roomy for something so small. And it did make parking much easier. He reached into the back seat and grabbed a couple of the cotton net bags they used for shopping, picked his camera up from the passenger seat and slung it around his neck before unfolding his long legs from the wheel well and clambering out.

He strolled into the market square and was immediately surrounded by the sounds and smells of the souk, a harkening back to Sicily's Arab roots. The air was filled with voices rising and falling in animated debates, bordering somewhere between argument and agreement, as local residents haggled over prices. He paused and closed his eyes for a moment as he breathed deeply through his mouth, almost able to taste the aromas of herbs — garlic, oregano and chili, as well as a number he couldn't quite identify. Then he moved on, wandering slowly from stall to stall as, in halting Italian, he bargained for broccoli, a bunch of chard, chicory, a small pumpkin, tiny potatoes and a handful of grapes, all of which would go into the vegetable tagine he was planning to prepare for dinner. It would be good company for the freshly caught dentex he hoped to find in the fish market. In his mind, he could smell it, cooked to perfection in his cast-iron grill pan. He and Charlotte liked this locally caught fish that was remarkably similar to snapper. He passed by the lemons and oranges since their own trees were still heavy with fruit but paused in front of a stall selling stems loaded with tiny artichokes. He'd deep fry those twice, once for tenderness, and a second time to crisp them and then sprinkle them with coarse salt and chopped parsley and finish with a quick squeeze of lemon. He and Charlotte could nibble on those as the tagine did its thing in the oven. He'd sip a glass of wine, and she her ginger beer as she looked longingly at his glass, her eyes begging for just one tiny sip. He'd give in eventually, since the doctor had said that a little mouthful now and then during these final weeks wouldn't hurt the baby.

His stomach gave a loud growl, and he realized that the picnic breakfast of fruit, bread, cheese and a hard-boiled egg that he'd washed down with a small thermos of coffee at the summit of Mt. Etna was hours in the past. With his shopping complete except for the fish, he followed the smell of food frying in the open air. Soon he came to the area that served a variety of cooked food. There were the chickpea fritters known as *panelle*, which are usually served in large sesame-seed coated flat breads. As he had hoped, there was an enormous pile of *crocché*, his favorite potato and parsley croquettes fried in oil as were the *melanzane fritte*, the deliciously delicate fried eggplant that always tasted best when eaten right there at a table in the market. On he moved, this time to the stall that sold *pesce cicreddu*, tiny, crisp, fried fish. With his hands full of food and a glass of local red wine, he found a place at a standing table and set down his lunch. *I'm sure all this fried food can't possibly be healthy,* but with a shrug of one shoulder, he dug in anyway, feeling virtuous after his strenuous morning walk.

After popping the last bite of *cicreddu* into his mouth and washing it down with a final sip of wine, he wiped his fingers on a napkin, making absolutely sure his fingertips were clean of the last bit of oil from his lunch, before gathering up his trash and dropping it into a tall container not far from his table. He raised his camera, and with the lens cap dangling from its tether, took several shots of the stalls loaded with fruits and vegetables, as well as some close-ups of the stall keepers. That it was possible to buy such a variety of fresh fruits and vegetables in late December never ceased to astonish him. Perhaps when they'd lived here another five or ten years, he'd become accustomed to it, though he hoped not. He looked down at the small window on the camera to review his shots. While he was fastening the lens cap back in place, the woman he'd seen earlier wearing a tightly belted red trench coat and fashionable ankle booties, net bags similar to his dangling from her fingers, sauntered past as bold as could be, her hips switching slightly from side to side, her chin up as she gazed ahead confidently, her auburn hair gleaming in the bright winter sunlight.

His groin tightened ever so slightly, and without thinking, he began to follow her, never quite letting her out of his sight. He clenched his hand around the handles of his bags as he imagined what it would feel like strangling her. It had been a long time, actually, since he had killed the young woman in Budapest. And Lydia? That had been self-defense. She'd figured out who he was. Remy had been just a dreadful mistake, one he'd regret for the rest of his life. He moved closer until he was only a few steps behind the young woman, his anticipation growing. He hoped she would take the right turn up ahead into that little alley that wound around for blocks. Tracey often used it as an alternative to the main street because it seemed no one else ever walked that way. With each step, his heart pounded more rapidly, and he inhaled and exhaled through his nose to control his harsh breathing as he imagined what it would be like. Coming up behind her, looking around to make sure they were alone. Putting his right hand over her mouth and nose like when he first strangled his mother – *his arousal began to press at the front of his jeans* – his left hand closing around her throat. Pulling her close – *his breath grew ragged* – tightening his grip. The way she would struggle, would writhe against him, like when the prostitute in St. Petersburg realized what was happening – *he bit back a moan* – the excitement he felt every time when he knew the end was near. The way he felt as he laid them gently on the ground. Stroking their hair back from their faces as he might stroke the face and hair of a lover. Finally, taking an earring from their right ear. The pleasure he'd feel later when he held the earring and touched himself.

Tracey stopped abruptly, his eyes narrowing, as a handsome man with tanned skin and dark, curly hair gave a wave, stood up from his table at the edge of the market square and strode over, taking the woman in his arms and kissing her passionately. She wound her arms around him and returned the kiss with equal passion. Their hands strayed downward, pressing their bodies together.

He turned away slowly.

*

Back at the car, Tracey put the bags into the cooler in the back of the Mini and sat for a moment regaining his composure. He went to the settings on his phone and turned off airplane mode to call Charlotte. He always turned his phone off when hiking, maybe not the wisest thing to do, but he hated to be disturbed while out in nature.

"I'll be home in two hours or so, my love. Is there anything else you've thought of that you need?"

After disconnecting the call, Tracey pressed Fong's mobile number, and his stomach churned when Remy answered. "Remy. Hello, how are you?"

"Hi, Tracey. We're fine. It's good to hear from you. Any sign of the baby yet?"

He switched the phone over to speaker, started the engine and turned on his blinker, pulling out into the late afternoon traffic. "No, but she's so ready to be done with being pregnant. The nursery is nearly done. Gia and Frannie are here now putting the finishing touches on it."

"I can hardly wait to see it. Frannie emailed me with their plan but swore me to secrecy."

"Of course she would. By the way, thanks for the camera recommendation. I took some great photos during my hike on Etna this morning, and I got a few decent shots of food and people, I think, at the market here in Catania."

"Oh, that's splendid, Tracey. Send them to me if you don't mind. I'd love to see them."

He told her that she sounded great, wonderfully relaxed. When he asked how she was feeling, she replied that physically she was doing better but that she still had gaps in her memory. He said that having memories out of reach must be frustrating.

"Yes, there is before and after, but there's still that big blank in between when the accident occurred. Thank goodness my memories of friends and family have come back, though. In the end, that's what's most important."

"Yes. And hopefully, it will all come back with time," Tracey said, hoping that it wouldn't, as he thought about how he'd been interrupted with his hand around her throat, how she'd struggled and then stopped, and how he'd hurriedly shoved her overboard into the wintery Danube as the river boat pulled away from Budapest. But she hadn't died. He was safe, for now, as long as her memory didn't return, but if it did— He couldn't make his mind go there. *I wish I'd never tried to kill my good friend's lover. I wish—*

Remy's voice cut through his thoughts, "Here's Fong now. Take care, Tracey, and give my love to Charlotte."

"I will… Hello, Fong."

"Tracey, it's good to hear from you." He told Tracey how happy he and Remy were to be back in Slovenia at Sasha's house in the vineyard, how good it seemed to be for Remy, the sunshine and fresh air, Sasha's wonderful cooking. They'd had a splendid holiday with Remy's family, who'd gone back to Berkeley the day after Christmas. Frannie had left for Sicily the next day to meet up with Gia, and Sasha would go back to work early in the new year. He and Remy would stay on for a while to give her a chance to recover from her accident.

"That's always the place that you go, isn't it?"

"It's a good place for healing."

"Is Remy still planning to move back to the States?"

"She's decided to stay here."

Tracey carefully probed, "So, she says her memory of that night still hasn't come back?"

"It's been coming back in small pieces at a time. She often talks about how strange it is not knowing what happened. She says it's like when you have something hovering on the fringes of your memory, on the tip of your tongue. The harder you try, the further it seems to recede. The doctor recommended that she try to relax and not think about it. Obviously, that's easier said than done."

"What about you two?"

"She's the woman I was telling you about when you were last here. The woman I fell in love with."

"Do you hear from Lee anymore?" Tracey asked.

"Now that we're divorced, there's no need to communicate with each other."

"That's so sad. You seemed like the perfect couple."

"On the surface, perhaps." Fong paused, "At first, it was like a fairytale. We had so many interests in common. Art, food, our lifestyle. She worked very hard to make me happy, and I think she was happy at first. She supported me while I grew my business and began to travel. She stayed home, in Paris and then in Ostia, and found work there that I thought fulfilled her." Fong paused, and Tracey heard him take a deep breath.

"Years before I met Remy, when I began to take longer trips, I started cheating on Lee. She always knew when it happened. She'd send me away to sleep in the other room until she could bear to take me back into her bed. I didn't pay attention to how it hurt her, Tracey. I bear most of the responsibility for the failure of our marriage. I don't know what would have happened if she had continued to call me out on it. But she didn't, and so sleeping alone for a week or two was just the price I paid for what I allowed to happen while I traveled. But then I met Remy and fell in love with her. If Lee hadn't left me, I would have asked her for a divorce."

"I didn't realize…" Tracey's voice drifted off, and they were both silent before he continued, "If we could all see the future, a lot of things might be different. I wonder what my life might have been like if I'd met Charlotte earlier." *Perhaps I wouldn't have felt so abandoned by my mother. Maybe I wouldn't have started killing.*

Fong gave a chuckle, "You'd probably have a whole passel of kids, maybe even enough to field an entire baseball team."

"I'm not sure Charlotte and I are up to any more pregnancies, much less raising that many children."

The Interview

In 2013, Dr. Jane Mitchell had graduated from the University of North Carolina in Raleigh where she'd studied film and psychology. Her interest in what makes people tick, what makes them do the things they do and how that affects others was the reason she'd decided to explore why people cheat in relationships as the topic for her doctoral dissertation. She'd created a powerful documentary, examining not only why people cheat, but also the impact it has on the aggrieved party. As a result of her work, she'd received many job offers and had ultimately accepted a position as a production assistant with a local television station, hoping that its small size would yield more opportunities to learn and advance quickly. In that job, she handled all nature of paperwork, made copies and did administrative work in the studio offices. During shootings, she helped move equipment, took and delivered food and coffee orders and accompanied talent around the set. She'd been told that if she worked hard, she would eventually be noticed and offered a more challenging position. Even though the work was boring, she'd liked her colleagues, and she'd used the opportunity to familiarize herself with the many aspects of the page-to-screen process. But after working there for a year, Jane had realized that moving up in a small station was only going to happen if someone quit or was fired – and no one seemed to be leaving. She'd felt stuck, as though her creativity was being stifled. She'd grown anxious to find something else. Then she'd stumbled upon a once-in-a-lifetime opportunity, one she couldn't resist, and she took a huge leap of faith and quit her job to become an independent filmmaker.

It had taken sixteen years to finally discover that the serial killer, known as the Parking Lot Strangler, was retired Judge Tracey Lauch. After Raleigh investigative journalist, Edgar Spring, had broken the story about Tracey, other newspapers had vilified him, called him a monster and listed in great detail all the women he had killed. Newscasters focused on the murderer and the victims and speculated about why he would have killed all those women. In late 2014, after the killer and all of his victims had been identified, Jane decided to produce a documentary that would explore the emotions of the survivors, the ones who'd been left behind to come to terms with their losses. How had they survived and gotten on with their lives? What was the impact of the murders on them?

Once she'd completed her research into the PLS victims, she interviewed many of the survivors. But when she began to edit her material, she'd realized there was a facet she hadn't addressed. How would Tracey react to hearing about his victims? What had caused him to kill ten women in six countries on two continents? How had he felt as he committed the murders? What was the impact of those actions on him – and on his family and friends?

Using the phone number she'd gotten from a member of the investigative team, she called Tracey. They discussed the documentary and the interview she hoped to do with him. She told him that she felt the real casualties were the people who'd had to go on with their lives, and that she'd wanted to explore how they had dealt with the gaping hole that had formerly been filled by a friend or family member or a co-worker or just an acquaintance who was gone forever. The victims were still a part of these people, but never again could they turn around and make a casual comment or share a laugh or cry together. She told him that she planned to share their reality with him and observe how he reacted in turn. Jane had been surprised when Tracey agreed and even seemed to be anxious to tell his version of the story. Something he said to her in their phone call came back to her, "Each act performed by anyone inevitably changes another's life, and it's not often we know the impact."

In this case, everyone will have the opportunity to understand the impact of his actions and how it changed everyone's lives, including his.

She breathed in deeply several times. This afternoon, she will finally meet him in person. She knew she would have to struggle to remain objective, to maintain her composure and never show how deeply this work had already affected her.

She paused and drew another deep breath before entering the room where she would conduct the interview. *I have to get it right. I only have this one day, this one shot. I promised myself I would maintain a balance between compassion for the victims and survivors and objectivity toward his responses. I can't let him get to me… this is a documentary, not an exposé,* she cautioned herself. After a brief glance around her, she spotted him seated in the corner near the window. She took another deep, calming breath and forced herself to walk toward him with her usual confident step.

Rising from his chair, gesturing to the place opposite him, he said, "Dr. Mitchell, I presume," and stuck out his hand toward her. Startled, she hesitated for a second before reaching out to him.

She looked up at him solemnly as they shook hands, "Tracey, thank you for agreeing to see me." While his grasp was firm, he kept their handshake very brief. He was taller and much thinner than she'd expected from the pictures she'd seen, his hair had more salt than pepper and was cut very short, the creases around his eyes and on his cheeks were deeper and new lines had etched themselves on his forehead. From his deep tan, she assumed he'd been taking advantage of the amount of time he was able to spend outdoors.

She set her oversized, yellow leather tote on the floor next to the chair, and after sitting down across from him, glanced at her watch. It was precisely two o'clock. She reached into her bag for her equipment and laid out the microphone and her camera with its folding tripod on the table in front of her.

The room was overly warm. Tracey sat fanning his face and neck, silently watching Jane's petite hands as she set up her equipment. She focused the camera, so the picture was tight and close to create a sense of intimacy with him. Then, with her right hand, she unfastened the leather strap and removed her inexpensive wristwatch, folding it, propping it to her left so she could keep an eye on the time.

Finally ready, with her list of questions in front of her on the small square table, she pressed the red button on the camera and tapped lightly on the top of the microphone. Satisfied that it was recording properly, she took a last deep breath to center herself and looked up at Tracey.

Then glancing down, she read from the sheet of paper, "This recording with retired Judge Tracey Lauch is being made at two p.m. on August seventeenth, 2015, as part of a series of interviews for the documentary film, *After the Killings*. For the record – is it okay if I record you?"

"Sure, I have nothing to hide anymore."

"Let's begin, then." She looked across at him, "Have you ever spoken to anyone about the murders?"

He gave her a wry smile and laughed, "Who would I talk to about the women I've strangled?

Chapter Two

Penelope's phone vibrated and flashed. She picked it up and glanced at it, *12:10. Bobby Figg. Of course*, before flipping it face down on the highly polished gray concrete bar. *It's only been thirty minutes since I was fired. Can't a girl sulk in peace?*

"Midday drinking, alone?" said Pete, the bartender, who'd worked there at In The Alley since she started at the academy. He set a glass of beer on a cardboard coaster in front of her, "That's never a good sign."

Penelope's phone vibrated again. She tipped it up, saw that it was Figg – again. With a roll of her eyes, she gave Pete a rueful grin and shook her head, "Sometimes it's just necessary."

She shredded a bar napkin into a pile in front of her as she thought back to that evening in April 1998… On the way to her car after a dinner with friends, Raleigh Police Officer Penelope Huber had found the first victim of the Parking Lot Strangler and called 911. Detective Emily Bissett, who had trained Penelope as a rookie, had arrived on the scene to take charge. While Emily's career had advanced and she'd been promoted to detective, the two women had remained close. At the crime scene that night, Emily had asked if Penelope would like to shadow her, hoping to entice her to give up patrol and join the Major Crimes Unit. From that evening, until Penelope's retirement from the police department in 2012, she had solved many murders, but four strangulation cases in particular, remained unsolved – four murders so similar that they pointed to a serial killer – a killer that Penelope was obsessed with catching. If Emily could have had a dollar for every time Penelope said, "The bastard is still out there somewhere," she'd have been able to stop working altogether.

Emily had retired from the police force years before Penelope and had built Haypress Security, a company with a specialty in supporting river cruise lines. Her business had grown rapidly, and she'd needed more senior-level leadership. Since Emily knew Penelope well and trusted her implicitly, after Penelope's retirement from the Raleigh PD, Emily had snapped her up. Penelope became Emily's second-in-command, her operations manager, and everything had been going great – until it hadn't.

She sat sipping her beer as she thought about how angry Emily had been. Every one of her words had humiliated Penelope as she'd chewed her up one side and down the other for twenty minutes, ranting about how she had broken her trust. Emily had never spoken to her like that. "*Why,*" Emily had shouted, hadn't Penelope contacted Bobby Figg when they figured out that the Parking Lot Strangler had killed in a second state? She was supposed to have given her analysis to him before she retired so the Raleigh and Trigg Pass PDs could work with the FBI – and she hadn't done it. It was over a year later, and she still hadn't passed it on. "*Why?*" she'd shouted again.

Instead, Penelope had taken home the evidence from Emily's office. Unfortunately, even after she'd retired from the PD, she'd neglected to pass that information on to Bobby, who was her boss and head of the Major Crimes Unit.

Emily had been angrier about that than Penelope had ever seen her, and she'd seen her get mad and lose her temper a few times when they'd both been working for the department. When she had finished berating her, Emily had taken a deep breath, and in a level voice, she had told Penelope she was fired, to collect her things and leave – immediately. Penelope had found it hard to meet Emily's eyes, she had let her boss, mentor and friend down by not following protocol, and the only words she was able to say were, "I'm sorry, Em. I really fucked up. I'm so sorry."

She sniffled and rubbed the heels of her hands under her eyes before taking a deep breath and then a final, long swallow of her beer, "Mmmm, that's good." She caught Pete's eye and tapped her glass.

He set a second beer in front of her. After she gave him 'The Look' that told him not to go there, he simply said, "Well, let me know if you need anything else."

She nodded and picked up her glass, tipping it slightly toward him.

A movement behind her caught Pete's eye. "Hey, Bobby Figg. You're a sight for sore eyes." They exchanged a firm handshake, and Pete said, "It's been way too long, and—" he made a sound of commiseration, "Bobby, I was so sorry to hear about Hallie."

"Thanks. It's hard to believe she's been gone for almost two years." He gestured toward Penelope with his head, "I'll have what she's drinking," and he hooked the stool next to her with his foot, pulling it out from the bar.

"Imagine that," Bobby grinned at him. "One Anchor Steam coming up." Pete glanced at the two of them, remembering how often they'd come in as a group, Bobby and his wife, Hallie, and Penelope with her husband, Hugo. Later it had been just Bobby, Hallie and Penelope – after Hugo left. But it was always the same beer, always on tap, never from a bottle or can.

While they were talking, Penelope reached across the bar and snagged a couple of cocktail napkins and blew her nose, hard, as if that would cure everything.

Bobby turned to look at her. She never cried. From the minute they'd met at the police academy, there'd been something between them. They'd had a never-ending string of inside jokes. And it seemed as though sometimes they could read each other's minds, they knew what the other one would do or say almost before it happened. They were a couple of blue-eyed blonds who looked like they were California surfers who were fiercely competitive with each other. Penelope was good at the physical stuff, like handling firearms, defensive techniques and driving cars backwards as fast as possible. Bobby was more intellectual and excelled at criminal law, procedures and operations, and report writing. Even when she was upset, she never cried.

He'd spent four years in the Marine Corps and then used his GI benefits to pay for his degree in Criminal Justice. At just over eight years older than Penelope, Bobby had found himself attracted to, and oddly protective of the scrappy young woman as they competed for the top spot in their class. He'd begun calling her kid to get under her skin, to make her take notice of the fact that he was both older, and in his mind, wiser than her. Eventually, it was what he called her, just as she'd always called him Figg.

Bobby leaned over to kiss Penelope on the cheek, their usual greeting, but this time she didn't kiss him back. He put his hand on hers, "I haven't seen you in a while."

"Yeah, not since I retired – what, eighteen months now, Figg. But even before that, after Hallie died, you pushed me away. I was your friend and Hallie's best friend, and you kept me at arm's length, even at work. If it wasn't work, you weren't there," she tapped her forehead lightly.

"All I did was work and go home. I couldn't do much more than that. Sympathy would have made me fall apart. I've never thanked you for everything you did for Hallie at the end, kid," he rested a hand on her arm for a moment.

Penelope and Hallie had been best friends all through high school. They were both raised in middle-class, blue-collar households and had been there for each other through all the ups and downs of high school drama. Hallie had gotten a scholarship and went on to college, and Penelope had married Hugo and had been hired by the police department, first as a cadet, and when she was old enough, she got into the academy where she met Bobby. Then Penelope had introduced him to Hallie.

Hallie had admired their friendship, the way they bickered like a couple of siblings but always had each other's back when things got tough. The way Bobby called her 'kid'. They were a solid unit, Penelope and Bobby. Hallie loved them both deeply, her husband and her best friend, and as Penelope often commented, she was their biggest cheerleader.

By the time Penelope found out she was dying, Hallie had already sold her goats but continued to make her special homemade soaps, candles, jams, jellies and dried herbs right up until the last few weeks. At that point, Penelope had packed up all the inventory in her store – with Hallie looking over her shoulder, giving her instructions every step of the way – and converted it back to a dining room because Hallie knew Bobby wouldn't be able to deal with all of that.

"She was my best friend. Today I could have used her shoulder to cry on. She always knew what to say to make me feel better."

He brushed his knuckles across her damp cheek. She was the

toughest cop he'd ever met. Nothing seemed to get to her. He'd seen his male colleagues break down under pressure, but never Penelope. "You had a rough morning, huh?"

"Well, getting fired by Emily wasn't a kiddy roller coaster ride, that's for sure. I felt like I was being flayed alive. Are you here to give me shit too?"

"Nah. I'm sure Emily gave you enough for both of us."

Bobby watched Penelope finish her beer and signal to Pete for another. "Do you want something to eat?"

After she'd ordered a burger with fries and he'd ordered the same, they moved to a booth.

She stared at her amber beer, watching the bubbles rising up to the thick, creamy head, "So, why are you here?"

"I wanted to hear your side of things."

"When the Raleigh PD lab had matched the Parking Lot Strangler's DNA to the Trigg Pass murder, Emily told me to turn my information over to you to involve the FBI. But I didn't."

Bobby looked at her and shook his head the way he always did when people let him down. "Emily and I are very disappointed that you didn't. You're the *last* person we would think wouldn't follow protocol."

"Your lab had all that information."

"Don't make excuses," Bobby glared. "It was your job to make sure I knew."

"You're right."

"Damn straight, I'm right. We were shorthanded and so, as your boss, I asked you to be the PD's liaison to Emily's detective group. You were supposed to keep me updated."

"I'm sorry."

"Sorry doesn't cut it. It wasn't the lab's job to tell me what they found. It was yours, and you didn't do that before retiring."

"I should have told you."

"Yes, you should have. And because you didn't, I was blindsided when Emily called to tell me there had been a murder of a skateboarder in Budapest that was similar to the Raleigh and Trigg Pass murders. That Trigg Pass murder was news to me."

"I guess I was too caught up in the investigation and lost sight of the rules."

"Yes, you did. It's a good thing you'd already retired because otherwise there would have been some serious disciplinary action."

Pete placed their burgers in front of them. Penelope squirted ketchup on her plate and started to pick at her french fries. "So, is this your kinder, gentler version of chewing me out?"

"I can keep going and be harsher if you want. Just say the word."

Penelope raised her head to look at Bobby. Then her lips turned up slightly at the corners, "I'll pass."

He bit into his burger and chewed thoughtfully. "We don't have what's in your head, and we need to tap into that. We just need to figure out the best way to do it."

He took a long swallow of his beer. "So, let me ask you this. Did you like working for Emily? I never imagined that you would have wanted to work at a desk job."

"It was an easy transition when I retired to become Emily's operations manager. I got a fair number of opportunities to travel. But I was still obsessed with solving the Parking Lot Strangler case." She turned to Bobby, "You know I kept working on it in my free time, even though it belonged to the Raleigh PD."

"I figured you would. After all those years of working together, I also figured you would share with me when you had something."

"Well, now you know everything that I know. The killer has obviously expanded his reach. I can't believe he's killing in Europe. What are you going to do?"

"Involve the FBI."

"I'll miss that case."

"Unfortunately, Penelope, it's not your job anymore."

"Yeah," she said sadly, "I guess I have to finally let it go."

"Yes, you do."

"Maybe we should change the subject."

"Would you go out to dinner with me?"

"*Wow*, that was a change of subject. You mean go on a date with you?"

"Do you want it to be a date?"

Penelope thought about how at the academy, she'd always had a thing for him and was pretty sure he had a thing for her too. But she'd married Hugo, her high school sweetheart, right after graduation. Their marriage had always been up and down, but even though she'd been tempted sometimes, she would never have cheated on him. Penelope had supported him through med school. It wasn't until he wanted to go away with Doctors Without Borders that it had all fallen apart just as fast as it had started. In the meantime, she introduced Bobby and Hallie, and that was that.

Penelope laughed, "Sure, why not."

"Don't get all enthusiastic on me."

"I can't decide if it will be awkward or not."

"Well, let's find out. How about tonight?"

She finished her beer, washing down the last of her burger. "I guess I should go get my run in. I'll have to take it easy after all this beer and food," she said with a grin.

"I'll pick you up at seven."

*

That evening, after a quiet ride to the restaurant, both of them a little self-conscious at being on a date with one another, Bobby pulled into the strip mall parking lot and drove to the far end where he slipped his car neatly into the last empty spot, directly in front of Saint Michel.

"This spot's for you, Bob." Penelope quipped, recalling the Nissan Sentra commercials from the 1990s.

Bobby chuckled, "I haven't thought about those ridiculous ads in years."

He waved his hand at the small restaurant in front of them. A few weeks earlier, he'd read about its incredibly good food and extensive wine list in the weekend section of the paper and had been looking for an opportunity to try it.

"French?"

"That okay?" he asked.

"I adore French food, but for some reason, I didn't realize you were into it too, Figg. I just read a review of this place, and it immediately went on my to-try list."

"Probably the same one I read. I seem to remember you liking French cuisine – though maybe not quite as much as the 'freedom fries'," he air-quoted, "and burgers we had earlier – so I thought I'd take a gamble on this place."

Penelope leaned over slightly and gave him a light punch on the bicep. "I've grown up a lot since the Hugo days when it was all about the three B's—"

"Beer, Burgers and Barbecue," they said in unison and laughed at the memory.

"Stay right there," Bobby said before he got out. She gave him a puzzled look and then grinned as he walked around to open her door. *I guess we've both done some growing up.* After helping her out of the low-slung car, he tucked her hand under his arm. Surprised, Penelope found that she liked it, Figg treating her like she was someone special.

She glanced back at the pristine, metallic silver Corvette and finally made the comment that had been on the tip of her tongue the whole ride over. "Big black Escalade is beat out by shiny silver sports car, huh?"

"The Escalade belongs to the department, and this evening definitely does not qualify as work. It's pure pleasure."

She leaned into him, "Pleasure? I can go for that, Figg."

As they entered, the maître d' greeted them and escorted them to their reserved table by the window. He seated Penelope and switched the white napkins for dark ones.

Penelope said to Bobby, "I love restaurants that pay attention to what you're wearing. There's nothing worse than to have a linty, white napkin on your lap when you're wearing dark clothes." She looked at the maître d', "Thank you."

He smiled, "Of course." He lit the candle and then asked, "Would you like to start with a cocktail?"

Bobby raised his eyebrows at her.

"Yes, please."

A few minutes later, the waiter brought over their drinks on a silver tray. "Campari on the rocks with lime," he said to Penelope, and to Bobby, "Your very dry vodka martini, sir."

Penelope picked up her drink in a silent toast.

He touched the rim of his glass lightly to hers with a smile.

"But, looking back for a moment, tell me what it was like working at Haypress Security. I always thought Emily was a shrewd businesswoman, so her success was no surprise. And she certainly didn't suffer fools when she headed up that squad of detectives at the PD. But how was she to work for as a civilian?"

"As a matter of fact, she was a great boss. She gave me free rein to manage my job. No politics. If she said 'yes' to something, we just moved forward. Doing river boat security is a lot different than chasing the Parking Lot Strangler. I thought I would be bored, but I wasn't. It's not like being a security cop, standing guard at the top of the gang plank, with my weapon on my hip and my cuffs on the back of my belt." She moved her shoulders in an exaggerated swagger, imitating a stereotypical security guy.

Grinning, Bobby watched her.

"It's fun. Or it was. It's undercover. Only the senior staff on the boat know who you are, that you're not a passenger or a member of the crew. We find opportunities to improve their security, and then make formal written recommendations to them."

"You? Writing reports?" he snickered, and she laughed with him. "So how do they take that? Being told about their failures?"

"It's not negative. We do it in a very positive fashion."

They continued chatting about some of the trips she'd taken.

The waiter brought two small plates to the table. They looked up in surprise as he said, "*Amuse-bouche*, compliments of the chef."

Bobby looked down at the delicate arrangement of salmon and avocado perched atop a tiny swirl of sauce on white porcelain spoons and gave a smile of anticipation, "Salmon is one of my absolute favorites."

"Mmmm. Mine too."

As they ate the tiny bites of salmon, Penelope grinned at Bobby and said, "Did you know," she paused, knowing that he'd studied Spanish in school because he felt it would be useful for his job. She had done three years of Spanish herself and sometimes had spoken it with Hugo, and then she'd taken French during her final year of high school. She was fairly certain Figg hadn't learned any, except maybe a little cooking French. It was a gamble to ask the question.

"What?"

"*Amuse-bouche* means to amuse the mouth. It is supposed to tease your palate and serve as an example of the chef's cooking."

"Well, this little bite has certainly teased me." He took his little finger and touched the tip of it to the remainder of the sauce on his spoon and closed his eyes, savoring the flavor. Then he looked at her with a raised eyebrow, "All these years I've known you, and you continue to surprise me."

"Languages have always come easily to me. I know a little of this one and a little of that. But, beyond reading menus, I only know enough French to carry on a basic conversation without getting myself into trouble."

"Thank goodness you do because I'm going to need some help."

When the *amuse-bouches* were finished, he said, "Salmon always reminds me of my trip to Maine with my college roommate the summer after our sophomore year."

Penelope propped her head on her fist as he continued. "We drove up along the coast in the rusty old VW beetle my parents had passed on to me when I started college. Neither of us had much money, but it was a wonderful adventure, stopping and staying in cheap motels, eating local food. The evening we arrived in Maine, we went to my roommate's grandparents' house for dinner. They were two old-school New Englanders in their eighties. He had done something with the CIA – back during World War Two, when it was still the Office of Strategic Services. And she was a painter, a pretty good one, as I recall. Her name was Marge – I remember her telling us we were having 'sahlmon' for dinner." He chuckled as he tried to imitate her, "She spoke just like Katherine Hepburn."

"And?"

"So, Marge picked up the phone and called a local fisherman. He put his hand to his ear in the sign used to indicate a telephone, "Isaac, I'd like a *sahlmon* for dinner... Ohhh no, Isaac, twenty pounds would be *faaaahr* too much. Ten pounds would be just *pahr-fect*." So, Isaac got into his rowboat, rowed out to the *sahlmon* pens, reached in, pulled out a fish, hit it over the head with the handle of his oar, rowed back, and brought it to Marge's back door. She cut off the head, cleaned it, dropped it in her steamer with Diet Sprite in the bottom, covered it with lemon slices and stuck it in the oven for a few hours."

"Ooooh, that sounds fabulous. I should try it."

"The *sahlmon* or the rowing?"

Penelope laughed, "Or knocking the fish on the head? Ha-ha, Figg. Cooking salmon that way, of course."

"Marge served it with two different types of potatoes – boiled and a German-style potato salad and some fresh string beans from her garden. It was the best *sahlmon* I've ever eaten, and in the morning we had it again for breakfast, cold that time."

"Shall we?" Bobby nodded at the dinner menus lying discreetly alongside their plates.

After the *amuse-bouches*, they agreed they didn't need appetizers, but dessert was a must for them both. Penelope studied the dessert menu carefully and said, "I'm tempted by the *Smorêve en chocolate*. All that dark chocolate and marshmallow inside a graham cracker crust will make me feel like a kid."

When the waiter returned, Penelope ordered braised duck with young carrots and roasted parsnips, and Bobby a rack of lamb with new potatoes that would be roasted with garlic and rosemary. Both opted for a simple butter-leaf lettuce salad with thinly sliced tomatoes, minced onion and a light vinaigrette. They asked the waiter to recommend a bottle of wine that would pair well with her duck and his lamb.

At the end of dinner, Bobby said, "Turning back to this afternoon for a minute."

"No, no. Please, enough is enough."

"About your run, I mean." He looked her up and down with half-closed eyes, "You're in fine shape, kid. Even better than when you worked for me."

"Maybe because in my spare time, I've been training for a triathlon," she flirted cautiously. "Now, I'll have lots of spare time to train even harder."

Penelope put her hand over her mouth to disguise a huge yawn, "Too much wine and all this training. I obviously need more sleep."

"Let me take you home," he said, reaching over to cover her hand with his.

*

When they arrived at her townhouse, he took the key from her hand and unlocked the door.

"Would you like to come in for a glass of wine – or a beer? And I want to show you what I've been working on – my war room, so to speak."

"I'm not sure another drink would be a good idea – I can see the headlines, *'Police Lieutenant Totals Car. Blood Alcohol Level .083.'* But I would like to see what you've been doing."

Penelope led the way upstairs, opened the door at the left on the landing and flipped on the overhead lights. Bobby noticed that she had replaced the sleeper sofa with a large table and several chairs in the middle of the room, and one wall filled with photos of victims, crime scenes and evidence, a long strip of paper with a timeline and a lot of scribbled sticky notes.

He walked along slowly, pausing now and then to look at the photos and read her notes, absorbing the comprehensive research she and the team had done. "Wow, seeing all of this in one place has so much more – impact – than just reading through the files."

"I look at it every night, trying to find a way to solve the murders. But that's over now." She began taking down items that had been attached to the wall with reusable Blu-tac putty. "I can deal with being fired. But this…" she swallowed hard, looking at the papers on the walls and then at the ones she had clutched in her hands.

Bobby gently opened her fingers, took them from her and laid them on the table. He wrapped his arms around her and held her against him. She buried her head against his chest, and as she began to cry, he pulled her closer. "It'll be all right, kid."

"Chasing this bastard has been such a huge part of my life

for so long. It seems so final to pass it off. I just wish I had been able to catch him." She put her arms around his waist and held onto him as she sobbed.

With a gentle hand, he stroked her hair and kissed the top of her head, "Shhh, shhh. It'll be okay." He leaned his cheek against her hair, the fine, silky strands catching in his three-day beard as he breathed in the citrusy smell of her shampoo.

His kiss on the top of her head, the touch of his hand and the slow inhale of his breath against her hair, the little sigh she thought she heard, caught her by surprise. She'd seen how affectionate he had been with Hallie. But before that evening, while they'd flirted with each other outrageously even as they'd competed for the top spot at the academy, he and Hallie had always been her good friends – and she'd been married to Hugo. It had been Hallie, not Figg, who'd been there for her when Hugo left, but when Hallie'd died and it had been time for her to be there for Figg, he'd pushed her away, along with everyone else.

This time, everything seemed softer, gentler, more romantic. She looked up at him, uncertain. And he looked back, considering – and then took her face between his hands and kissed her, passionately, certainly not the kiss of a good friend.

Her hand in his, she led him across the landing and into her bedroom. He slowed as, with his elbow, he nudged the door partway shut. Penelope giggled, "There's no one here to see us."

"But there's something strange about doing what I think we're about to do with the door wide open."

She grinned at him and tipped her face up to continue where'd they left off. This kiss went on for an even longer time before Penelope broke away with a laugh, "I think we need to sit down, Figg. You're so much taller than me that I'm getting a crick in my neck."

He pulled her toward the bench at the foot of the bed with his hands tangled in her hair and his eyes on hers. When the bench bumped against the back of his calves, he picked her up and sat her on his lap, her legs straddling his hips, pressing her against him. His eyes were still locked with hers when he leaned in, pausing for a moment, teasing this time, and then he kissed her again, a slow, deep kiss that left them both breathless. He leaned back ever so slightly and rested his cheek against hers.

Her heart hammering, her breath short and fast, Penelope waited a moment and then asked, "Are you having doubts? Is this what you want?"

"You? Is it what you want?"

"Figg, I've been attracted to you for a long time."

He wiggled his hips against her, "In case you haven't noticed, I'm attracted, ahem, very attracted to you as well." He pressed himself against her.

She gave a little wiggle back, "Well, that's some attraction," before she asked in a voice so quiet he could scarcely hear it, "Do you have any protection?"

"I was hoping this would happen, so as a matter of fact, I do." As he reached into the pocket of his slacks and pulled out a string of several small square packages, he gave her a slow wink.

A happy smile curved her lips as she gave a sigh of relief and pleasure and anticipation.

Bobby stood, picking her up with one hand cupped beneath her bottom, the other against the center of her back, and laid her carefully on the bed. Her hair spread across the bedcover, and the short skirt to her black sweater dress rode up her thighs. He stroked his hands through her hair, across her face, up and down her body, his thumbs grazing her breasts, her waist, her hip bones, his eyes following his hands as they wandered down her thighs, seducing her with looks and light touches. "About that attraction..." Bobby murmured as he slowly reached for the button at his waist.

Penelope moaned, "Please, Figg, you're tormenting me."

"I want to see you all hot and bothered. I want to see you squirming on the bed while you watch me take off my clothes." He lowered the zipper and removed his slacks, laying them carefully on the bench. He unfastened the buttons on his shirt and placed it on top of his slacks. Then his t-shirt.

Her eyes lingered on the bulge in the front of his underwear. She panted, "I want to kiss you and touch you and take you in my hands. I want you to kiss me, long, hot, sexy kisses and take off my clothes and put your hands all over me and make love to me. I want to make love *with* you, Figg. Please…" she moaned again.

*

In the morning, Bobby got up first and took a shower. With a towel wrapped around his waist, he made coffee and brought the cups into the bedroom.

Penelope was slowly waking as he entered.

"Good morning, kid."

She looked at him with sleepy eyes. "And don't you look – attractive," she giggled. "Oh my God, that coffee smells heavenly."

"I'm the coffee maestro!" He handed her a cup, sat next to her and ran a finger along her thigh, along her long, lean runner's muscle.

The Interview

August 11, 2015

Jane took a sip of water before glancing down at her list of questions, "Tracey, let's talk about your third victim, Zoe Abrams."

"Parking garage, four blocks from the Lauch Art Museum. After the annual gala, New Year's Day 2005," Tracey added in a flat, emotionless voice as he looked down at his hands folded on the table in front of him. "She was a pretty thing. She was one of the regular bartenders at the galas."

"And you knew her name?"

"My entire life, I've been good with names. Funny thing about names. As a child, I called everyone from my parents' generation 'Mr.' and 'Mrs.' and never by their first name. From the moment they adopted me, my parents and grandparents raised me to be polite and considerate." Tracey smiled, "As I grew older, they told me using people's names was a sign of respect. I was always warm to our staff and called them by name, but to be honest with you, I never would have recognized them away from their jobs."

She gave him a quick glance, "Getting back to Zoe. Her family is very well off, although not as wealthy as yours. They didn't want to be interviewed. Her best friend, Edie Jeffers, told me they are still, after all this time, grappling with her death. They don't socialize anymore. They stay at home all the time. They had warned her repeatedly that her lifestyle would lead to no good." Jane cleared her throat and took another sip of water. "Edie told me that Zoe's parents always thought she could do much better for herself. Edie's also a bartender. They were part of what they referred to among themselves as an elite group, female bartenders who worked high-end events – like your family's annual fundraiser gala at the museum.

"Do you want to know what Edie told me about the aftermath of Zoe's death?" Jane narrowed her eyes as she watched him. She went on, speaking slowly, without waiting for his answer, "Fear. Other than the loss of her dearest friend, the enduring impact of Zoe's death is fear. That's what her friend still suffers from… overwhelming… fear."

"I never meant to frighten anyone." After taking a deep breath, he continued in a low voice, "I wanted to stop. Back then, I wanted to stop killing."

"She works late, and since Zoe's murder, she's frightened. Strange men at night have become bad people. She never parks in a garage or in a lot anymore. She always parks on the street. Even if she has to walk farther. She always tries to find a place under a streetlight."

Tracey looked down at his coffee, picked it up and took a sip. He grimaced. It had become tepid.

"Zoe and Edie are real people with family and friends and colleagues whose lives you ended or changed… forever. For ten years, Edie has lived with that fear… day in and day out." Each time Jane said their names, she looked directly at Tracey.

He winced, "How difficult that must be. I'm sorry I hurt her." She almost thought she heard a slight quaver in his voice.

"That type of lingering effect of her murder wasn't what I was expecting to find in my interviews. I was thinking more about sadness or anger or denial. I hadn't thought about women in that same situation carrying that fear with them *all* the time." Jane thoughtfully tucked the tendril of hair that always seemed to escape firmly back into her topknot. "Now, I'll always carry around a little bit of that fear when I'm out alone at night too."

He shook his head, "All I thought about at the time was my desire to strangle her. I didn't think beyond that moment."

Chapter Three

Tracey walked into the nursery from the adjoining master suite. Charlotte, who was remaking the small crib for the umpteenth time, looked at the little bear in his hands, "Are you sure that bear is for Baby Sarah? You seem to have been carrying it around a lot ever since it arrived."

"I had one when I was young. Not a Steiff bear, of course," he said, examining the steel button in its ear that held in place a tiny white tag with red writing designating this bear as one of Steiff's limited editions, "but my teddy was a lot like this one. His arms and legs had joints, and his head could turn as well." He stroked his fingers against its face, "I never needed a security blanket because I had my bear. I carried him everywhere with me, and of course, he slept under my covers at night. I was devastated that he got left behind when Child Protective Services came and took me and Sarah away. I cried for him for months. Every child should have a teddy." He looked at Charlotte, "Do you really think Baby Sarah will like it?"

Charlotte took the bear from him and caressed its soft mohair fur. "What's not to like about this little guy? Steiff bears are so sweet." With a gentle tap on the bear's nose, she moved his legs into a sitting position and set him on the windowsill with his front paws posed in his lap and his head turned as though he were looking out at the world.

Youthful laughter sounded through the second doorway, the one that led into the great room. "That must be Frannie and Gia now," said Charlotte as she walked over to give Tracey a kiss.

He slid his arm around her non-existent waist, "Everything is ready for breakfast." He gave her belly a gentle pat, "Let's go feed you two."

The day before, Gia and Frannie had prepped the nursery walls with creamy white paint and the ceiling with a soft blue. Once breakfast was over, they stood in the small, airy room with Charlotte and Tracey, listening one more time to Tracey's explanation of what he thought should be included in the mural.

"It has to have Charlotte's little turquoise car, a volcano in the background, and the whole group of us together at Sasha's vineyard harvesting grapes."

Charlotte rolled her eyes, "A baby doesn't want to look at that stuff. Think newborn, Tracey, newborn. Baby animals and grass and flowers and her home. We want our Sarah to look at sweet, innocent, happy things. Not a volcano that could erupt at any moment." She chortled, "Or a bunch of debauched adults drinking and dancing around a fire on the edge of a vineyard."

Laughing, Gia and Frannie shooed them out of the room. "Go. Go get some fresh air and sunshine. It's lovely out today," said Gia. "You'd scarcely know it's already late December."

Frannie picked up the small bear from the windowsill and gave it a kiss on the top of its head before tucking it into the crib and covering the whole thing with the drop cloth that Charlotte had removed earlier that morning so she could remake the bed yet again.

With soft music playing in the background for Gia, they unrolled their sketches on top of the well-covered changing table, chuckling quietly at the suggestions that Tracey had made. They agreed that their drawing, which bore remarkable similarities to Charlotte's preferences, was much more appropriate for a small baby – a village street lined with little stone houses with puppies and kittens and small children playing in front gardens. Winding up the hillside would be a driveway with grass and flowers growing along either side with goats and sheep grazing happily, and at the top, a house that was identical to Tracey and Charlotte's stone house. The hillside, covered with more flowers, would fill the background. All this would wrap around two walls of the nursery, and the fluffy clouds in the sky would drift from the walls across the ceiling.

Frannie dashed over and locked the door to the master suite. She signed to Gia, "We don't want them walking in and spoiling the surprise."

"Good thinking," Gia said as she signed back. "Let's get started."

After a few adjustments to their drawing, they began to work, quickly sketching on the walls the mural they would come back around and paint. Hopefully, they would finish it by the end of the next day.

At the edge of the great room, outside the other closed door that led into the nursery, Charlotte whispered, "I just want a peek. What about you?"

"Well, we did promise – but okay, let's do it," he whispered back.

They stood close to the door while Charlotte slowly, very slowly, pressed down on the handle and cracked it open. Since that door was normally never closed, they were surprised at the small creak of the hinges. She glanced at Tracey and made a face.

Gia jumped when she heard the sound and ran over to stand in front of them. Pushing them back into the great room, she scolded, "No, no, no, no, no! You'll spoil the surprise. Scoot. Off with both of you. Get out of our hair."

Charlotte gave a fake pout, "Well, we know when we're not wanted." She turned to Tracey, "Let's escape to the great outdoors."

Gia grasped the door handle, "Good idea. Why don't you spend the next eight hours outdoors in the sunshine? Or go to lunch in town. Do anything to amuse yourselves so long as it takes you away from this room. We need to get this done before Baby Sarah makes her appearance." Noticing that Charlotte suddenly seemed to be carrying the baby lower, she added, "Which could be any day now, it seems."

Tracey took Charlotte by the hand, and when they heard the door lock click emphatically, he said, "Let's go up the hillside and look at the view – of the sea, of course." He quirked an eyebrow and ran his eyes over Charlotte's body with what he hoped was a lascivious look. "Now that the plants have grown a bit, we'll be out of sight, so that should satisfy Gia."

Charlotte chortled, "Who are we satisfying and about what?"

When they reached the upper terrace, Charlotte sat down heavily on the couch they'd bought because it had been so comfy when they tried it out. "Whew, that's become quite a climb for this old pregnant lady." She shifted her weight, trying to find a comfortable position.

He slid his arm around her shoulders, rested the other on her very large, round stomach and drifted kisses over her face and neck. The baby kicked, bouncing his hand lightly. He pulled back slightly, "Good lord, she's going to be a world-class soccer player." He stroked Charlotte's belly, *This family, my wife and my child, this is what I want in life. Nothing more.*

Charlotte wriggled out of his arms. "There's not enough room on this couch. I'm so big and uncomfortable. And I can't even kiss you properly," she said fretfully. She felt him pull away and reached over and put her hand on the front of his trousers where his desire had become quite evident. "But I could help you out."

He slipped his hand under her dress and caressed her leg, "Or I could help you out."

"Yes, please, that would help, I think."

He pulled a cushion off the couch and knelt in front of her. He lifted her skirt. She gave a long moan of pleasure in response to his fingers and his mouth.

Charlotte lay back, her eyes half-closed, thoroughly satisfied by Tracey's ministrations. With a smug smile at his prowess curving his lips, he stood up, tossed the cushion back onto the couch and sat down on the chair nearest his wife. He stroked her knee gently and then picked up his pipe and pouch from the table where he'd laid them earlier.

Charlotte watched him as he stared off into the distance at the sea while he went through his usual ritual, placing a pinch of tobacco into the bowl of his pipe, tamping it down with the little tool specially designed for that, all in preparation for lighting it.

When he'd lit it and ensured it was drawing to his satisfaction, he lifted the pipe in her direction, as if he were giving a toast, "You know, this is my last pipe. I've decided to give it up."

"Glory be," she rolled her eyes to the sky and clasped her hands. "I never thought I would see the day." She broke out into laughter, "So you do love me and Baby Sarah even more than your pipe?"

"Well, it's very close but…"

"You know, that makes me so happy."

He squinted at her through the smoke and smiled, "I know."

Tracey picked up the French phrase book that lay on the table next to his tobacco pouch and began reading sentences aloud.

"I so enjoy listening to you speak French. It's very romantic. And you have such a lovely accent. But don't you think you should be working on your Italian as well?"

"But French is more useful for cooking and for traveling – and for seducing my darling wife. Besides, I'll have the rest of my life to improve my Italian."

"Unless, when we get to Raleigh, you decide you don't want to come back here," she said with a note of uncertainty in her voice.

Tracey looked at her with shock, "I thought it was a done deal. After the baby is born, go there to sell my house, take care of my belongings, go to the gala and come back here after the holidays."

"It's just my hormones talking. Of course, that's what we'll do."

"*This* is our home, Charlotte."

Chapter Four

Penelope lay with her head on Bobby's shoulder, twirling her finger through the soft blond hairs on his chest.

"Mmmm, that feels good," he murmured.

"What we were doing before felt good too."

They'd never had sex at his house before. Even if this time it was in the guest room, it was a step toward him overcoming the natural awkwardness of bringing another woman into "his and Hallie's" home. Ever since that first night when Bobby had revealed his "attraction" to her, it had always been in her king-sized bed.

When Figg had led her into the guest room earlier that evening, Penelope wondered if being in his bed would have felt like he was betraying Hallie. Her mind had flashed back to the days when she'd helped Hallie decorate this room, right after the newlyweds had bought their dream home, an old farmhouse just beyond the edge of town. It was perfect – Figg liked to putter around and fix things, and Hallie had wanted to raise goats and have a large garden full of flowers and herbs and vegetables. The two friends had cleaned and sanded the old wrought-iron bed frame, a real find that they had come across in a junk shop, and then painted it a bright white. Hallie'd wanted the small room to be all done in shades of whites and creams to make it feel light and airy. She'd said that flowers would provide the color. Centered on the antique dresser – another find they'd carefully restored to its current gleaming state – she always had a vase filled with hydrangeas in the summer and in the winter, roses. But that night, when Figg and Penelope had sex at his house for the first time, there were no flowers.

Bobby propped himself up on his elbow, "I think I'm falling in love with you."

"How could you? We've only been together for a few days. Nobody even knows about us yet."

"But we've known each other for years. Why do you want to keep our relationship behind closed doors?"

She tipped her head toward the door, "Excuse me? I think

it's you who prefers to have the door closed."

He chuckled, "I know, I know. It's just odd, making love with doors wide open."

Amused, she shook her head.

"After Hallie died, I didn't think I would ever care for anyone again." He leaned over and kissed her, "What we have is different. But why do you want to hide what we have? It's beautiful. I want to shout it from the rooftops."

"I like to keep my private life private, so no shouting, Figg. I don't want to share it until I figure out if I'm ready for all this commitment. Let's just ease into this."

"Wow, Hugo really did a number on you, didn't he?"

Embarrassed, Penelope looked away with a nod of her head.

"So, for right now, let's just stick with sex and good times." He stroked her hair, "Will that work, kid?"

"Yeah," she said with a sigh of relief, "sex and good times."

Chapter Five

After pushing the sleeves of her light sweater up to her elbows, she folded the financial section of the newspaper she'd been reading and used it to fan herself.

Tracey gave her a quizzical smile, "Hormones?" His eyes went to her belly that had pushed her dress into an ungainly mound.

Charlotte nodded, "This little one has my body all confused." She idly caressed her stomach with one hand while with the other, she tapped the newspaper on her knee, "I'm worried about my investments, Tracey."

He looked up from his sudoku, "Hmmm, you mean with all the rumblings about Britain leaving the European Union?"

"Effin' Brexit. I have a lot of money invested in the U.K. Do you think I should move some of it?" She winced suddenly, shifted her position in the chair, gently rubbing her abdomen.

"Are you all right?" Tracey looked over at her anxiously. "Is it time to go to the hospital?"

"No, my love, I'm fine - just another bloody Braxton Hicks," Charlotte grimaced. "I wish I'd gone into labor when Sarah dropped, but apparently, that's the privilege of women who've had babies before, not first-timers like me. So here I am, still – ooof," a sharp kick interrupted her, "waddling around and playing goalie to our future soccer player." She placed her hand over the spot where a tiny foot had just given her a vigorous kick, "and tormented by these false contractions to boot."

"More ice water?" His face reflected his frustration at being unable to do anything to make his wife more comfortable. "A cool cloth for the back of your neck?"

"No, thanks. If I drink any more water, I'll float away." She gave him a little smile as the cramp eased, "Ahhh, that's better." She fanned herself again.

They were sitting under an umbrella in wicker chairs at a small table on the pea gravel patio in the back garden. "I wish I could waddle myself all the way to the upper terrace to catch a little breeze. I love the view from up there, and I just feel so confined down here." She glanced at Tracey, "Sorry, my love, I'm awfully grumpy today. I just can't seem to get comfortable at all."

"Shall I go get your fan from the upper terrace? You're doing quite a number on that poor newspaper, waving it around like that."

She scowled and fanned herself more vigorously, "This paper is just fine."

"Well then, back to your question about moving your money, I've been thinking about it too. My money is mostly invested in the U.S. And when we sell my house in Raleigh, I'll need to do something with that money as well. Maybe it's not a bad idea to diversify. We don't have anything to speak of invested in Europe, and we live here."

"Even though I want to live here in Sicily forever, I don't think I want all my money tied up in Italy. The government and their economy have always been too unpredictable for my comfort."

"There are a lot of other places to consider. That's the job of our financial advisors."

Suddenly, she turned toward him with a grin, "Just think, when you sell your house, you won't have to pay upkeep and property taxes. That means when we go back a few times a year for things like the museum gala and Sarah's House fundraisers, we can stay in a posh hotel and be pampered."

He looked over at her with a raised eyebrow, "Mmmm. While we're discussing houses and upkeep and taxes, are you sure you don't want to sell the Whidbey Island house?"

"Not in a heartbeat! We need a foothold somewhere in the U.S. for tax purposes. Besides," she said with a twinkle in her eye, "what if you cheat on me and I have to divorce you. I'll need a place to run away to." She lifted his hand and pressed a kiss into his palm.

"Cheat? Not likely," he said, standing suddenly, and leaning over her from behind, he stroked her throat with his fingers and thumbs in a touch that she said always sent thrills of pleasure through her body. Then he put his mouth on hers in a long, sensual kiss.

"I love you beyond belief, Tracey Lauch," Charlotte sighed with contentment. "You know, I'm so excited that we've decided to settle here permanently." She looked around at her house and garden – and her husband and her huge belly, "I have everything I want here."

Chapter Six

"I'm at the hospital, I have Charlotte on speaker. Sarah's arrived, Fong. Our baby girl is perfect even though she came a couple of weeks early. Ten fingers, ten toes and a full head of fuzzy red hair."

"Congratulations, Daddy."

They heard Fong's muffled voice talking to Remy, "It's Tracey and Charlotte. Sarah was born." His voice became clear again, "I'm putting my phone on speaker so we can all talk."

"Congratulations to you both. This is so exciting," said Remy. "Charlotte, how are you feeling?"

"Tired, sore, so happy not to be pregnant anymore. Mostly, I'm just thrilled to death. Our Sarah's absolutely beautiful."

"Red hair?" asked Fong. "Who does she get that from?"

"There's no red hair on the French side of the family. Mine's from a bottle," Charlotte laughed. "It has to be from Tracey."

"You would never know it from my dark hair. But my birth mom had beautiful red hair."

"I can hardly wait to meet Sarah," said Remy.

"Hopefully, you'll get to meet her very soon. We'd like the two of you to be Sarah's godparents," said Charlotte.

In unison, Fong and Remy replied, "We would be honored."

A muscle flicked in Tracey's jaw, *I just hope Remy's memory of that night doesn't come back. Ever since she was found alive, I've been looking over my shoulder, waiting.*

They talked about the baby a little longer, and then Remy said, "Well, we have some exciting news ourselves. We've decided to stay here in Slovenia."

Fong chimed in, "We've made an offer on a small vineyard and cottage that's just come on the market. It's right next door to Sasha. The cottage is tiny but livable. It stands on a hillside that overlooks a dilapidated stone wall marking the boundary between what will be our vineyard and Sasha's."

"Oh, how wonderful. We would like to have the christening there at the old church across from Sasha's vineyard, wouldn't we, Tracey? When we hang up, we'll give him a call to share the good news and ask him if he would host us."

"You know how Sasha is. I'm sure he'll be thrilled to have it here."

In the background, Fong and Remy heard the fretful cry of a baby.

"Sorry, I have to go. Sarah needs to be fed. We can talk later about who to invite," Charlotte said. "Bye Remy, bye Fong."

"Congratulations again," said Fong.

*

A few days after they'd returned home, Tracey followed Charlotte through the door from the great room into the nursery. He picked up Sarah's teddy bear from the rocking chair and set it in the center of the windowsill before he sat down. Charlotte laid the fussy baby in his arms and handed him a bottle of breast milk.

"This stuff looks absolutely disgusting," he said as he slipped the nipple into the baby's mouth. She immediately began to suck on it eagerly. Tracey rocked the chair ever so slightly with one foot as he looked tenderly into his little girl's eyes. "Yummy, yummy," he said and made a face.

Charlotte chuckled as she moved the small bear to one side and leaned against the windowsill, watching the two of them, father and daughter.

Chapter Seven

Sasha was back at work in the bar on board the *Terre Verte*. It was the evening before Valentine's Day, and he smiled to himself as he thought about the baptism celebration, the celebration of life he would host at his vineyard next month.

Because she was working on her first cruise with Spectrum since she'd finally gotten the security contract, Emily had stuck to sparkling water with dinner. But before she headed back to her cabin to call it a night, she'd stopped in the bar for a glass of wine and a chat with Sasha, whom she'd met a few years earlier when she'd first been pursuing that coveted contract. Her cheek rested on her hand, her drink in front of her. She took a sip and savored its rich flavor while she toyed with the crane he'd set on the edge of her glass when he served her. She held it up to her wine and noticed that the reds were precisely the same color.

They chatted while she watched Sasha folding and placing cranes into a copper bowl on the counter.

"I remember that first evening when you came into the bar on the Ukraine cruise, coming up on four years ago," he said. "You introduced yourself to me and told me you were determined to land a security contract with Spectrum. You gave me your business card. I stuck it away in my journal. I imagine it's still there." He grinned at her as his fingers continued to make intricate folds in the paper. "There was something about you, an air of… an air of persistence, as though you wouldn't give up." His eyes twinkled at her, "I guess you didn't."

"I nearly did, on several occasions," she said. "And then, one day, out of the blue, they called me and made me an offer."

"Good things come to those who wait," said Sasha with a smile.

Emily's face lit up as she gave him a huge smile in return. She toyed with the small crane for a moment, making its wings move and then asked, "Are they red for Valentine's Day?"

"Yes, in part. Because, among other things, red represents love and joy."

"You look so sad when you say that."

"As you did, most people will think these are simply for Valentine's Day. But in fact, I'm folding a thousand cranes in memory of my friend, Isabelle Ronaldo. She was murdered two years ago tomorrow." He took a few of them from the bowl and set them in a row on the counter as he spoke, "Isabelle brought so much joy into everyone's life. I can still hear her playing the piano over there." He motioned toward the baby grand that stood across the room. "It was her way of relaxing. And it gave me such pleasure to listen to her."

"So, tell me about Isabelle and what happened."

"She was the first female captain working for Spectrum. She and her wonderful partner, Victor, had four young children, all girls. She was on her last cruise before she retired, but when she left the Valentine's Ball in Strasbourg that evening, she was strangled in an alley. They never found the killer." His fingers slowly caressed the small birds as he picked them back up from the counter and placed them in the bowl.

"How very sad. I'm so sorry, Sasha." She rested her fingertips on the back of his hand for a moment. "I'm surprised no one's mentioned this to me. You know, I'm here to watch for and investigate security issues on the Spectrum Line."

"There was no connection to the boat. It didn't happen here. It was in an alley in town."

"You said she was strangled, correct?"

Sasha nodded and said quietly, "That's right."

"In an alley in town, correct?"

He nodded again.

"Two years ago, correct?"

He nodded yet again and looked up at her, "I feel like I'm on a witness stand."

"Oh, sorry. This is making the hair on the back of my neck stand up. Tell me, what color was her hair? How old was she?"

"Dark blond. Early thirties. What's this all about, Emily?"

"Bear with me, I just have one more question. You wouldn't happen to know if she was found... minus anything, like an item of clothing or something you'd expect her to have on her person but didn't?"

While Sasha wasn't enjoying dredging up the painful memories, he responded to the urgency in Emily's voice. "Well, actually, yes, I think the police said there was a missing earring."

Emily said slowly, "Isabelle's murder sounds eerily similar to ones committed by a guy we've been chasing across the U.S. for years, but his victims have all been redheads. We recently found another murder in Budapest that has the same MO as the U.S. killings, red hair, strangled, isolated location, missing an earring. It occurred a few months after Isabelle was killed. It's quite possible that he's moved on to kill women here in Europe. Isabelle was strangled in an alley at night, she was fairly young, and an earring was missing. Even though she was blond, I wonder if her murder is also part of this series."

"It was very dark and rainy that night, so maybe he didn't notice she wasn't a redhead."

Sasha folded another couple of cranes in silence. When he looked up, he noticed that Emily's glass was almost empty. He held up the wine bottle. She put her hand over her glass and shook her head.

"I think I should tell you about the murder of Mari Oliver," Sasha said slowly. "She was killed four years ago this summer."

Emily touched her glass, "It sounds like I may need that refill after all."

He poured her several ounces of wine and then a glass for himself before he went on, "I don't know if you will remember her. She was the concierge on our cruise to Ukraine."

"Lovely young woman, vibrant personality, auburn hair?" Emily took a gulp of wine and said with a self-deprecating move of one shoulder, "I'm a former police detective. They paid us to remember details."

"Mari was also killed, strangled, in an alley in Zaporizhzhya. But in broad daylight."

"Oh, my, as passengers we didn't hear anything about that. I do recall noticing that Mari wasn't with the cruise after that stop, and I just assumed that she had left for personal reasons."

"Again, it occurred off the boat, and everyone thought that she'd run into some unsavory character who'd killed her." He paused and closed his eyes briefly, remembering the day he'd been told about Mari's death. "I heard later that her right earring was missing." Looking at Emily intently, he asked, "Do you think both women were killed by the same person?"

"Those are too many coincidences for my comfort. I need to pass on that information to the investigators back home. I'm only tangentially involved."

He finished folding another crane and put it in the bowl. "These are for Isabelle. I'll fold another thousand for Mari in August." Sasha told Emily about how it felt, having lost two dear friends in addition to his partner, all in recent years. He was coming up on fifty-five. He was feeling older than he thought he should at that age. "Maybe," he said, "it's finally time to retire and go live and work full-time in my vineyard in Slovenia. Maybe, I'll take my journals and turn them into a book. I want to be in my home, in my vineyards, on my land. It's magical there."

Emily said, "It would be nice to have the closure that solving their murders might bring, healing for you, for their friends, for their families."

Sasha nodded silently.

The Interview

With her eyes on Tracey's face as she spoke, Jane recited, "Isabelle Ronaldo, 2012. She was your eighth victim. Her partner was Victor Tomas. They had four daughters, Frankie, Lily, Iris and Rose."

"Strasbourg?"

Number eight was Strasbourg. As soon as I said, "the eighth victim," he immediately knew the location. Jane nodded.

"I thought she was someone else. She wasn't the woman I intended to kill. She wasn't supposed to die."

She opened her mouth and closed it again without saying anything. *Are any of us supposed to die like that?* She took a deep breath and let it out slowly before taking a swallow of water. "She had four small children, and their father was left to care for them by himself. Do you ever think about your family and the effect this has had on them?"

His face flushed red as he leaned toward her, putting his hands flat on the table. His voice was taut, "You've… crossed… a line. This is not about *my* family."

Jane tilted her head quizzically, "That question was partly hypothetical because I see Charlotte and Sarah both as survivors and as victims." She paused, "We're talking about the stories the survivors told me about what's happened in their lives since the murders."

Tracey sat back with his heart still pounding and gave a short nod.

"Victor used to worry about whether or not Isabelle's murder was intentional or just a random act of violence. He said there's always been a nagging worry about his daughters' safety, if they would be the killer's next victims."

Tracey swallowed hard, and pictures of his small daughter flickered in his mind. *What if someone were to threaten her?* His stomach churned.

"When I asked him if knowing who the murderer is has changed how he feels, he told me it has and it hasn't. He was glad to know that the murderer would not be targeting his children next. But at the same time, knowing who'd killed Isabelle didn't make any difference. She's dead and nothing will bring her back. It doesn't matter to him or his children who it was."

Her voice cracked, "He still keeps so many of his emotions inside – to protect the children, he says. He's lost the love of his life and the mother of his children. He told me they were supposed to have the rest of their lives together, but instead, they'd only had eight years."

"I also spent some time with Isabelle's oldest daughter. Frankie is twelve now, and she tries to keep up all the family traditions that began with her mother. She's helping her three sisters cope by keeping her mother's memory alive. Victor told me it seems as though she's trying to fill her mother's shoes." Jane paused and repeated, "And she's only twelve."

He listened with half an ear as Jane went on to describe how Frankie helped the younger children cook dinner at night and clean up after. How Isabelle and Victor always had the children participate in family chores, even if they didn't do very well at first. How Frankie had taken over bath time for the three younger ones, though Victor insisted that he still be the one to read to them every night.

Tracey thought about how he'd always tried to look after his sister. He'd felt very protective and done his best to take good care of her. Even at a young age, he'd reminded her to brush her teeth and pick up her toys, and he always retrieved the red ball from under the bed when they played together.

Jane continued, "Frankie wears her mother's necklace. A necklace that Victor had made for Isabelle from a pear leaf he'd given her when he found out she was pregnant with Frankie."

Tracey clenched his hand around his coffee cup.

She jabbed her index finger toward Tracey, "You know what he says he misses most?"

Tracey closed his eyes.

"He misses using the words *'we'* and *'us'* in the present tense about his relationship with Isabelle. He has pictures of Isabelle, he sees her in their girls – he says he hears her voice through them. But he struggles because he feels like he's already losing his memories of her touch and smell."

Looking off at some spot over Jane's shoulder, Tracey said in a quiet voice, "I miss using those words too. I miss my wife."

Jane heard the pain in his voice, but at that point, she didn't care. *Objectivity be damned!* She wanted him to hurt for what he'd done to Isabelle and her family.

"But Charlotte's not dead."

Chapter Eight

Slovenia, Late March 2014

It was a bright Sunday morning when the friends gathered in a loose semicircle in front of the altar facing the priest. Each of the women held a few stems of white flowers that Charlotte had handed them when they entered the church, and she'd tucked a single flower into each man's buttonhole. Sarah's parents stood on one side of the baptismal font, the godparents across from them and the rest of the party a few steps behind. Remy had examined the font before the service, certain that it must be as old as the church itself. Tracey looked over at her, forcing himself to meet her eyes and smile. This visit to Slovenia was the first time he would have spent in her presence since the cruise. Since the night he thought he'd killed her.

The beautifully carved wooden font held a silver bowl in its center for holy water. As the sole acolyte assisting at the service poured water from a silver ewer into the bowl, the priest recited the words sanctifying it for Sarah's baptism. Charlotte handed him the baby, and cradling her in his arms, he used a small, silver shell to pour water over Sarah's forehead, saying the words that would make her a member of the church.

At the end of the service, the priest gently lifted Sarah in her white lace christening dress and bonnet, supporting her head in his hand, "Sarah Olivia Lauch, meet your family." He turned her carefully from left to right so everyone could see her. When they all applauded, she began to wail. Tracey took her from the priest and put her up against his shoulder, patting her on the back.

"There, there, my little one." She calmed considerably as he talked to her in his low, quiet voice but continued to snuffle and whimper, turning her face back and forth against him. Tracey shifted Sarah from his left to his right shoulder so he could shake the priest's hand, "Thank you, Father."

"Yes, thank you," Charlotte added. "It was lovely."

The priest took a narrow wooden box from the table where the ewer and shell sat and handed it to Charlotte. "It is a tradition that our congregation gives each new member a rosary to remind them of this day and that they are members, not only of the Holy

Church but also of this congregation. It will bring focus to her prayers and solace in times of pain and sadness."

"Thank you," said Charlotte. "What a very special gift. We'll keep it safe until Sarah is old enough to look after it herself, and we'll certainly bring her to services whenever we're here visiting." She peeked into the box at the simple turquoise and jasper rosary, adorned with a small wooden cross and tipped it for Tracey to see. "It's beautiful. Thank you again, Father."

As the rest of the small group slowly began to move toward the exit, the priest said, "There is one more thing we need to take care of today." Fong and Remy moved closer to each other.

"Oh, of course. We all need to sign the baptismal register," said Tracey.

"Yes, we do need to do that," the priest said with a smile.

Fong said, "But there's something more."

"Fong and I have decided to get married."

"Ahh, congratulations! I can't say it's a surprise, I just hope we're invited to the wedding," Gia said, looking closely at Remy, whose face glowed with happiness.

"Tracey, will you be my best man?" asked Fong.

Remy turned to Charlotte, "And Charlotte, will you be my matron of honor?"

"Of course, just tell us when, and we'll be there, wherever *there* is."

Fong took Remy's hand, "Well then, how about right now, right here?"

They all looked around at one other in excitement.

Charlotte gathered the flowers from all the women. Pulling a decorative ribbon from Sarah's baptismal bonnet, she tied them into a wedding bouquet and handed it to Remy, who took it with an excited grin. The bride and groom moved to stand in front of the priest. Gia took Sarah from Tracey so he and Charlotte could join their friends.

The priest turned the pages of his prayer book to the Ceremony of Holy Matrimony and began to read the familiar words, *"Dearly beloved, we are gathered here in the eyes of God…"*

After hugs and congratulations all around, led by the bride

and groom, the group slowly walked down the aisle paved with stones worn by thousands of feet, past the hand-carved wooden pews, and toward the heavy wooden door that stood between windows of stained glass. At the last moment, Tracey reached over and picked up Remy's camera and bag from the front pew.

"Photos out front in five minutes," Remy said, turning to thank him with a smile and a wave of her bouquet.

"Would you like me to set up your equipment or take some of the pictures, Remy?" asked Tracey as they emerged from the church. "You're the bride."

"And you're the father of the child who has just been baptized."

They both laughed as she thanked him, "But I know my equipment, so it will be faster if I set it up."

Relieved, he watched her walk away to set up her tripod and camera in the front of the small chapel. *Just remember, she doesn't know it was you. You're the only one with guilty knowledge.*

With everyone out front in the warm March sun, Remy began positioning them for the photo, "Baptism pictures first."

"Everyone, we want Father to be on the bottom step, centered on the door, holding Sarah. Charlotte and Tracey to the left of him. Fong, you're on the right, and I'll jump into the picture after I set the camera's timer. Then behind them, Frannie, you and Leo, Sasha, Gia and Sal."

After rearranging the group for the wedding photos, Remy took another series of shots. Tracey and Fong shook the priest's hand and thanked him again. He apologized for not being able to come over to the house for the celebratory meal, but he had to take communion to a sick parishioner. The group of friends walked down the gravel drive from the church and across the road, following the low stone boundary wall to Sasha's driveway.

Before handing Sarah to Charlotte, Tracey said, "Daddy is going to go help our friends make us a big meal. Be good for Mommy." He kissed the top of her head and went on into the kitchen with Gia and Sasha to help prepare the baptismal meal, which would now also serve as a wedding feast.

Sasha peered over Gia's shoulder as she put yellow flowers

on the cake she'd iced with white buttercream. She elbowed him gently, "Sasha if you joggle my arm, these yellow roses might just turn into yellow honeysuckle instead." She turned to kiss his cheek and saw a disappointed look on his face.

"It's white," he said.

"Don't worry, Sasha, the cake is chocolate. And that white buttercream, it's actually white *chocolate* buttercream."

He smiled, "Mmmm, double chocolate. It is a double celebration, after all."

Gia pointed to her stomach, "It's a triple celebration," she whispered.

He raised his eyebrows.

"Two months."

"Well, you and Sal aren't wasting any time. Congratulations!"

"We've wasted enough time already, so now, we're getting down to business. We plan to have a big family."

Sal wandered up behind her and slid his arms around her waist, resting one hand on her abdomen, "We'll never catch up with Joseph and Anusha. They have four kids and one more on the way."

"Joseph and Anusha?" Tracey asked, overhearing their conversation.

"One of my best friends," said Sal. "We all grew up together, me, Joseph and Raul. Raul and David have one daughter."

"At two-and-a-half, it's pretty obvious that she'll be as much of a prankster as David is," Gia giggled.

"We were all confirmed bachelors, and now we are all dads," Sal laughed. "Or in my case, in the process of becoming a dad."

Fong looked at Leo, "Do you want to help me get the wine? Sasha keeps a magnificent cellar." Leo nodded his agreement, and they headed off.

Sal looked at Frannie, "So, Frannie, do you and Leo plan on getting married and having kids?"

Frannie replied, signing as she spoke carefully, "Oh, we've only been dating a few months. We're not ready to commit yet. Look how long it took you and Gia to decide."

"Good things come to those who wait," Sal smiled, thinking

about the bumpy road he and Gia had traveled to get to marriage and the verge of parenthood.

*

After dinner, Tracey and Fong invited the others to come join them on the patio, but everyone turned them down.

Charlotte had gone off to feed Sarah and catch up with Remy. Even though they talked regularly on the phone, it just wasn't the same as seeing each other in person. They missed the closeness they'd had when Remy was still living in Florence, before Remy and Fong fell in love, before Lee and Fong divorced, when they had been the group of five, all living in Italy.

Gia, Frannie and Leo had jumped in and offered to clean up from dinner. Sasha had insisted on drying the dishes and making sure everything was put away in the right place. The rumble of his voice followed by laughter from the young people carried out onto the veranda.

Tracey suspected that Sasha was giving him and Fong time together as best friends who were every bit as close as Charlotte and Remy, despite the physical distance between Sicily and Slovenia.

On the way out, Fong and Tracey reminisced about the days when they used to smoke together on the river cruise where they'd first met and made up stories about Henri, the art thief. And now, Tracey had given up his pipe for Charlotte and the baby, and Fong had stopped smoking for Remy when they had come to Slovenia together in December.

"At least we can still enjoy a good glass of cognac," said Fong, tilting his snifter toward Tracey in a toast. "Do you miss your pipe?"

"At times like this, yes. After a good meal with a nice drink in my hand and good conversation, I miss my pipe then." He looked over at Fong, "It's not a shotgun wedding, is it?"

"Oh, no, no, Remy's not pregnant."

They walked side by side across the grass to the fire pit. Fong lit the wood, and the two of them sat down with their glasses in their hands.

In response to a question from Tracey, Fong picked up the conversation they had begun months earlier after Tracey's climb on Mt Etna. He talked about how he had come to understand the different types of love he'd had with the two women in his life. He had been in love with Lee and in love with their lifestyle.

"I think that perhaps Lee loved me more than I loved her. She accepted me, warts and all. I took for granted that she always would, and so whenever I was unfaithful to her, I assumed she'd go on accepting it and loving me." Fong paused, considering, and then went on, "What I have with Remy is more balanced. After her accident, we wanted to get married sooner instead of later. Things like that make you realize how fleeting life is. We didn't want to spend any more of our lives apart."

"How is she doing? Her memory, I mean."

"She's still having problems. The doctor says the memories are there, it's just that she can't connect to them. There's a piece missing. Sometimes, when I tell her about things that happened, she remembers, and she'll tell me more about that memory, something that she knows or feels that can only come from inside her. So obviously, she's actually remembering. Then there are other times when she still can't make that connection."

"Does she ever remember things, you know, without prompting?"

"Sometimes. There are times when fragments come back on their own."

"What a fascinating topic that is, how our memories work. We all hope for the best for her."

"The pieces she worries about most are the hours around that period when she fell overboard. She may never get that memory back because no one was on the bow of the boat with her to describe what happened and to help connect her memory of the event."

Tracey leaned back, watching the flames, worrying whether the more time he and Charlotte spent with Fong and Remy, the more likely her memory of that night would surface. Of him coming up behind her, putting his hand over her mouth and the other around her throat, of him pushing her over the rail into the river. A look of pain crossed his face as he thought about his double life – one life as a good friend, husband, father, founder of Sarah's House – and the other as a serial killer, filled with a litany of lies and pretense.

Sasha wandered across to the fire pit with the cognac bottle in one hand and a snifter for himself in the other. As he refilled their glasses and then poured one for himself, he said, "This is obviously where the old guys hang out. Leo has gone off with Frannie. Sal went up to take a shower. He's the cleanest young man I know. And Gia is deep in conversation with Charlotte and Remy. They've left me to my own devices."

Tracey looked into his glass and then over at his friends. He told them that he felt he was spreading himself too thin – Sarah's House, the art museum board, fundraisers – and his life in Sicily. "Quite frankly, my life in Raleigh isn't as important to me as it was before Charlotte and Sarah. They should be my focus now." He went on to tell them about their planned trip to Raleigh where he'd sell his house, find someone to take over his duties on the museum board and then set up a trust for Sarah's House. "I want Sarah to make the decision when she's old enough, if she wants to run it or continue to let the trust handle it."

"It seems as though you are divesting yourself of your old life pretty thoroughly," observed Fong. "Does it feel like the right long-term decision?"

"I think so," said Tracey, "and nothing, after all, is completely irrevocable."

"Well, except for the sale of your house," Fong chuckled.

"Even that, enough money could probably buy it back. But it isn't as though it's been in my family for years. I bought it because it reminded me of my grandparents' house and because it had a cottage at the back of the property where my housekeeper and her husband could live at no cost." He leaned back and took a sip of his cognac. "Times change, what we want from life changes."

Sasha added, "I suppose, when you have a family, you find that your priorities change."

"Well, one of my priorities right now is to get my finances

reorganized. Charlotte and I have been talking about diversifying." He told them they wanted safe investments, worldwide so that if the economy plummeted in one area, it might be stable or up in another.

Fong reached into his pocket, pulled out his phone and clicked a few keys, "Here, I'm sending you the contact information for my financial advisor, in case you want to get an opinion from someone outside the U.S. I'll let him know that you may be reaching out to him."

Tracey gave Fong a thumbs-up as his phone pinged. That meant that finding another financial advisor was a task he wouldn't have to deal with.

Chapter Nine

Pulling into her driveway in his black Raleigh PD Escalade that they allowed him to take home at night, his eyes were on Penelope, or more precisely, on a certain part of her anatomy, as she stretched against her garage doorframe. He imagined giving that anatomical part a little swat as he glanced at the dashboard clock. *She's just leaving for her run, not back already, all sticky and sweaty and anxious to get inside and shower.*

"Morning, Figg. Didn't anyone teach you not to block the sidewalk when you park?" She pulled her earphones out and swung them gently by the cord.

He grinned, "And good morning to you too, kid. I'd give you a kiss, but, you know, no PDA. Someone might see us."

She made a face, but no amount of teasing was going to persuade her to 'go public' – not yet, anyway.

"How far are you going to run today? And are you biking or swimming too?"

"I'm doing a little of everything. I'll do a five-mile run, then come back and bike the long way around to the community pool for a swim, and then I'll bike back home. I'll be at it the rest of the morning." She glanced at her sports watch, eager to get on the road.

"So, other than biking and swimming and running impossible distances, do you have any other plans for the immediate future?"

She looped the headphone wire around her neck and returned to stretching, "One of these days, I'm going to look into volunteering with kids. Maybe go back to school. After this triathlon, of course. But we've already talked about all this."

"No, like tomorrow. What are you doing tomorrow?"

"Huh? Are you asking me on a date? You don't have to ask. You know I'm available."

"If the date is at home," they said in unison and laughed.

"No, I'm serious. What are your plans?"

"Nothing specific. Why?" she asked curiously.

"Have I got a deal for you," he said with a grin.

Penelope looked at his crotch and rolled her eyes, "I'm

always up for those deals, but I've gotta run first. And don't you have to go arrest someone or something? You're still a working stiff." With her earphones back in place, she took off at a slow jog down the driveway, detouring around his SUV.

"Wait. Pens, wait. You haven't heard my offer yet," he called out to be heard over her music.

"What?" she said impatiently as she turned around and jogged backwards, beckoning for him to run and talk with her.

"How would you like to be back on the case again?" he called out.

Penelope stopped dead in her tracks and walked back toward him. "Did I hear you right? I'm not goin' back to my old job. I'm retired. And I'm not goin' back to work for Em. She fired me." She started to turn away to get on with her run.

Bobby reached out and grabbed her wrist, "Wait Pens. How about as a consultant? It looks like there might be two more PLS victims in Europe. Raleigh PD wants to get credit for solving the case. The FBI has agreed to provide support as needed. Things are heating up, kid, and I've managed to get a year's funding to hire a consultant to work it."

"Whoa – two more victims? A consultant? Whadda you mean?"

"I want to hire you to work exclusively on this case. With no other responsibilities. You'd report directly to me, but you could consult with the FBI to draw on their expertise or get things expedited, and you just need to keep them and me in the loop," he looked at her sharply. "If we haven't solved the case in a year, then it goes back up for review with all the other cold cases, and the FBI can do what they want about it."

"You're serious?"

"Dead serious."

"Can I work from here," she pointed to her house, "or do I have to work out of the PD?"

"Here is fine."

"What's the salary?"

"At least what you were making as a detective. Come in this afternoon, and we'll get all the administrative stuff worked out.

Interested now?"

"Yep, definitely, but I have one condition. I need to share everything with Edgar Spring."

"But he's the press. Why does he need to be involved?"

"He looks at things differently. His ideas have been so useful all the time we've been working together on this case. And he's very discreet."

"I dunno," Bobby said doubtfully. "He certainly doesn't fit into my budget."

"He's a freebie. He'll do it for the intellectual challenge – and exclusive rights when we break the case. If I can't have Edgar, that's a deal breaker."

"Well, free, no deal otherwise. I guess you can."

She threw her arms around him and hugged him tightly for a moment. He looked around, "Do you think anybody saw you?"

"Can't a friend hug another friend?"

"There's one more thing. I'll be your boss, so we can't sleep together."

"That's gonna be tough," said Penelope, already hoping that today wouldn't count.

Bobby felt relief that she felt the same dread for the challenge ahead. "But we can do this," he said, almost to himself. "It's only a year." *It's going to be really tough.*

"Then we better get inside. One last fling before we start that year."

*

Later, as they snuggled together in her bed, they discussed how to deal with the upcoming year.

"But what if I don't want to date other people?" Bobby's voice was grumpy.

"You haven't been with anybody else but me since Hallie. You need to date other people so if we get back together, you know for sure you're ready for something serious." Penelope sat propped against the headboard, covers pulled up around her, Bobby's head in her lap. She stroked her fingers through his hair, "It's perfect timing for us."

"*If* we find other people we want to date while we're taking this time off, so be it. If we don't, we don't." Bobby pulled her back down beside him, "Before you go off on that date…"

Chapter Ten

Emily leaned back in her office chair, admiring the bonsai tree that stood on the table beneath her window. She'd bought it when she first started Haypress Security in her hometown of Raleigh, North Carolina, following her retirement from the Raleigh Police Department. She hadn't expected it to survive this long given the limited sunlight in her office. Nonetheless, she'd been meticulous about trimming, watering and feeding it exactly as the gardener at the Japanese nursery had shown her, meticulous like she was about everything in her life and particularly in her business. She gazed at the small tree for a few more minutes, organizing her thoughts and then picked up her phone to make a quick call to Bobby since she'd promised to let him know when Tibor was in town.

Tibor Papp, a private security consultant based in Hungary, had told her about the Budapest murder following the security conference they'd both attended the previous December. The back of her neck had prickled as she'd listened to his description of the murder of a young red-headed woman that had taken place up in the hills above Budapest. He had convinced the Hungarian police to share the DNA results with the Raleigh PD. Meanwhile, Bobby wanted to meet Tibor, to pick his brain about their case. Just before they hung up, he'd told her that he had hired Penelope as a consultant to work on the case for a year, and he'd like her to come along to the meeting Emily had scheduled for late the following afternoon.

*

It was after her normal business hours when Emily unlocked the front door of Haypress Security. Penelope stepped inside, nervous about this first encounter since she'd been fired. "I never thought I would be coming back in here."

They walked down the hall side by side as they used to. "Yeah, I was pretty rough on you."

"But I deserved it."

"Bobby told me he's hired you to work on the case."

"I'm excited and so grateful for the opportunity. He told me Tibor is here," she gave a quick sideways glance at Emily. "He said you thought we should all meet."

Emily pushed open the hallway door to the conference room that also connected to her office. A tall, slender Black man stood staring out the window with his back to the room, one hand against the nape of his neck, the other hanging loosely at his side. He was dressed in that smartly casual way that Penelope had noticed was adopted by many European men. When they entered, he turned with a smile.

"Penelope Huber, I'd like you to meet Tibor Papp," said Emily. "Tibor, this is Penelope."

They shook hands. "I've heard a lot about you," he said as they sat down.

Emily looked over at Penelope and grinned, "Good stuff. Among all of us, you have the most knowledge about the murders and the victims. I'm glad you're joining us. Bobby just went to get some water. He'll be back any second." As she spoke, he appeared in the doorway, balancing a tray with four glasses of water.

"Hi, Pens," he said, handing around the glasses.

"Now that we're all here," Emily said, "let's start. You've all heard about one another, but let's go around the table and introduce ourselves."

"Just like in big government meetings," Bobby said with a wink for Penelope and a quick grin for the others. "I'll start. I'm a lieutenant at the Raleigh Police Department and head of the Major Crimes Unit. The Parking Lot Strangler case falls under my jurisdiction. We're bound and determined to get it solved, and we've hired Penelope as a consultant to work it exclusively."

Penelope picked up from Bobby, "My role is to be the point person for the PLS investigation. I won't necessarily do all the legwork. Edgar Spring will be helping me in a volunteer status, but I'll still be very busy. My contract is for one year, and I'm hell-bent on getting this bast – guy identified by then."

"You all know who I am, and once we finish the introductions, I have some new information to share," said Emily. "Now that Raleigh PD has re-engaged on this case, my involvement isn't necessary. Although I'll always be interested in the details," she finished with a grin.

With a smile at the others sitting around the table, Tibor introduced himself, "I'm a private security consultant. I've known Emily for years. A few months ago, I described the murder of a female skateboarder in Budapest to her. When I gave her the details, she said it was uncannily similar to the PLS case you're working on. The Hungarian police have engaged me to help them work their case. The Budapest lab should be sending the results of the DNA tests they ran to the Raleigh PD." Tibor turned to Bobby, "I guess that means you. Apparently, there was some kind of snafu with the testing, and they had to rerun it."

"Same problem everywhere," said Penelope.

"Emily told me that in light of the Budapest murder, you would like to know if there are any other murders in Europe that match the MO of the PLS. Right now, no one else seems to see any urgency to this. But since I'm officially working on the Budapest killing, I've reached out to some pretty good contacts I have with Interpol. They won't want to be directly involved until the DNA comparison of the Budapest and U.S. murders is complete. If there's a match, then they'll weigh in if necessary."

Bobby leaned toward Tibor as he spoke, "I'm betting there'll be a match. There are too many similarities."

"Penelope, earlier this month, I happened upon something interesting that may be related. I've shared this with Tibor and Bobby already. I've found a couple more murders that are very similar." Everyone's eyes turned to Emily as she shared the information about Mari and Isabelle. "It's informal, and while no one has connected these murders to the Parking Lot Strangler, I think the next steps are to reach out to the police departments in those cities and to get the manifests for the Strasbourg and Zaporizhzhya cruises from Spectrum."

Emily continued, "I'm passing this off to Bobby since I'm no longer involved in law enforcement, but if you'd keep me in the loop, informally of course, I'd appreciate it."

"Of course," said Bobby and Tibor at the same time.

"Let me know, if you want me to take the lead and get those

manifests from Spectrum." Tibor said. "I assume you would want both passenger and crew lists. Maybe, as someone officially connected with the investigation, I'll be able to expedite that for all of us. And now that we have dates and locations and victim names, it should be no problem to get copies of the police reports for those murders."

"That would be good, Tibor," said Bobby. "Penelope'll update me formally each week by memo, laying out any progress on the case, and I'll use that to keep my boss and the Bureau in the loop. They don't want to be blindsided by anything. Would you mind providing your updates to Penelope so she can integrate them into those memos?"

"I'm happy to do that," Tibor replied. "Depending on what I find, Penelope, we may generate new leads to be followed up on."

She nodded at Tibor and turned toward Bobby, "I'll get the memo to you by close of business each Friday if that works."

"That works for me if it works for Tibor. You'll need to fold in his information as well."

"That's fine, Penelope. I'll have my input to you every Thursday by the end of my day."

They all stood up and shook hands. Emily said, "Tibor if you could stay behind a minute."

On the way out, Penelope walked over and bumped shoulders with Bobby. "How about we meet on Fridays at In The Alley? I'll give you my memo, and then we can discuss the case."

"Good idea. Away from curious eyes at the PD," he grinned at her.

"Right – it'll give us time together at least. Even though we're not officially together right now." With her head, she pointed at the others and whispered, "I've never seen Em like that."

"What do you mean?"

"I think she's in love, head over heels in love. Didn't you see the way she looked at him?"

As Penelope and Bobby closed the front door, Tibor put his arm around Emily. They walked into her office together, and the lock on the door clicked.

Chapter Eleven

MEMORANDUM FOR THE RECORD

TO: Lieutenant Bobby Figg, Major Crimes Unit, Raleigh PD

CC: Tibor Papp, President, Security Consulting International Ltd.
Edgar Spring, Investigative Journalist

FROM: Penelope Huber, Consultant to Raleigh PD

DATE: March 28, 2014

SUBJECT: Parking Lot Strangler Investigation – Memo #1

This memo covers the week of March 22–28.

The team for this investigation is Penelope Huber, consultant to Raleigh PD; Tibor Papp, President of Security Consulting International Ltd. from Budapest, Hungary; and Edgar Spring, investigative journalist with the *Raleigh Weekly News*.

This memo is a recap of what is known at this time.

The evidence suggests the following individuals were murdered by the Parking Lot Strangler:

1. April 1998, Maggie Wilson, Raleigh, NC
2. January 2002, Ruth Sampson, Raleigh, NC
3. January 2005, Zoe Abrams, Raleigh, NC
4. December 2007, Sheila Kovacs, Raleigh, NC
5. March 2011, Sophie Jones, Trigg Pass, WA
6. May 2012, Katalin Arany, Budapest, Hungary

Other than the evidence cited below, nothing significant has been found; a search for video footage around the area of these murders yielded nothing useful.

- The first five victims were found in or next to parking lots (hence the name of the investigation).

Page 1 of 3

97

- Each victim was strangled by a left-handed person, probably a male based on the size of handprints on victims' necks.
- An earring was missing from each victim's right ear.
- Each victim had red hair.

The laboratory completed analysis and found matching DNA from three of the six murder scenes:

- Abrams, foreign hair combed from the victim's coat.
- Jones, skin cells retrieved from the inside of a single sock, owner unknown.
- Arany, skin and blood collected from under the victim's fingernails.

European Developments

Tip regarding two possible connected murders provided by Emily Bissett, owner of Haypress Security, Raleigh, NC. In February 2014, Bissett was working on the Terre Verte, a Spectrum River Cruise Line boat, when she learned, via conversation with bartender Sasha Martinescu, of the murders by strangulation of two of his female colleagues. The killings bear striking similarities to the PLS murders. Papp will examine the case files to confirm or discount connections. The two victims are:

1. August 2010, Mari Oliver, a concierge for Spectrum, killed during a one-day stop in Zaporizhzhya, Ukraine.
2. February 2012, Isabelle Ronaldo, a captain on a Spectrum cruise on the Rhine River, killed in Strasbourg, France. She was the only blond-haired victim, but her name will be kept on the list because of the other similarities.

Note

The serial killer has expanded his killing locations beyond parking lots to other isolated locations. This will be added to the profile.

Next Steps

Papp will reach out to the police departments to review the Strasbourg and Zaporizhzhya murder files.

Papp will reach out to Interpol to do a sweep for murders of a similar MO; this is a huge task and dependent on the goodwill of local law enforcement agencies. He is also getting in touch with his contacts across Europe for similar information.

Quantifiable data, such as names, dates, locations, descriptions, etc. is being entered into the Investigative Data Analysis System (IDAS) as it is received, overseen by Huber. Here's what is being entered so far:

- *Individuals Interviewed:* The names of individuals originally interviewed during the course of the investigation have been entered into IDAS.
- *MJW Expressions:* Wilson was the owner of the gallery, which had a guest book presumably signed by all visitors. If her killer was stalking her, it is possible he may have visited the gallery at some point and signed the book. All signatories are being entered into IDAS. Additionally, all gallery employees', artists' and students' information are being entered.
- *Lauch Art Museum:* On the night Abrams was murdered, she was working as a bartender at the 2004 New Year's Eve Gala at the museum. Her assailant may have been at the gala, so the names of all guests, volunteers and staff are being entered into IDAS.
- *Trigg Pass Golf Course:* While they don't have the names of all golfers, the full or partial names they have and the names of the employees are being entered into IDAS.
- *Spectrum Boats:* Once the manifests for the river boats that Ronaldo and Oliver were working on are received, the passenger and crew names and itineraries will be entered into IDAS.

The Interview

"In 2010, you murdered Mari Oliver, she was your fifth victim. Everyone who boards a Spectrum boat is greeted personally by the concierge. She was the concierge on the cruise to Ukraine that you took and would have greeted you as you came aboard."

"She was a lovely young woman."

"And you killed her. How do you feel about that?"

"I'd gone to Europe to try to stop killing. She was the first one outside of Raleigh. Even though I wanted to kill her, I struggled so hard not to. I tried to talk myself out of it. I thought I had it under control. I was on my way back to the boat when I ran into her, and I gave in." Tracey's voice was dispassionate as he replied.

"Let me tell you about my conversations with Sasha Martinescu and Gia Delgado, about their friendship with Mari. They're your friends too, aren't they?"

"I haven't seen them in a while," he said quietly.

"Gia had known Mari all her life. When she was an infant, Mari would feed her and look after her whenever Gia and her mom would visit them. Mari taught her about fashion and makeup and gave her advice about boys. She said they were like sisters. She's still grieving. Mari helped her get her first job in Madrid and later a position on the Spectrum River Cruise Line. They were out together in Zaporizhzhya the morning you murdered Mari."

Jane paused, watching Tracey.

"Sasha had only known Mari for a few years. He's gay, and she was bisexual. She said he was the only one she could talk to about her lifestyle at first. Mari was one of the people Sasha reached out to when his partner died. Now, Mari's dead too. Sasha is recovering from her death, but he is still in pain."

Jane looked at Tracey to see if she could detect any reaction, but he sat so still, his face blank. She decided to deviate from her list of questions.

"So, when did Sasha change from being just a bartender, just part of the staff, to becoming a close friend?"

Tracey was caught off-guard by her question and thought for a second. "I met Sasha on that Ukraine cruise. We spent hours talking in the evenings, and I could tell that he was genuinely interested in my perspective on life. And," Tracey gave her a quick grin, "he was instrumental in me meeting my wife. It was through my friendship with Fong, a couple of years later, that I really connected with Sasha to become friends as well. He's a very wise man."

"But you killed Gia and Sasha's friends, Tracey. How does that feel?"

Tracey winced.

"Gia and Sasha are both survivors of Mari's murder. And you knew her too. That makes you a survivor."

Jane paused and took a sip of water and a long breath. "What I'd like now is to share with you some of Mari's favorite things. She was more than just a concierge."

After he had shifted positions and settled back in his chair, Tracey asked, "Why? Why are you doing this, Jane?"

"I want you to hear about the women you killed. You need to know them as real people whose lives you ended when you put your hand around their throats and squeezed the life out of them."

Tracey shut his eyes. *Is hearing these stories my penance for killing those women? What if I just get up and leave?* He drew a deep breath and tucked his shaking hands between his knees.

"Gia told me about Mari's true passion in life – flamenco dancing – about how much she practiced, how her dress had to be perfect, and the musicians she worked with had to be equally perfect. Gia showed me videos of her when she competed. She was a beautiful dancer.

"She and Gia and Sasha all worked together – but you know that. Did you know that they loved to get together in the evenings over food and wine and discuss their days, the passengers and life in general? They called these get-togethers their 'midnight soirees'."

"I've heard them talk about the midnight soirees."

"Did you know her favorite drink was Perrier with lime? That she liked to come into the bar in the early afternoon and have a quick chat with Sasha and the regular passengers before she went back to work? She said the conversations refreshed her as much as the drink."

She paused for a moment and leaned forward across the table, "Did you know those things about her, Tracey? Did you? *That* is Mari, the woman you strangled."

Tracey shoved his chair back, "Excuse me. I need to take a break."

Chapter Twelve

MEMORANDUM FOR THE RECORD

TO: Lieutenant Bobby Figg, Major Crimes Unit, Raleigh PD

CC: Tibor Papp, President, Security Consulting International Ltd.
Edgar Spring, Investigative Journalist

FROM: Penelope Huber, Consultant to Raleigh PD

DATE: April 11, 2014

SUBJECT: Parking Lot Strangler Investigation – Memo #3

This memo covers the week of April 5–11.

The data entry for MJW Expressions and the Lauch Art Museum into IDAS is now complete, and it has yielded dozens of corresponding names. There are too many at this stage, and work continues to narrow down the pool of potential persons of interest. It's very likely that the killer is somewhere in this list.

The three-step analytic process being used is outlined below:

1. *Data Entry:* The data must be added to IDAS with great care. The MJW guest book is handwritten, and the names can be difficult to read.
2. *Data Accuracy:* This step requires combing through the data and verifying first and last names. Names can be misspelled, or they may be nicknames versus given names. Any differences are identified and researched to see if there is more than one person by this name, and then, depending on the results of the research, the data may need to be corrected. All permutations of names and spellings will be entered.
3. *Data Analysis:* Finally, the data is analyzed using the functionality in IDAS to identify patterns and trends. This is iterative, and during this step, at times issues are found and the data must be rechecked for accuracy and reanalyzed.

European Developments

Papp is still working through red tape to obtain the case files from the police departments for Oliver and Ronaldo. The police departments in Zaporizhzhya and Strasbourg are reluctant to share their files. They don't feel that there is sufficient evidence indicating that the murders in their cities are part of the PLS case. His contacts have informed him there is political pressure from their departments not to jump to conclusions about a serial killer from the U.S. now killing in Europe.

Next Steps

As Papp's informal resources have not been fruitful, he is escalating his inquiry into the European cases with Interpol.

He will continue to liaise with his contacts throughout the European law enforcement community to see if additional murders with the same MO have occurred.

Huber to draw up a schedule for interviewing persons of interest or potential witnesses and start contacting individuals.

Spring to research media, especially, northern European news, to seek out similar murders which may be connected.

110

Chapter Thirteen

Tracey and Charlotte settled back into their comfortable first-class seats. The flight attendant had fastened a bassinet to the bulkhead in front of Charlotte, and Sarah was lying sprawled on her back, one hand closed around the satin edge of her soft baby blanket, her little bear clutched in the other. They'd noticed that she fussed far less when she had the small toy nearby. So, while parenting magazines and even their pediatrician recommended against toys in the baby's bed, they'd agreed to ignore that advice. They'd braced themselves for a rough flight, thinking the bear had been left behind when they packed for their extended trip, until Tracey discovered that he had absentmindedly tucked it into his jacket pocket. Crisis averted.

He held a flute of cold champagne in his hand. She picked up her own glass, filled with ginger ale, from the console between them and touched the rim to Tracey's, "To our future."

"To us."

She leaned over to look at Sarah, and with her free hand, tucked the blanket around her more snugly. "It's going to be a busy few months in Raleigh, my love. Do you want to talk about it?"

He smiled gratefully, "I know I've already said all this before but thanks for putting up with this need of mine to talk about this over and over." He loosened his seatbelt and turned toward her, "I've had that house for years. It'll be wrenching to see it go. But it's less about selling my house than disposing of all the belongings that have been in my family for generations. Some we can have shipped to Sicily – I need you to help me decide on those. Some of them will obviously go to Sarah's House. Some of the art can go to the museum. And some of it we'll sell."

While the flight attendants served their meal, they once again reviewed the lists in the little red notebook that Charlotte pulled from her carry-on bag.

Over coffee after dinner, Charlotte said, "We'll walk through the house together, over and over, until you're completely comfortable that we're making the right decision about each piece."

Once Charlotte had tucked the notebook back into her bag, Tracey took her hand, "I've also been thinking about my other commitments. As important as it is to me, as near to my heart, it's just not practical running Sarah's House from Sicily, you know, being on the phone with them every day. I'm not familiar with all the kids like I was when I was living in Raleigh, when I knew them all by name. It might be time to hand that off to someone else, someone local. I have a few people in mind."

"I know how much you've loved doing that." Charlotte leaned over and kissed his cheek, *Oh, how he badly needs to talk this through again.*

"I'm sad that I can't be there for those children anymore," he rubbed a hand over his face. "And being so far away all the time means I don't know what's going on in Raleigh, so I have less and less to contribute to the museum board. Frankly, though, my board position is something I'm looking forward to divesting myself of. It isn't something I've ever enjoyed the same way my parents and grandparents did."

"Nonetheless, Tracey, you're very good at it. No one would ever know that you don't enjoy every minute that you spend on museum matters."

"I guess we all have our little secrets," he said with a chuckle.

"That's a lot of changes you're planning to make."

"My whole life has changed since I met you – new friends in Europe, our home in Sicily, our new daughter, all the traveling we do…" Tracey reached up and twisted the stud in his left ear, thinking about his trip to Budapest with Fong, and the young woman he killed in the hills there, the one who had all the piercings. How he would be glad to tuck her tiny gold hoop away in the elaborately carved wooden box in his dressing room in Raleigh with the rest of the earrings he'd collected.

Tracey watched as Charlotte took her tablet from where she'd secured it beside her leg during takeoff, and then set it on the tray table in front of her. "More news articles about true crime?"

Charlotte chortled, "It's just for fun. It's grimly fascinating that people will kill other people for no apparent reason." She turned on the screen and began to type.

He watched her search before he continued, "I know you've been pushing me – gently mind you – to go talk to that young man, Mikey, who was mentioned in that newspaper article and may be my half-brother. When we get to Raleigh, I think I'll do that."

"Oh, you're going to have a DNA test?"

"No, remember that Edgar Spring interview you found online in the *Raleigh Weekly News* with all those pictures of Maggie and her family? And how I told you that she looks so similar to the way I remember my mother." Tracey had come to hate all the lies he had to tell to cover his killings. He was afraid at some point, he'd trip himself up, in particular when it came to Maggie. He'd known she was his mother the night he'd killed her.

Charlotte pulled up the article again and looked at the pictures, "I can see the resemblance between you. It's something about the eyes in particular." She nodded her head.

"Those pictures make me remember how she looked and smelled, her sparkly earrings, her perfume. She looks so familiar. I think that's enough reason to go talk to Mikey and see if we are related." He sipped his champagne and glanced at Charlotte, "I think it's time to see if Baby Sarah and I have any relatives on my side of the family."

Chapter Fourteen

Seated at the large worktable in the middle of her home office, Tibor and Penelope discussed the information about a St. Petersburg murder that one of his contacts had sent him. The local police had collected a lot of DNA from the scene, but since the woman had been a sex worker, they hadn't spent much time sorting through it or investigating her case. Sex workers were frequently killed in that area by the river, and often, no one knew their names or where they came from. The police had assumed her killer was just another client who'd gotten carried away during a bout of rough sex. With more than a little disgust, Tibor told Penelope that the St. Petersburg police claimed to have other priorities to deal with.

"I asked them to send the DNA results to Raleigh PD for comparison," said Tibor. "Meanwhile, I've been trying to get those manifests from Spectrum for over a month now. No luck so far, but I'll keep working at it. Personally, I think they are afraid that two of their employees being murdered in mid-cruise will taint their reputation."

He tapped his fingers lightly on the table, something she'd noticed he did when he was impatient, "After Emily's tipoff about her conversation with Sasha, I requested the case files for Mari Oliver's murder. Everything's the same as all the other murders – redhead, strangled by a left-handed person – likely a man from the size of the marks left by the killer's hand – and her right earring missing. And the details in the file from Strasbourg were almost a complete match as well – except that the victim didn't have red hair."

"I think we should keep the Strasbourg case on our list," said Penelope, "because, as Em pointed out, it's nearly identical to our murderer's MO."

Tibor gave a brief nod of agreement.

They looked up as Edgar used his shoulder to nudge open her office door, his arms full of rolls of paper. Once he'd dumped them on the end of the worktable, he walked around to where Tibor sat. Sticking out his hand, he said, "Edgar Spring,

119

investigative journalist for the *Raleigh Weekly News*."

Penelope pulled one knee up and rested her head on it, laughing to herself at Edgar and thinking back to how much he'd changed from when she'd first met him, when he stuttered and blushed and was scared of his own shadow – and of her as well.

Tibor put his hand out to Edgar, "Tibor Papp, European liaison for this case. Penelope mentioned you would be joining us."

"Nice to meet you, Mr. Papp." Edgar shoved his glasses up on his nose and pushed the items in the middle of the table to one side. He picked up a European map from the pile at the end of the table and unrolled it.

"Please, it's Tibor. We'll all be working as a team."

Edgar nodded absently, his mind already on the next subject. "Pens, I had this 'aha' moment last night – I called you but you didn't answer. So, I wanted to share it with you first thing this morning. When I knocked at your front door just now, and you didn't answer, I let myself in." He walked over to the cabinet that held a mini fridge. Opening it, he pulled out a bottle of water and asked over his shoulder, "Anyone else want water?" Without waiting for an answer, he handed each of them a bottle and came over to lean against the table.

"So, Eddie, what's this 'aha' moment you had?"

"After I thought about the St. Petersburg murder, it came to me. So, I went to this used bookstore near my house. They have a whole map section. Some of the maps are really old. Anyhow, I dug around until I found a European map. I didn't need a brand-new one. This is an old school map – see how it still has the staple holes where it was attached to the wood dowels? These are the coolest maps."

"Eddie…" Penelope shook her head and said to Tibor, "Just be patient. This is how Edgar processes information."

"Okay, okay. I wanted to see where all the international murders took place in relation to one another – to see if there's a connection. I could barely get to sleep after realizing this."

"This?" asked Tibor, his fingertips drumming on the table top.

"Well, you know all the U.S. murders were in Raleigh, except for the one in Trigg Pass. We have a lot of information about those, so I focused on the ones in Europe. See the bright green dots on the map? St. Petersburg, Strasbourg, Zaporizhzhya and Budapest. Do you notice anything?"

"Rivers," Tibor said in a low voice.

"Rivers," echoed Edgar affirmatively. He picked up another roll and flattened out a U.S. map beside the first one. "And Raleigh has a river too, the Neuse River. Then I looked closer at the location of Trigg Pass and what do you know?" He pointed to the bright green dots, first on the East Coast and then on the West.

"The Trigg River. I went out there last month to see the crime scene. I would love to go back there and go tubing," said Penelope.

"Yep, there's a river there too. Maybe our murderer is a fisherman, a kayaker, or just likes water sports. Maybe he finds his victims while he's there on vacation."

"We can't rule that out, but these European rivers are much, much larger." Tibor traced his finger along the Rhine River, "There is a lot of commercial traffic on them, they aren't just for recreational use."

"What kind of commercial traffic?" asked Edgar.

"Barges, ferries, cruise boats…"

Edgar smiled, "Oh… my… God. Like Spectrum?"

"Precisely. Let's see who's on those Spectrum cruise lists we've already requested," said Tibor, "before we broaden our search."

The Interview

When Tracey returned, Jane was looking down at her notes, rapidly clicking her pen with her thumb. As he sat back down, she put aside her notes and the pen. "There were three sets of responses," she said, making hard eye-contact, "that I found unusual because they didn't fit my preconceptions. There were some family members who had written off the women you killed even before they were murdered."

Tracey watched her silently.

"I went to St. Petersburg, to the place where the sex worker was strangled. I couldn't talk to her family because the police had never been able to discover her name. Her body was never claimed. She had become just another whatever Russians call a Jane Doe in their system. It's as though, somewhere along the line," Jane said with a hitch in her voice, "she'd ceased to exist. I wondered if the situation was the same with her family, if she no longer existed to them either. Didn't they worry about her? Didn't they wonder where she was, what had happened to her?"

"She was a prostitute who approached me on the street. I tried to resist her advances. I sent her away. Then, suddenly I had an overwhelming urge to strangle her. So, I called her back. She's the only one to that point who I interacted with socially. I had a drink with her." A tiny smile touched the corners of his mouth for a moment as he recalled her confusion over the name of her drink. "She wanted a Manhattan, but she told me she wanted New York."

Jane wrinkled her forehead at his smile but stayed silent.

"Afterwards, she took me to an isolated place beneath a bridge abutment. We had sex. And then I strangled her," he said matter-of-factly.

"I can only presume that she was a woman who happened to work in the sex trade to support herself." Her voice shook at his nonchalance.

"I left her a hundred euros. She couldn't use it, but I guess I figured she'd earned it. I'm afraid she didn't matter much to me either." He sighed and whispered almost to himself, "What does that say about me? Quite a sorry indictment, I'm afraid."

"Indeed it is. And the woman you killed in Budapest? Katalin Arany."

"Ah, the young woman with the skateboard."

"Her family said Katalin's lifestyle would catch up with her. All the piercings, her tattoos, her whole attitude toward life, living for the moment— Her parents were sure her bohemian ways had her rubbing shoulders with the less savory side of society, drug dealers, gang members, that kind of thing. They weren't surprised when she showed up dead. They didn't seem to care." Jane looked down and swallowed hard, "I found that incredibly sad."

Tracey reached out across the table as though he wanted to comfort her, but unsure about how she might react, he pulled his hand back and rested it on the table in front of him.

She continued, with her head down at first, as though she were reading from her notes, "Even Zoe Abrams, the bartender you murdered after the gala, her family were saddened but not surprised. She apparently didn't listen to them when they gave her advice. They felt she had made a whole series of bad decisions." Jane looked up at Tracey, "In their minds, her bartending job was just one of those poor decisions. Being out late at night, serving alcohol to strangers. It wasn't even in a regular bar with a regular clientele, people who might know her, look out for her, notice something out of the ordinary. Her jobs were different events with different people each time and no one to care."

Tracey's eyes were sad as he looked back at Jane, "How unfortunate that some of the women's families cared so little about them. That they seem to have written off their daughters because they chose to live their lives in a way their parents objected to."

"You voice such compassion for these women. Why do you think that is?"

"Perhaps because they were abandoned by their families – like I was."

"Do you regret it? Do you regret killing them?"

He noticed how sad Jane's face had become and leaned forward, "In response to your question, yes, I do regret it. I wish I'd never started. When my wife got pregnant and then our daughter was born, I realized I couldn't continue killing. But it's hard, very hard to stop. Every now and again, when the right woman's gone by, I've still been tempted."

Slumping back in his chair, he went on, "It was an addiction, the sexual excitement I felt – when I strangled them, and—" he paused, his face reddening at the memories of the intense pleasure when he climaxed holding an earring in his hand, "—and when I relived it later. I couldn't stop."

Chapter Fifteen

MEMORANDUM FOR THE RECORD

TO: Lieutenant Bobby Figg, Major Crimes Unit, Raleigh PD

CC: Tibor Papp, President, Security Consulting International Ltd.
           Edgar Spring, Investigative Journalist

FROM: Penelope Huber, Consultant to Raleigh PD

DATE: April 25, 2014

SUBJECT: Parking Lot Strangler Investigation – Memo #5

This memo covers the week of April 19–25.

Within IDAS, dozens of names overlap from the MJW Expressions guest book and the gala list.

The investigation has extended to entering into IDAS license plate and vehicle registration data from private golf clubs throughout the Raleigh area. It is believed the murderer may be a golfer, because Jones was murdered in the parking lot at the Trigg Pass Golf Course in a similar manner to the Raleigh women.

We intend to narrow down our search by first looking at high-end, private clubs, in line with the profile of the potential suspect (likely to be high status and well-resourced), before moving on to municipal courses if need be.

European Developments

Papp has made significant progress this week. With the assistance of Interpol, he obtained copies of the Oliver and Ronaldo case files. In Oliver's case, the pattern was the same as all the other PLS murders. Ronaldo wasn't a complete match (victim profile deviation - hair color).

There was no video footage from the area of the Oliver murder. However, there was a camera covering the street from the front of the Hotel Le Fleuve to the entrance to the alley where Ronaldo was strangled. A man approximately six feet tall was seen in the footage just prior to the murder. He exited the bar across the street from the hotel and crossed over, where he entered the alley just after Ronaldo turned into it. However, his hat was pulled low against the rain and obscured his face. Strasbourg's case file stated that they interviewed the employees in the bar, but no one remembered the man. It was Valentine's night, and they were very busy.

The team has a new theory that, given the location of the European murders, the killer may be traveling on river boats. Therefore, in order to identify possible persons of interest, Papp has requested subpoenas for manifests, with particular emphasis on the passengers for the Spectrum river boat cruises that the victims were working on at the time of their murders.

Papp's contact in St. Petersburg identified an unknown sex worker who was murdered under a bridge in the same manner as the other Parking Lot Strangler victims. From everything he heard, the MO of this murder is identical to that of the PLS murders. Investigators in St. Petersburg said DNA was found at the scene of the crime; they agreed to send copies of the case file and DNA results to Papp after some pressure for cooperation from Interpol. At present, there is no connection between this murder and any river boats.

Factoring in this new information and placing the deaths in chronological order (recent discoveries shown in bold italics), one can speculate that the PLS has moved his killing to Europe and simply made a trip back to Washington when he murdered Jones:

1. April 1998, Maggie Wilson, Raleigh, NC
2. January 2002, Ruth Sampson, Raleigh, NC
3. January 2005, Zoe Abrams, Raleigh, NC; DNA
4. December 2007, Sheila Kovacs, Raleigh, NC
5. *August 2010, Mari Oliver, Zaporizhzhya, Ukraine*
6. March 2011, Sophie Jones, Trigg Pass, WA; DNA

Page 2 of 3

7. *August 2011, Unknown Sex Worker, St. Petersburg, Russia; possible DNA*
8. *February 2012, Isabelle Ronaldo, Strasbourg, France*
9. May 2012, Katalin Arany, Budapest, Hungary; DNA

Next Steps

Continued collection, processing and analysis of data, overseen by Huber.

Continued search for additional victims by Papp and Spring.

Papp to continue to pursue the Spectrum manifests.

Once Papp receives the DNA results from the St. Petersburg murder, they will be passed to the PD to compare with that found at the Abrams, Jones and Arany crime scenes.

Chapter Sixteen

Laying the memo describing the river connection on the table in front of him, Bobby spoke thoughtfully, "Originally, I didn't think there was any way we would solve this. Not a snowball's chance in hell." He winked at her, knowing how Penelope loved to sneak a cliché in wherever possible. Then, moving the memo with the pads of his fingers, he continued, "Now I think there's a real possibility we'll be able to get this guy. You know, it never would have occurred to me that there might be a river connection. That's good work by your team."

"Thanks. See, having Edgar around was a good idea."

"Thank goodness we're not paying him, though," they chucked companionably.

Bobby looked across at Penelope. He'd missed her so very much over the previous month. Yeah, they still met weekly for lunch to discuss the team's progress on the case, but that was work. He missed her. Her shiny hair that she'd cut a bit shorter, so the front parts framed her face, making her look younger than her forty-three years. The feel of those silky locks sliding through his fingers. Her fresh, clear skin that tinged a rosy red when they made love. Her fingers on his chest and back and— He felt his heart beat faster, his face flush, and he leaned toward her. *These weekly lunches just aren't cutting it. What I really want—* He saw Penelope's face light up, but quickly realized it was at something behind him. Curious, he turned his head to follow her gaze.

"I see you two are hanging out at the same old place," Hugo shook his long-lost friend's hand. "Hey, Bobby – s'been a long time, I was so sorry to hear about Hallie." He motioned for Penelope to move over in the booth and waved to Pete for a beer. "I'm afraid I haven't been very good at keeping in touch with anyone."

"No shit," Penelope muttered under her breath.

"Thanks. It's been a tough couple of years. I'm coming out of it though." He looked over at Penelope, and his eyes softened.

Hugo caught his look, "Hey, are you two an item?" He bumped his leg against Penelope's. She looked at Bobby and then at Hugo and scooted away.

Bobby opened his mouth to acknowledge to his old friend that, yes, he and Penelope were becoming an item when she broke in and said, with an emphatic shake of her head, "No, we just work together. In fact, I'm working *for* Bobby right now."

"We were becoming an item when Pens came back to work for me, and we had to take a break." Penelope glared at him for sharing that. "Are you just back to visit your family?" Bobby asked hopefully.

"Actually, I've taken a job at the hospital. In the emergency room." Hugo took a swig of his beer, "And since you two aren't together, you won't mind if I cut in on you."

Bobby watched the way Hugo looked at her, at the way she responded to him. An itch of annoyance scratched under his skin at her refusal to be open about their own relationship. In fact, that she hadn't acknowledged it at all really burned him. Hugo had just waltzed in, ready to snatch her up, pick up where they'd left off, and her face looked like she might welcome that. And he couldn't do a damn thing about it because he was her boss.

Penelope said, "So does this mean you're back for good? Because I've never heard you say anything was 'for good'."

"Except you," Hugo said suggestively. "So yeah, it could be. People change. D'you mind if I come by tonight? I need my stuff. Maybe I'll even take you to dinner."

Bobby watched as Penelope bristled at Hugo's attitude and gave himself a mental grin, *Let's see how that goes.* "I've got to get back to the office." He picked up the memo, "Thanks for the update, kid. If I don't see you before then, I'll see you here next Friday." Bobby glanced back at the two of them, alone together at his and Penelope's table, and fingers of jealousy clawed at him.

While he was settling their bill with Pete at the bar, Bobby overheard Penelope losing it at Hugo, "Where the hell do you get off assuming that we'll pick up right where we were before you left? That I'll even be home tonight for you to come by and get that stuff you left with me when you went off unannounced? What makes you think I kept your stuff? For fifteen years, Hugo! *You* divorced *me*."

They're already at it. Bobby shared a grin with Pete, *Maybe I have a chance after all.*

*

Penelope returned from her afternoon run and jumped into the shower. As she stood, wrapped in a towel, blow-drying her freshly shampooed hair, she said to herself in the mirror, "How much effort do I want to put into this? He walked out on me and now…" She glanced down at her curling iron, "I don't want him to think I'm excited to see him," she grumbled, still annoyed at his attitude at the bar. Her training session hadn't managed to ease her indignation. She looked at the curling iron again, "Nope. Too much. Another day – if there is one."

She pulled open the drawer to the vanity and took out her mascara. Then she flipped through the bin of makeup and chose her palest eyeshadow and a tube of natural lipstick. She leaned close to the mirror as she applied her makeup, still talking to herself, "What I want is to look good, but not like I've done it for him. A woman needs her pride after all."

She pulled several sweaters out of her dresser drawer and held each one up against her, "Nope, too dressy. No, this one is too heavy. This one is too old. This one makes me look huge." She picked up the final two and looked at the pale blue and peach cashmere sweaters. "Cashmere says I care about me. But it's soft and feels nice, just in case. Def the peach one with the lower V-neck – it makes me look prettier and a little sexy." She tossed the blue sweater onto the bed with the others.

She pulled the peach one over her head and slipped on her favorite skinny jeans and then wandered over to her closet. She stood there indecisively for a moment, "Flats or heels? Heels. They make my legs look longer." She told herself it had nothing to do with the fact that Hugo always liked them. She picked up her fave pair of beige heels.

Downstairs, she checked to see that the door was unlocked and tossed her shoes under the table in the front entry, the table with the mirror she'd bought in Mexico, the spot where she always dropped her purse and keys on the way in and checked her hair and makeup on her way out. She and Hugo had agreed that a designated drop zone for all the little bits of stuff they both carried, keys, wallet, purse, phones, would keep that kind of clutter in one small area. The little table that they'd picked out together was one of the few pieces of furniture she'd never bothered to replace. It really was perfect in that spot.

She went on into the kitchen and took a beer from her fridge before wandering into the living room, where she propped her bare feet on the coffee table and flicked on the TV. As she drank her beer and rolled through the channels, Penelope was nervous, excited and annoyed that she cared enough to do all this after he dumped her, that she cared enough to hope again. *Maybe,* she thought, *I should have just left the key for him under the front door mat and not been here.*

From the beginning of their affair, Penelope had felt that with Bobby, there had been a chance of something solid. *But, this is Hugo. Is he gonna drop back into my life, I fall for him again, and then he's gone, and I get hurt – again?* "And why do I feel like I'm cheating on Bobby? We agreed to date other people during our break. That's what this is, right?" she muttered to herself.

Penelope heard the front door open and stood up slowly as he came in. Hugo walked over and leaned down to kiss her, but she turned her cheek toward him.

"So, what, you think I have cooties?" he said. They both laughed at the old joke between them that had started because when he came home from work in the hospital, Penelope didn't want him to kiss her or touch her until after he'd showered and she was sure he didn't have any germs that he would share with her.

"You just drop back into my life after all this time and think you can pick up where we left off?"

"It's worth a try."

"But you divorced me – through the mail no less. You didn't even have the decency to tell me to my face that you wanted a divorce."

"You wouldn't move with me."

"Why would I give up the ten years I had already invested in my career with the PD?"

"Because we were married?"

Do I really want to get into this? She pointed toward the basement door, "Your stuff is down there."

After he'd finished loading up his SUV, he grinned, "So I guess I should buy you dinner as a thank-you for taking care of my stuff all this time. What do you think?" He took her hand and gently rubbed the inside of her wrist with his thumb.

Oh no, he always used to do that because he knew it made me weak in the knees and ready to fall into bed with him. "Don't!" She pulled her hand away slowly, reluctantly. "Just dinner, Hugo."

Chapter Seventeen

Tracey pulled up in front of the Wilsons' house and turned off the ignition. He leaned back in the seat and closed his eyes. As he'd promised Charlotte, once they'd settled into the house in Raleigh, he'd made the phone call to Michael Wilson, who'd told him he goes by Mike now. They chatted briefly and set up a meeting. *Why am I here,* he wondered, *other than to satisfy Charlotte's curiosity?* She'd wanted so badly to come along. He chuckled to himself – at least now, she'd finally stop pressing him to make contact.

He hadn't told Mike much, other than who he was and that he wanted to talk with him and his son, Mikey, about Mike's late wife, Maggie Jackson Wilson. He'd said it was too complicated to discuss over the phone. Admittedly, he was curious about what kind of young man Mikey had grown up to be. The only other time Tracey had seen him, he'd been four years old and had been crying for his mother. At that age, he hadn't understood that she was dead and never coming back. In the quotes Edgar used when he interviewed him years later for his series about the victims of the Parking Lot Strangler, Mikey had sounded thoughtful and intelligent.

Here he was, about to come face to face with his half-brother – his mother's other son. As he pulled the key from the ignition, Tracey ran through what he would tell them. This would be the first time he would share the lies he'd spun for Charlotte, that he thought that Maggie might be his mother, that he'd recognized her from the newspaper interview. These were the lies he would now need to keep straight in his conversation with the Wilsons.

Tracey realized he had been parked in front of the house for several minutes, lost in his thoughts as he tried to figure out what he was going to say when they opened the door. From the corner of his eye, he saw the curtain in the living room window move slightly and realized it was time to get on with it. He set his phone to airplane mode and then opened his door and climbed out of the car. On his way up the long brick walkway to the modest ranch house, he unbuttoned the cuffs to his shirt and turned them up twice, trying for a slightly casual look.

Before he'd done more than raise his hand to knock, a man of average height with a graying walrus mustache, kind eyes and a little pot belly opened the door. He was an older, slightly more tired version of the man whom Tracey had met at Maggie's funeral. Behind him, with his hand on his father's shoulder, stood a tall, lean young man with red hair and green eyes – an adult version of what Tracey remembered from the funeral. The young man bore a marked resemblance to Maggie.

While still standing on the front porch, Tracey introduced himself and said that he was on the board of the Lauch Art Museum where there had been an exhibition of Maggie's work many years ago.

"Well, let's not just stand here," said Mike. "Come on in. I've just put on a pot of coffee."

They settled on chairs in the living room, and Tracey picked up the thread of his story. "I was looking at one of Maggie's paintings shortly after the exhibition opened when a lovely, red-headed woman walked up and stood next to me. I said something like, 'I really admire this artist's work.' She thanked me and told me she was the artist. I asked her about her other pieces, and we had a lengthy conversation about her art. She was truly gifted. It was such a privilege to spend that time with her."

Mike paused for a moment as he thought about his first wife, "She told me about meeting you and how knowledgeably you spoke about abstract art when the two of you talked, about her choice of media and the meanings behind her work. She was impressed that you, as a member of the board, would spend so much time with her. And she appreciated that you came to visit her gallery after that." He looked over at Tracey, "I'm sorry that I never thanked you for coming to her funeral. It meant a lot to me."

"It meant a lot to me too," replied Tracey. "We spent a long time together that afternoon at the museum. There was something very familiar about her." Uncomfortable with what he was about to say, Tracey cleared his throat, "But at that time, I wasn't able to put my finger on it." He shifted awkwardly in his chair. The truth was that when he had met Maggie at the Lauch Art Museum, he had immediately recognized her.

Instead, he explained that his wife, Charlotte, had come across an article, written by Edgar Spring, with photos of Maggie. In the pictures in the article, he said it was something about the way she held her head and leaned toward Mikey, something in her eyes that made him think she might be his mother as well. She looked exactly as he had remembered his mom, Tracey said – red hair, kind, green eyes, sparkly earrings, leaning toward him in that same loving fashion. He told Mike and Mikey that he had absolutely no documentation to prove that he was Maggie's son. Just an overwhelming feeling of familiarity based on the newspaper pictures accompanying Edgar's interview. He said it was the same sense of familiarity he'd felt that afternoon years earlier when he met her in the museum.

Tracey looked at Mike, "I hope together we can figure this out."

Mike stood up, "Let me get that coffee. Keep going, I can hear you from the kitchen."

Tracey went on, speaking a little more loudly for Mike's sake. After the birth of their daughter, Charlotte wanted to know more about his family background and pressed him to reach out to the two of them. She hoped that Tracey could finally find out more about his past, even if it had been many years since his mother's death.

Mike brought the coffee on a tray with cups and saucers and small spoons, a bowl of sugar and a pitcher of cream, and they talked about Maggie and her life before she met Mike. Pieces fell into place in Tracey's mind as Mike told them that she'd been a sex worker for a time, and the night she'd been arrested, the two children had been taken away by Child Protective Services.

Mikey gasped, "Why am I just hearing this now?"

Mike reached over and touched his son's knee, "There was never a good time. And I didn't want that short part of her life to define her – she did what she had to do to bring money in, and I think she was extraordinarily selfless in doing so. As well as being an artist, she taught art classes for underprivileged young women.

It was a way of passing on the support she wished she could have had, she'd said."

Tracey sat very still, feigning astonishment at Mike's words.

Mike looked first at Mikey and then at Tracey, "I'm sorry to have shocked you both." He motioned to the coffee table, "Let's drink our coffee before it gets cold. There's more I need to tell you." Mike filled the cups and handed them around.

Using the sugar spoon that lay on a saucer beneath the bowl, Tracey added two cubes to his cup and returned the spoon to its place. As he reached for the cream pitcher, his shirt sleeve pulled up.

"Man, that's some birthmark!" Mikey pointed at the two vivid red streaks on Tracey's forearm.

Tracey gave him a quick grin, shrugged one shoulder, lifted his hand slightly and pulled his right sleeve up farther. He glanced down at it, "Yeah, it is, isn't it?"

Mike looked at Tracey's arm thoughtfully, and after a long moment, he raised his index finger, "Hold on. I've got something to show you."

While he was gone, Mikey and Tracey sipped their coffee and made uncomfortable small talk.

Mike came back into the room with an old box in his hands. Setting it on the coffee table, he riffled through it and pulled out an envelope of photographs. "Here. I knew I'd seen a birthmark just like that before." He handed Tracey a photo of a young blond girl with big blue eyes and a boy with brown hair and green eyes showing off his birthmark, with Maggie grinning in the background.

Something shifted inside and a feeling of warmth filled him as Tracey held the small photograph by one corner, tapping it lightly against his fingertips. Cautiously, he shared what he remembered about the day the photo had been taken. "My mom kept telling me how special I was to have that mark on my arm. No one else had anything like that. She asked one of our neighbors to take that picture of the three of us – me, my sister, and our mom – celebrating my birthmark. She made me feel so proud of it – until later, when I got teased about it in school."

"So… you're my… brother? Awesome! I have a brother."

"I think so," Tracey nodded his head. "And that would mean that somewhere out there, you and I have a sister, my twin." He looked at Mikey with a smile, "Her name is Sarah. When I founded Sarah's House, I named it after her."

Mike gave Tracey a quick look, startled that he knew Sarah's name. "I have to confess, I'm still a bit skeptical about you being related to Maggie." Mike's voice drifted off, and he looked back and forth between Tracey and Mikey with troubled eyes.

"What's wrong, Mike?"

Mike stared down at the floor, and then, with his eyes filled with compassion, he looked at Tracey, "I said there was something more I had to tell you – assuming you're related to Maggie, I'm sorry to tell you that she wasn't your mother."

"I don't understand," Tracey shook his head. "I have so many memories. I remember her so clearly. What about the pictures?"

"Dad, what? He's not my brother? So, now, I don't have a brother? This is getting very confusing. What's going on, Dad?"

Mike explained that Tracey's mother would have been Maggie's younger sister, Anna. She had gotten pregnant out of wedlock, her parents had kicked her out of their house, and she and her sister had gone to live in Raleigh. When Anna died, her twins were still infants, and Maggie continued to take care of them. The sisters were the spitting image of one another, so Maggie had them call her Mommy – it was just easier for her that way.

"She said she had planned to tell them when they were older," said Mike.

Tracey's face turned deathly pale as the reality of his actions struck him. He shook his head in disbelief, "So… you're telling me the woman I thought was my mom… was my aunt?"

Mike nodded.

Like a video tape, Tracey's life rewound and then replayed with the new reality.

Fuck. I didn't kill my mother. I killed my aunt…

"Can I get you a glass of water?" Mike asked Tracey.

He nodded, "Please."

After Tracey recovered somewhat from his shock, they continued to talk about Maggie and Anna. Looking through the items in the box slowly, one after another, they talked for a long time. And as they talked, Mike became more comfortable that Tracey was Anna's son and Sarah's brother.

Tracey and then Mikey had a lot of questions for his father, and as Mike answered one question after another, Tracey felt his head begin to pound in a familiar headache, one like he'd often suffered ever since he'd hit his head on the rock on the playground as a young child, headaches that came on when he was under a lot of stress. The longer the conversation went on, the worse he began to feel, and finally, he excused himself.

*

When they'd closed the door behind him, Mikey said to his dad, "I'm so excited to have met Tracey, even if he's not my brother. And I now know I have a female cousin too." He grinned at his dad with the exact same grin as Maggie's. "I know Tracey made it clear that he won't do a DNA test—"

"It seems pretty clear that he's related to Maggie and Anna, but without DNA to confirm it, in my mind, we can't be completely certain."

"How many birthmarks like that are out there? And he knew Sarah's name before he even saw the birth certificate or even looked at the back of the picture. I saw how surprised you were at that. I'm sure it's him, Dad."

A little sarcastically, Mike said, "Well, it's not like I'm writing him into my will or anything."

"I think he's an interesting guy. I'd like to get to know him better."

Mike looked at his son and grinned, "I know you'll do what you want."

"Hey, you know what's really weird? A few weeks ago, I submitted a sample to MyDNA for a forensics class. Since Tracey and I are," he paused, his eyes twinkling with excitement, "cousins, or most likely cousins, then maybe I can find Sarah. And," he looked at his dad with a grin, "that would mean that Tracey would find his sister."

"Don't you think you should talk to Tracey about this?"

"No, I don't want to disappoint him if nothing comes of it. But, Dad, think how surprised he'll be if we find Sarah."

*

Tracey hurried down the long walkway to his car, feeling like he might throw up at any moment. He'd promised to call Charlotte as soon as he'd left the Wilsons' house and tell her how it had gone. But his head was throbbing and his mind raging. He just needed some time.

My mother died? And the woman I killed was my aunt? Fuck!

He turned the key in the ignition and pulled away from the curb. Driving aimlessly through Raleigh's streets, he ultimately found himself in front of the building that had formerly housed Maggie's gallery. He pulled to the curb and turned off the car, leaning his face in his hands, recalling how he'd parked there the afternoon of Maggie's funeral.

Over and over, memories of the night he murdered her ran through his head. And memories of all the women he'd killed since then. *I wonder if I would have killed them if Maggie had told me, if she'd brought me home to meet her family. Fuck! My aunt?*

He shook his head violently, trying to get rid of the thoughts. But that only made his headache worse. *I wonder if my life would have been different if I'd known that she wasn't my mother. If I'd known that my mother had died, and Maggie had raised us for four years? If I'd known that she'd done her best. If I'd known that Maggie was arrested for prostitution and didn't abandon us? If Sarah and I hadn't been separated. I wonder if I would have killed my... Maggie. I wonder what—*

Sick to his stomach, feeling as lost and confused and alone as he had at four years old, he put his arms on the steering wheel and buried his head in them and wept.

Chapter Eighteen

MEMORANDUM FOR THE RECORD

TO: Lieutenant Bobby Figg, Major Crimes Unit, Raleigh PD

CC: Tibor Papp, President, Security Consulting International Ltd.
Edgar Spring, Investigative Journalist

FROM: Penelope Huber, Consultant to Raleigh PD

DATE: May 9, 2014

SUBJECT: Parking Lot Strangler Investigation – Memo #7

This memo covers the week of May 3–9.

There continue to be dozens of redundant names in IDAS. It is anticipated they will be narrowed significantly once the Spectrum data is entered, checked and analyzed.

European Developments

Papp is still waiting on DNA results from the St. Petersburg police department regarding the murder of the unidentified sex worker. There have been a number of delays getting this evidence, and he is trying to find someone in St. Petersburg who can cut through their red tape.

Additional data to be added to IDAS:
- The manifest for the Spectrum cruise that Ronaldo was working on has just arrived.
- Spectrum has agreed to provide the manifest for the cruise Oliver was working on. It is expected to arrive next week.

Papp has reached out to all of his contacts throughout Europe. If they come across anything new, they've agreed to contact him.

Next Steps

If the DNA from the St. Petersburg sex worker matches the other DNA, the team agrees that four matches in three countries will be sufficient to try to get a warrant approved for MyDNA. MyDNA is the largest worldwide familial genetic testing company with the largest database of DNA. The team recommends the Raleigh PD submit a written affidavit for a warrant to a judge in Indianapolis, Indiana, where the company is headquartered.

The Spectrum data will be added to IDAS as it is received. To be overseen by Huber.

Papp recommended that the net be cast wider to include all manifests, not only for Spectrum boats but all river boats that stopped in Zaporizhzhya, Strasbourg, Budapest and St. Petersburg on the days of and four days surrounding the murders. He pointed out that most cruise lines have more than one boat docked in a location during the same timeframe. This frequently happens when one boat is traveling downriver while another is traveling upriver. To be spearheaded by Papp.

Page 2 of 2

156

Chapter Nineteen

Seated in their regular booth at In The Alley, Bobby and Penelope had been discussing the PLS case and the information in her latest memo. As Pete set their lunches in front of them, Bobby concluded their discussion, "You know how much I appreciate all the background information on your thinking. It helps me sound smarter to my bosses." He grinned at her, "And we all want to sound smarter to our bosses, don't we?"

Penelope nodded.

"You seem to be a little distracted today," Bobby said. "Is everything okay?"

She picked up a french fry and swirled it through the puddle of ketchup she'd squirted from the bottle, raised it to her mouth and then dropped it back on her plate. Avoiding his eyes, she blurted out, "Hugo wants to see if we can make it work again now that he's here instead of thousands of miles away."

No way. "What do you want?" Bobby bit into his burger and waited.

Penelope pulled the top of the bun off her burger and slowly removed the lettuce and tomato, leaving just the bacon and cheese. With a slice of bacon in her fingers, she said thoughtfully, "What we have is so good right now. He's considerate and not such a macho guy anymore. He asks my opinion about what we do together. He never used to do that. I think Hugo has changed." She crunched down on the bacon, enjoying the smoky flavor. It was crisp, just the way she liked it.

With his mouth full, he rolled his eyes, then he swallowed and said, "Or he's acting like he's changed. Really? How long do you think that will last?"

"You can roll your eyes all you want, Figg. You know full well how lost I was when Hugo left. I was so young when we got married. I was such an idealist. And then he just left me."

When Hugo had gone off to join Doctors Without Borders with virtually no discussion of her reluctance to join his adventure – after ten years of marriage, mind you – and then divorced her with no communication a few months later, Penelope had been devastated. She'd been so in love, investing all her emotions in their relationship, supporting him through medical school and his internship, while at the same time, putting years of hard work into her own career. When he left, she shut everyone out and just curled up inside herself. She swore off men and didn't let herself date or become emotionally involved again. It hurt too much. If she could have Googled it back then, she'd have chosen the word "bereft" to describe how she felt.

"I thought I was fine with settling for work," she said, looking down at the remains of the perfectly good strip of bacon that she'd slowly demolished between her fingertips, "and my friendship with you and Hallie."

Then Bobby was there, wanting more from her than she was able to give. But when he'd agreed to "just sex and good times", she'd thought it would be okay. She'd thought that maybe someday, she'd even be able to let go and allow herself to care for Bobby.

But Hugo had shown up.

She looked up at Bobby, pleading for his understanding, "I thought I had dealt with it over a decade ago, but I didn't realize until I saw him again that he'd left me still wanting him. I need to figure out if it's just a memory of what we had or if it's real. There's so much unresolved stuff between us. I need to make sure there are no ghosts, whatever choice I make."

"And you said *I* needed to date other people?" He crammed several fries into his mouth and chewed hard.

"I think I said that we both should. I never dreamed that Hugo would be back for good."

Bobby picked up his beer as his spine stiffened, "And you're willing to open yourself up to being hurt again – after what he did to you last time?" He took a long drink and set the glass down hard on the table, sloshing the beer perilously close to the top.

"I have to try. It's unfinished business right now. No matter which way it goes, I have to make sure." Penelope held her beer in her hand, making concentric circles on the tabletop with the moisture from the bottom of the glass.

Bobby shoved a coaster her way. "Here, you're making a

mess." He broke a fry in half and put one part in his mouth, "I figured you were seeing him again. I saw his SUV in your driveway the other morning. It was early." He popped the other half into his mouth.

"You're spying on me?" Penelope snapped.

"I was just driving by," he mumbled and looked at her with eyes that showed how badly seeing that Hugo was there had hurt him.

"Driving by? There's nothing out there to drive by except a bunch of houses, including mine. It isn't on the way to anything. Are you jealous, Figg?"

"So, I'm jealous," Bobby shoved his plate away. Suddenly, he'd lost his appetite. He counted to three like they'd taught them in his conflict resolution classes, "I want to be the one with you, not him."

"That is so not fair. You can't come and tell me that you're jealous that I'm dating when we've agreed to date other people."

"There was nothing in our agreement about getting back together with ex-husbands. And *you* agreed. I'm not sure I ever did." Bobby took a huge gulp from his glass and then another.

"There was nothing in that agreement that said I couldn't."

"It's only natural for me to be jealous," he said in a low voice. "I've already said I'm falling for you."

Frustrated that he just didn't seem to understand where she was at, that he didn't seem very concerned about her happiness, she asked, "And what happened to just sex and good times?"

He waved to Pete for the bill and pulled out his wallet, "What happened to sex and good times? There's no more sex and good times for me in this. This serial killer – and fucking Hugo – have taken care of that."

Chapter Twenty

A week later, Penelope stood at the sink in the bathroom at In The Alley. These meetings with Bobby had always been a chance for them to see each other in a less formal way than in his office. Before Hugo came back, Bobby used to sit in the booth across from her and find an excuse to touch her arm or hand or find her foot under the table with his. His looks had been flirtatious, and she'd thrilled inside at those unspoken thoughts. She missed the way Bobby always used to call her kid. He didn't do that anymore.

Then she looked in the mirror and shook a mental finger at herself, "Penelope, what's going on? You're acting like a teenager who can't make up her mind between two boys. You want to have your cake and eat it too? Well, you can't. You say you've chosen Hugo – but you still lust after Bobby. You went for years with just work. No distractions, just work. Now, you have two hard-to-say-no-to male distractions – and a deadline to solve the murders with all the support you need to do it. Get it together, Pens. Being back on this case with the luxury of no other work is what you wanted." She glared at herself, and with her shoulders back and her chin level, she walked back to their booth and slid in.

Bobby looked up and said in a cool, impersonal tone, "Anything else before I head back to the office?"

With one hand holding the back of her neck, Penelope shook her head to clear it, "Uh, yeah, one more thing." She checked her watch. "I got a call from a Judge Tracey Lauch. He said he had some information he wanted to share with me, but he wouldn't elaborate. The only connection I can find between Judge Lauch and the investigation is the 2004 museum gala and the murder early the following morning."

"Maybe he has some additional information about Zoe's murder," said Bobby. "Maybe he's remembered something he saw. After all, he and his family hosted the gala, and we know he was there the night she was killed."

Penelope explained that he'd come up during the investigation, but after his call, she'd done some digging into the judge's past. Speaking rapidly, glancing at her watch again, she summarized, "He was adopted at about the age of five. When his grandparents downsized, they donated their large estate on the outskirts of Raleigh for the private foster home called Sarah's House that he founded. He'd been a compassionate lawyer who'd specialized in family law, and apparently, he'd carried that compassion over for the brief years he served as a judge. His family had tons of money, and after his grandparents and then his parents died, he inherited everything. He's obscenely wealthy and retired about four years ago. Now, for some reason, he wants to talk to me."

As she slid out of the booth, Bobby said, "Let me know what he has to say."

"We're meeting at his house this afternoon at two o'clock." She looked at her watch yet again, "Oops, now, I've really gotta dash."

*

She stopped at the bottom of the steps to Tracey's house, touched her hair to make sure none of it had slipped from its ponytail and checked her watch, "One fifty-eight. Two minutes early. Well done, Pens," she murmured to herself as she looked up at the broad porch with its groupings of white rockers on either side. Enormous ferns hung from iron hooks on the row of two-story pillars that spanned the width of the porch.

I wonder if he'll have anything new to tell me, anything I don't already know, something that might provide the break we need. A frisson of excitement tingled along her spine as she put her foot on the first step.

At her knock, a tall, trim, middle-aged man with salt-and-pepper hair opened the door. Startled at how young the woman in front of him appeared to be, he gave a slight frown before introducing himself. "I'm Tracey Lauch. You must be Penelope. Come in."

"Penelope Huber," she stuck her hand out and gave him a firm handshake that matched his. Mirroring his look, she frowned slightly, looked him up and down and, standing ramrod straight, said in her most official, police-officer voice, designed to intimidate witnesses, "Retired family court judge. Member of the Lauch Art Museum Board of Directors. Founder of Sarah's House. Right?" He grinned, recognizing the technique from his days as a lawyer, stood aside and gestured for her to come in. Penelope noticed his sharp gaze as she continued, "We interviewed you and your family at the time of the Abrams murder.

"I'm a retired police detective, currently investigating the Parking Lot Strangler case as a consultant for the Raleigh PD. You asked me here to talk about Zoe Abrams and her case, right?"

He gave her an odd look, "No." *Good Lord, how did I not know that?* His heartbeat increased, and he touched his fingertips to his temple to wipe away a drop of sweat.

Hmmm – If I play this right, it'll give me the opportunity to stay on top of any new developments in the investigation.

"Then why…?" her voice trailed off.

"Let me introduce Mikey Wilson."

A young man leaned around from behind Tracey and wiggled his fingers, "Hi."

"Wait, I just recently ran across a Mikey Wilson through MyDNA. We messaged and decided we should meet up soon, but we haven't finalized a date yet." She shook her head, "Are you the same Mikey Wilson?"

He nodded enthusiastically.

"Why are you *here*? Why are *we* here?" she pointed at Mikey and herself. "Are there some legal issues with our DNA results?" she asked, looking at the judge.

Tracey held up his hand, "Oh, no. No problem. But we need to take this from the beginning."

Just then, the sound of footsteps on the stairs interrupted them. They looked up to see a tall, slender woman with short, reddish hair coming down with a baby in her arms.

"Penelope, this is my wife, Charlotte," Tracey said as he went over and took the baby from her. "Come to Daddy, sweetheart." With one arm, he supported her against his torso so that she faced Mikey and Penelope. "This is our daughter. Say hello, Sarah." He took her hand in his and waved it for her. Penelope waved back uncertainly.

"I put a tray of iced tea in the kitchen for you," said Charlotte. "It's a beautiful day, so I thought you might want to take it out to the back patio. I know you three have a lot to talk about." She took Sarah back from Tracey, "We're off to a playgroup. Then I have some errands to run. I'll stop at the market on the way back. Do you need anything, my love?"

He shook his head, and after a quick kiss, she left, humming quietly to Sarah.

"That's her discreet way of telling us she'll be gone for several hours." Tracey went ahead down the hall. "The kitchen's back this way."

"What's going on here?" asked Penelope.

"Let's get comfortable first, and then we can talk."

As they walked toward the kitchen, she glanced curiously into the office and then the dining room. Mikey took a box and what looked like several picture albums from the counter while Tracey picked up a large tray with a pitcher of tea, a dish of lemon slices, one of sugar cubes and three tall glasses filled with ice. "Would you get the door, please?" he asked Penelope.

She held the door and then followed the two men out to a shaded brick patio. Several wrought iron chairs were arranged around a low table under an enormous Meyer lemon tree. *Nice place,* Penelope looked around as she trailed behind.

Tracey and Mikey set everything on the large table, and then Mikey flopped comfortably into one of the chairs. While Tracey poured tea and offered sugar and lemon, Penelope sat tentatively on the edge of another chair. *I wonder what this is all about.*

Once Tracey had handed the glasses around, Penelope watched Mikey look questioningly at Tracey, who responded with a tiny nod of his head.

"I know when we messaged each other after MyDNA informed us that we're related, we figured out that we are probably first cousins." Tracey cleared his throat, and Mikey glanced at him. "Like Tracey said, let's start at the beginning." Mikey swallowed hard, "My mom died when I was four years old, and I didn't find out I had relatives on her side of the family until last month when

Tracey came to see me and my dad – Mike Wilson. My dad told us about my mom's sister, and Tracey shared what he remembered about her. I found out that not only was Tracey my cousin, but he has a sister who he's been trying to find for years."

She opened her mouth and then closed it again.

"I know, it's shocking, isn't it? Of course this was before I got the results back from MyDNA. Penelope, now we know you and I are cousins… and Tracey and I are cousins…" Mikey said, glancing at him again. He was obviously bursting with excitement, though so far, he managed to keep his face solemn and his voice calm. Then, unable to contain himself any longer, he blurted out, "Tracey and I think we're *all* related," he circled his finger at the three of them, "all three of us."

Shaking her head in disbelief, Penelope looked at Tracey, "But why didn't *you* show up in MyDNA? Did you use a different database?"

"I would *never* do a DNA test," he replied, smiling. "But I am convinced that you're my sister."

Holy shit, did he just say his sister? Penelope's stomach felt like she'd just headed down a steep drop on an amusement park ride. "What? How do you know that?" She heard the shrill tone in her voice and felt her whole body begin to shake slightly. *Control, Pens. Stay in control here.* She gathered herself together and said in her stern cop voice, "You need to do a DNA test if you're going to make allegations like that. This is serious stuff. He's my cousin," she pointed at Mikey. "We know that because we have the DNA results to prove it. How do we know you're related to us? What proof do you have?"

Penelope watched him twist his earring round and round in his left ear as he said emphatically, "First of all, about those DNA databases, I don't want my DNA in any of them. I worry about identity theft with all the information they collect. I'm surprised, being in law enforcement for all these years, Penelope, that you, in particular, would make yourself vulnerable like that."

She looked from one to the other before she said in a tightly controlled voice, "What the hell is going on here? What proof do you have? Would one of you please explain?"

"Mikey has some pretty strong evidence of our familial relationship. In brief, our mother would have been his aunt. His mom, Maggie, raised us after our mother died when we were just infants. The material evidence," he said, using her cop lingo, "is compelling. Let us tell you the story, Penelope."

She concentrated on keeping her hands steady as she squeezed a wedge of lemon over her tea and took a sip before leaning back and crossing her arms, "Go ahead. Tell me. I'm waiting to be convinced." She breathed shallowly as she listened.

Mikey leaned toward her, speaking quickly, "Tracey saw the Edgar Spring article with the photos of my mom. The article he did for the series on the Parking Lot Strangler's victims. I'm sure you've seen it, since you're investigating the case."

Parking Lot Strangler? What…? Penelope noticed the odd look flit across Tracey's face again. She nodded, her eyes flicking back and forth between the two men. "Go on."

"He just called me and my dad one day, out of the blue," Mikey continued, looking over at Tracey.

She narrowed her eyes. *I wonder where he's going with this.*

Tracey repeated the story he'd spun for Mikey and his dad, that when he saw the pictures of Maggie, he was stirred by how much she resembled the woman who had raised him and his sister for nearly four years, the woman he had believed was their mother.

"Without DNA, how did you figure it out?"

"My dad commented that Tracey prepared his coffee exactly the way my mom did. First the two sugars and then a few drops of cream and then a quick stir with a spoon. They both tapped the spoon gently on the edge of the cup before putting it on a napkin. My dad said Tracey also has her eyes and her hands, and that it was uncanny, like watching my mom after all these years. He is so smart about things like that. He said there is a type of genetic memory where traits are passed on between generations, sometimes even skipping generations. He thinks they can be evidence, circumstantial evidence, of a relationship between two people.

"But without DNA…" she said skeptically.

Tracey took up the story again, "As I reached for the

cream—"

"I noticed his birthmark. It's so unusual," Mikey interrupted in excitement. "Show her, Tracey!"

He shrugged a shoulder, turning his palms upward as if to humor Mikey. Then, he pushed up his sleeve and held out his arm.

Penelope leaned forward to look at the red streaks on the inside of his forearm that looked as though they'd been made by the claws of a wild animal. They triggered a vague sense of familiarity somewhere in the back of her mind. "Go on," she said, a buzzing beginning throughout her body. She sat on her hands to calm herself.

"My dad had this up in our attic." Mikey scooted forward and rested his hand on top of the old box he'd set on the table before untying the twine holding it closed. "These are my mom's things from before my parents met." Perched on the edge of his chair, he saw Penelope watching him intently as he lifted the lid off the box. "My dad said this is stuff that my mom put up in the attic when they got married. She showed it all to him and then put it away." Mikey pulled out an envelope of old photographs, dumped them out onto the table and selected a picture of a little boy and girl in shorts and t-shirts, their feet bare and muddy. He passed it over to Penelope.

She looked at the two children and peered closely at the birthmark on the little boy's arm, "It's easy to see from this picture and that," she waved her hand toward Tracey's arm, "how you made the connection. But there must be more. Tracey, I can't imagine that you would be satisfied with that as the only evidence."

Mikey picked up another photo of Tracey and the little girl in swimsuits, his hair dark, hers blond, their arms slung around each other's shoulders, big grins on their faces. Handing it to Penelope, he said, "Here, you can see the birthmark again, much more clearly. These are the pictures that my dad recalled seeing, why he felt that Tracey was the same little boy in the pictures that my mom had. Especially when we put it together with all the information Tracey recalls about his childhood and the other information in the box. Aaand… Tracey told us his sister's name… before he even saw the birth certificates."

She pressed her left thumb and first finger against her eyelids.

Mikey reached out and touched her forearm gently, "Are you okay?"

She gave a little nod, "I'm just finding all of this hard to take in." She continued to look from the photo in her hand to Tracey and back at the small square picture. She turned it over. Written lightly in pencil on the back was Billy and Sarah, June 1973.

"Billy and Sarah? But—"

"We'll get there." Tracey reached over and riffled through the pile of photographs until he found one that appeared to have been taken the same day. He handed it to Penelope, "That was me and Sarah, when we were little, playing in the sprinkler in the front of the apartment complex. We would get so excited on the days that they watered the lawns. We had such fun running across the grass, jumping through the water, screaming at how cold it was and laughing ourselves silly. Maggie would sit on the steps, smoking a cigarette – that's the only time I remember that she smoked – and she'd watch us play. When she thought we'd had enough, when we were both shivering cold, she'd call us over to her, and she would wrap us in towels and take us inside and pop us into a warm bath. With bubbles," he grinned, "if she thought we'd earned a special treat."

A fragment of a memory caught at the edges of Penelope's mind. She had always thought that those images of running through the sprinklers followed by warm bubble baths were of her and the little boy from next door, who her mom babysat every afternoon until they started school. She and the boy had played together every day after she'd been adopted, while she and her parents still lived in an apartment before they proudly purchased the house they'd lived in for the rest of their lives. "Ooooh, I always thought..." she murmured to herself.

Tracey reached back into the box and pulled out a small red ball, "And here's the ball we played with whenever we had to stay in our room because of Maggie's visitors. We'd roll it back and forth. But whenever it went under the bed, Sarah would make me go get it because she was scared of what might be beneath there in the dark." He chuckled, "The only scary things were random dust bunnies that felt like spiders on my face." He held out the ball toward Penelope.

She took it from him and tossed it from hand to hand, not quite wanting to believe all of this. If she didn't believe it, there would be nothing to lose, and she wouldn't be hurt. "I think most kids have balls like this," she said in a cool voice.

"But not with a blob of sparkly pink nail polish on it. My sister sneaked into Maggie's bedroom one night while she was showering and took the little bottle so she could polish her toenails to be just like her. But she dripped it onto the ball and then cried so hard. She was afraid she'd get in trouble. I put the polish back on Maggie's makeup table for her." He leaned over and turned the ball in her hands to show her the spot where the polish had dried.

Memories of pink sparkles on her toes glittered as they floated to the surface. Tears glittered in her eyes.

He sat back in his chair and watched her caress the pink spot on the ball with her thumb.

Tracey closed his eyes for a minute. Then he looked at her for a long time before he said, "Penelope, I truly think you're my sister, the little girl in the photographs. DNA results connect you as Mikey's cousin. My birthmark and all this," he waved at the photos and memorabilia strewn around the table and then at the box, "indicate that I'm Mikey's cousin."

"Whew," she blew out a long, slow breath. "That's a lot to process. But now I understand why—" With her elbows on her knees and her head in her hands, she whispered to herself, "Sarah. Sarah."

Mikey opened his mouth to speak when Tracey put up a hand and shook his head, motioning to him to wait, to give Penelope some space to work through what she'd just heard.

She finally looked up at Tracey with damp eyes, "That would make you... my brother?"

"Yes, I believe you're my sister," he said solemnly.

Mikey laughed, "That's usually how it works."

Penelope shook her head. "So, is this Maggie in the photos, or is she—?"

"That's Maggie, my mom," Mikey said.

Tracey reached back into the box, took out a thin folder with a few papers in it and handed Penelope a birth certificate. "This is yours."

She looked at the document, and her voice shook as she read out loud, "Sarah Jackson. Born July 4th, 1970. Father – unknown. Mother – Anna Jackson."

Tracey's voice shook as well, "William Jackson. Born July 4th, 1970. Father – unknown. Mother – Anna Jackson." He handed it to Penelope.

Startled, she asked, "Are you William? That makes us twins?" *He looks so much older than me.*

Tracey nodded his head.

"Mikey," she turned to him, "what's the relationship between Maggie and this Anna Jackson?"

"Maggie Jackson Wilson was my mother. Anna was her younger sister."

Penelope's heart began to clatter in her chest, "Maggie – Jackson – Wilson?" Suddenly, the pieces fell into place, "The first victim of the Parking Lot Strangler? Oh shit! You're *that* Mikey Wilson?"

"Yes. Maggie was *my* mom. And her younger sister, Anna, was *your* mother. Their parents didn't have any other kids. My dad checked to be certain." Mikey handed Penelope the sisters' birth certificates and Anna's death certificate.

As Penelope scrutinized the documents, she asked Mikey, "What do you know about Anna?"

Memories of the night she'd found Maggie's dead body shot through her mind. *Shit. What are the odds that I'd end up being related to Maggie? Her NIECE! Oh shit! Oh shit!*

Her mind raced as she forced herself to listen while Mikey told her how Anna had gotten pregnant out of wedlock. Maggie was just a year older than Anna, and they were very close. So close that, when their parents kicked Anna out, Maggie left too and went to live with her in Raleigh. "According to my dad, my mom said that she and your mom had very little money. The only way they were able to support themselves and the two of you was to share a small, one-bedroom apartment."

Mikey told them that Anna and Maggie had been sharing that tiny apartment when the twins were born, and Maggie had looked out for them most of the time because Anna had never fully recovered from their birth. At first, the doctors had thought it was postpartum depression, but then, before they were even a year old, Anna had gotten very sick and had been admitted to the hospital where they discovered she had a rare blood disorder that had been triggered by the pregnancy. It's sad because if she'd had better care before and after the births, it might have been picked up and treated, but by the time she was diagnosed, it was too late and all they could do was keep her comfortable until she died. Maggie was left to raise the two children on her own.

She realized that, as a grocery store cashier, she couldn't support herself and two kids, pay for daycare, clothing, rent and food. She struggled to get by and applied for public assistance. It took forever to come through, so she found a second job with an escort service, a job that paid considerably more than the cashier job. One day, she went on a rare date with a man who'd flirted with her for months at her cashier counter. He always chose to come through her line. He told her he was married and just looking for a little something extra. He offered to pay her to have sex with him.

"He paid her well, and—" Mikey cleared his throat and paused, uncomfortable at telling this story about his mom, "after a while, she realized that there were men she met through the escort service who would pay her for those 'extras' as well. So, she quit her job as a cashier. That meant she could spend much more time with you two during the day."

"I saw that so often in the family court system, women doing anything they could to get by, to hold their families together," Tracey said softly, shaking his head. He picked up from Mikey, continuing the story he'd heard from Mike. "Maggie paid a friend who lived on the first floor of her building to keep us several nights a week. The woman knew what was going on, but she needed the money too. Finally, Maggie was earning enough to be able to move into a two-bedroom apartment in the same complex. It was still small, but it gave the two of us a separate room from her, and she was able to 'entertain' the men at home. That meant she didn't have to pay her friend to babysit anymore."

Tracey shared his vivid memories of what Maggie had looked like, her sparkling earrings, what her voice was like, of him and Sarah playing in the bedroom and of the men coming and going from the apartment. "Maggie locked us in our bedroom when she entertained men at night after we were supposed to be asleep. She told Mike she'd left us alone that evening, sleeping, to make a quick trip out. She suspected her friend had turned her in because she'd stopped using her as a babysitter. That night, when we were taken by Child Protective Services, Maggie was arrested for prostitution." He took a quick breath and said with a wry smile, "These days, we're politically correct and call them sex workers. Anyway, she fell apart, and for a while, she didn't care about anything. Finally, she straightened her life out, but by the time she looked for us, we had disappeared into the system. Eventually, she met Mike, got married and had Mikey.

"My adoptive parents tried to find you, Penelope, so they could take you as well. But you'd already been adopted, and the records were sealed. Later, the building they were stored in was destroyed in a fire," Tracey said. "My parents didn't even have a birth certificate for me, so they had no starting point to search for you."

Mikey broke in, "My dad told me that my mom said she'd felt she wasn't prepared to be left to bring up two children with no support. While she'd done the best she could, she'd resented having you dumped in her lap, and that consequently, she didn't think she'd done a very good job. She told him, in a way, she thought you'd be better off being adopted by someone who wanted you."

Penelope inhaled sharply.

"Are you okay?" asked Tracey. He reached over to take her hand in both of his and felt her pulse pounding under his fingertips.

She pulled her hand away and stood abruptly, "I'll be fine. I just need a few minutes to process this." She strode off across the yard and paced back and forth at the far end, out of sight of the patio behind a large hydrangea, thinking about how she had been looking for her mother and her brother off and on for decades, how devastated she'd been when she'd been taken away from Billy and had been adopted by two strangers. Now, she'd found her brother and learned what happened to her mother and… She dropped down onto her knees and wrapped her arms around the back of her neck and rocked back and forth, the same thing she'd done so often when she was little and dreadfully lonely. She wanted to believe all this was true but was afraid to. She wasn't sure how long she remained curled up, amongst the peaceful foliage, but finally, when her breathing had slowed and her mind calmed a little, she stood up, wiped her eyes, brushed the grass off her knees, and walked slowly back toward Tracey and Mikey where they sat chatting quietly.

When she returned to the chairs under the tree, she reached up and pulled a lemon from a low branch. She pierced the skin with her thumbnail and sniffed deeply. "I'm sorry. This is so overwhelming. I'm having a difficult time getting my head – and my heart – around all of it."

When she sat down, Tracey gave her a gentle smile and suddenly, instinctively, reached his hand over, offering his fingers to her and watched, incredulously, as she reciprocated, pressing her fingertips against his, their secret sign that everything would be okay. Penelope burst into tears.

Tracey stood up and went to her. He knelt beside her chair and took her in his arms, rocking her back and forth.

She cried harder. Billy had always done that, putting his arms around her and rocking her to comfort her when she was sad. She realized how much she'd missed it. Folding herself down as small as possible and rocking back and forth, as she had just done behind the hydrangea, was the closest she'd ever come to that after they'd been separated.

Finally, her sobs died down, and she hiccupped, "I never cried back then. Now I'm a hot mess." She laughed and said, "Tell me something funny before I melt down again."

"Maggie always joked that they set off fireworks specially for us to celebrate our birthday."

"Because it was the Fourth of July?" She shook her head, "I don't remember any fireworks. It's strange what I remember and what I've forgotten. I didn't know my actual birth date, and there was no birth certificate. All my parents knew was that I was five, so they used the date they adopted me for official purposes. When they told me I could pick a date to celebrate my birthday," Penelope laughed, "I misunderstood, and so every year I picked a different date. They went along with that, and as I got older, we all thought it was incredibly funny."

"Oh, your parents must have been sooo cool," Mikey said.

"They were. They died in a car accident a few years ago, and that's when I started looking for my birth family through MyDNA."

"I'm glad you did. Otherwise, we never would have found each other," Mikey grinned happily.

"It does seem like there's extraordinarily compelling evidence that we are all related and that you and I are twins, Tracey. I just wish we could convince you to do a DNA test to confirm it. You know, trust but verify."

His voice became agitated, "That's an absolute no. I told you, I am *not* doing a DNA test."

Penelope shook her head. She reached over and picked up a picture of Anna and Maggie. In the photo, they were very young women. Anna, visibly pregnant, had one hand cupped below her belly. The sisters had slung their arms across each other's shoulders. Penelope brushed the picture with her fingertips, "They look exactly alike. Tracey, you and Mikey look a lot like them too."

Mikey grinned, "I know. It's pretty weird. Do you see the mole above Anna's eyebrow? You have one in the same place."

"I've always wondered who I take after?" Penelope reached up and touched her mole, the one she'd always hated – until that moment. She caught the fragrance of the lemon she was still holding as she moved her hand near her face. She threw it up into the air several times, catching it effortlessly, before tossing it at Mikey who caught it easily.

Suddenly, out of the blue, Mikey said, "You work for the Raleigh PD?"

"Yeah, I've been in law enforcement since I was fourteen when I joined their Public Safety Cadet Unit. Even back then, I wanted to protect people," said Penelope, smiling at her cousin. "Especially women and children. Women's value to society is overlooked so often. They don't make a big deal about it, but they're actually the movers and shakers. They may not always be out there on the frontline, visible to people, but they make a difference, from the little, everyday things right up to big things like the whole women's liberation movement." She drew a breath, "I wouldn't go as far as to call myself a feminist, but while it's gradually changing, we still play a disproportionately large role in raising children and influencing how they grow up. So often, those women and kids struggle just to survive. I wanted to make sure they got a fair shake by taking their abusers off the street."

Tracey smiled at her passionate remarks, astounded at how similar her feelings were to his. "Do you have any children?"

"Nope. I was married for a while, but we were too busy with our careers to start a family. After my divorce, I threw everything I had into my job. There was more than enough work to keep me busy."

"What was it like being a cop?" asked Mikey.

"Good, meaningful, fulfilling." She looked at Tracey and Mikey, "This situation is unbelievably odd, because I was the one who found Maggie's body in the parking lot that night. The case fell into my lap, and I've worked it ever since. Not to beat my own drum, but I probably know more about the Parking Lot Strangler, or the murders at least, than anyone else."

Penelope saw Tracey rubbing his thumb against the arm of his chair. *That man has some serious stress going.* She noticed the way he clenched his jaw, how stiffly he held his shoulders, *I wonder what's with that.*

"That is weird." Mikey leaned forward, "You know what else is weird? Because of my mom's murder being unsolved, I decided to study forensic science. I chose Penn State because they offered me a full-ride scholarship. This summer, I'll be interning at the morgue here in Raleigh. We'll both be involved in law enforcement. And Tracey was a lawyer and a judge. Weird."

Mikey told Penelope who he'd be working for, and she said the guy was the best medical examiner in North Carolina. "He'll make you work hard, but in the end, you'll understand how to do the job right and why things are done the way they are."

Tracey asked about Mikey's scholarship to Penn State.

"It's an academic one, not one of those full rides for some sport or other. I had to work hard for mine, especially since I was," he paused, rolling his eyes in embarrassment, "an ill-behaved kid when I was younger. I had a lot of anger after my mom's death. My dad finally sent me away to military school to learn some discipline. Thank goodness, it worked, and I turned myself around. Still, I had to scramble to get my grades up, I had to do volunteer work for the community, *and* I was the captain of our lacrosse team. All those extras you have to do to qualify for scholarships."

"It's not just about grades anymore, is it?" Tracey commiserated.

"Nope," said Mikey. "Not at all. It's both stellar grades *and* being a well-rounded member of society, even at just eighteen."

"Your dad must be very proud of you," said Penelope.

Mikey stared off toward the far end of the yard, "He and my stepmom both are, but they've never cut me any slack." He looked at Penelope, "I want to know more about you – cuz."

"We didn't have a lot of money growing up. We were a typical blue-collar family. My parents both worked as soon as I was in school. We did lots of things together. We had picnics, we went camping, stuff that didn't cost much money. And we went to church every Sunday."

"Was your dad a cop?"

"He was an ambulance driver, and my mom went back to work as a school secretary when I was in first grade. We always had food on the table and clothes on our backs. They raised me with a strong understanding of right and wrong. Whenever I stepped out of line or did something hurtful to someone, they made me apologize or make some kind of restitution."

She smiled at Mikey, "I was an angry kid too, but the track coach at school got me into distance running, and that helped focus my energy. To be honest, I was usually too tired at the end of the day to have anything left over for anger. It's still there, under the surface, but mostly, I seem to have it under control."

"All three of us with anger issues as kids," Tracey looked bemused. "My family had a lot of money – old, family money. I had a nanny until I was about twelve. My parents were pretty hands-off until then. My mother told me much later that she and my father were not comfortable with little kids. Mind you, they were kind and loving, but remote." He glanced down and shook his head at the reddened spot on the thumb he'd been rubbing against the rough spot on his chair. "But I was just a kid, and I felt like I'd been abandoned by my mom, errr, Maggie. And then my twin sister went away." He looked at Penelope, "One day you were adopted, and you left and never came back. So, when my parents adopted me and handed me over to the nanny, I was angry that even they didn't seem to want me."

Penelope looked at him with tears in her eyes.

"Thank goodness for my grandparents, especially Granddad. He and I formed a special bond right from the beginning. For years, I wanted to be just like him. And then later, when I was old enough to interact with them at their level, I became very close to my parents as well."

He shook his head, "I didn't intend to go off on that tangent. I think I was heading toward a comment about being a bully when I was young. Because I was small, kids picked on me. Even though my granddad told me my birthmark made me special, I always thought they picked on me because of it. I don't know, maybe they just had a nose for vulnerability, but big, mean kids seemed magnetically drawn to me. That taught me that if you are bigger or meaner, you can get your own way. When I had a growth spurt in sixth grade, suddenly I was bigger than most kids my age, and I became very good at the more subtle ways of bullying. It was how I dealt with my anger."

"What did your parents do?" asked Mikey.

"They never knew. I'm not saying that because I'm proud of it. I was very sly and able to do things that only the person I bullied knew about. I made sure they were scared to say anything. I'm afraid I wasn't a very nice person growing up."

"Wow, what made you stop?"

"Before I went to Harvard Law, while I was still an undergraduate, part of my coursework included several psych classes. We all had to do some type of volunteer work, and I ended up working at a juvenile facility and saw firsthand the bullying happening there and the impact it had, especially on the smaller, more vulnerable kids. Seeing it from the outside like that, I realized I didn't want to be that way anymore, and I stopped."

"I think it's hard for people to change so dramatically," Penelope said.

"It is, but if you put your mind to it, it's usually possible," said Tracey. "Look at you. You figured out how to deal with your anger and so did our young cousin here."

"On a lighter note," she chuckled, "you're on the Board of Directors of the Lauch Art Museum – hmmm – that's a pretty obvious one since your family established it. But how come you just didn't sit on boards and do good works and philanthropic stuff – or play golf?" There was a slight tinge of sarcasm in her voice. "How did you end up as a lawyer and then a judge?"

"I do love golf," Tracey chuckled, and then his voice grew serious, "My family, not just my mom and dad, but my grandparents too, instilled in me that giving back to the community was important. So, I chose to be a lawyer, like my granddad, and then a judge. Public service has always been important to my family."

He explained that, because he'd been adopted and separated from his sister, he'd always wanted to watch out for children in the foster system, siblings in particular. "I remember very clearly the night we were taken from the apartment and the day we were separated. I was so traumatized. That's why I founded Sarah's House."

"Tell us about Sarah's House," Penelope prompted him.

"I never wanted brothers and sisters to be separated like you and I were." He smiled at her, "I named it after you, you know."

"Me? Oh, *Sarah*." She picked up her birth certificate again and read softly, "Sarah Jackson." She looked up at Tracey, "And your daughter? She's also Sarah."

"Yes, we named her after you." Tracey pulled out his phone and compared a picture of his daughter with one of the infants in a photo from the box. "Except for the hair color, I think you looked exactly like my little Sarah, don't you, right down to the mole above her eyebrow." He handed the picture and his phone to Penelope, and Mikey popped up to look over her shoulder.

Penelope studied the photos, "I guess so."

He pointed at his eyes which were filled with tears. "Must be getting old, this weepy thing going on." He continued wistfully, "Even though Maggie lost us, she hung onto all this stuff."

Penelope reached out to him and Mikey and held their hands for a moment before saying, "Let's see what else is in that box of yours."

Tracey pulled out several drawings and handed them to Penelope. One was of a red-headed woman holding hands with a little boy and a little girl. Penelope reached up and touched the blond hair on the little girl in the picture and then the brown hair on the little boy. Someone had written "*Sarah, 1974*" in the bottom right corner. The next was of a little blond girl and brown-haired boy playing with a red ball. "*Billy, 1973*" was written in the same handwriting, also in the bottom right corner. She ran her thumb over the names. "Is this Maggie's handwriting?" she asked.

"Yes. She did that to my drawings too," Mikey said, glancing at Penelope. "She always put my name and the year I drew the picture in that same corner."

"I'd like to have the pictures I drew and our mom's birth and death certificates, or at least a copy of those. And my birth certificate, of course."

"Absolutely," said Tracey.

Penelope turned to Mikey, "What else do you know about Maggie and Anna?"

Tracey sat back drinking his tea and watching the cousins, noticing the clear resemblances in their quick smiles, the way they tilted their heads as they talked, how they angled their bodies toward each other.

Mikey showed Penelope a photo album from when he was little. As they leafed through it, Mikey talked about how his mom had made a success of her life, become an artist, met his dad, had a family and her own business before she was murdered.

Then Mikey showed her the MJW Expressions guest book. "I took this out of her box. My dad must have stuck it in there."

They leafed through the guest book, looking at all the names of people who had visited her gallery. Penelope commented that the guest book the police had found when she was killed was only half full. She looked at the dates in the book she held. This one was an earlier one, and every page was filled. "Mikey," she asked, "do you mind if I borrow this? I'll make sure you get it back. But I think it might contain important evidence for my case. I know the bastard is still out there, and we're going to get him."

Tracey resumed absently rubbing his thumb against the rough spot on the arm of his chair.

"Oh, yes, tell us about the case," Mikey begged.

"I can't give you any details because it's an active case. But we're making progress. Slowly."

Penelope watched as Tracey lifted his thumb. A drop of blood had formed, and he put it to his lips to stop the bleeding.

He cleared his throat and said, "A beer before dinner would be good. How about you all?"

"I'm still underage for eight more months."

Penelope laughed, "Oh, I remember being that age. You count the months."

Tracey asked, "Does your dad let you drink at home?"

"Yeah, why?"

"Well, this is like being home, so I'll bring you a beer – if you don't think he would mind."

"But only one. I never drink and drive."

"Good man. Penelope?"

"Beer is my beverage of choice."

When Tracey returned a while later, he popped the tops of the three beers with an opener.

"Oh, there you are. We thought you'd gotten lost." He'd put a bandaid on his thumb, Penelope noticed. "How's the thumb? Did you cut it on your chair?"

"It's fine," Tracey replied tersely.

He handed the beers around and sat down, "Is the investigation your full-time job now, Penelope?"

"It is pretty much full-time, but since I work from home, my schedule is flexible. Gives me time to keep up with my running."

"Share something that hasn't already been in the newspaper articles," said Mikey.

"Hmmm, well, I think it's fair to assume the killer has a fixation with certain objects."

"You mean the earrings? They mentioned them in the article. Do you think he keeps them?" Mikey asked ghoulishly.

"I've done considerable research into this, and it seems that he's a typical trophy-keeper. Lots of serial killers keep objects from their victims." She looked at Tracey with a little shrug at Mikey's macabre interest and then gave Mikey a smile, "It's pretty interesting. A trophy helps them remember their victims. Sometimes it even enhances their ability to relive the killings, and for some, the trophies can actually become sexual objects."

"Ewww, women's earrings? The guy sounds like a real pervert."

Tracey stood up abruptly, "I'll go ask Marie how long it is until dinner."

*

Later that evening as they were leaving, Penelope said, "Hey, I know I had that melt down earlier – it's kinda been a bombshell sort of day. But honestly, I am so happy to have found you both," and then corrected herself, looking at Mikey, "Or that you found us."

"Well, if you want to be accurate, Tracey found me," Mikey laughed.

"Whatever, I'm glad it happened," she said, giving each one a hug. "Now we're a family, two sibs and a cuz. Imagine that!"

*

When Penelope got home, she went upstairs, but before going into the bedroom where Hugo was watching TV, she stopped in her office. She looked at the wall of evidence in front of her, at the pictures of the first woman she'd found dead all those years ago in the parking lot, letting it sink in that the woman in those photos that she had looked at for years was her aunt. *What a day! I found a cousin, I found my brother, and without knowing it, I've been investigating my aunt's murder.*

She picked up her phone and dialed Bobby's number. *I wonder if he'll think being related to Maggie is a conflict of interest. But... I never knew her...* Exhausted, she gave Bobby a quick rundown of the afternoon and evening. "But with all the evidence I saw, I'm convinced he's my brother. Wait until you see his birthmark."

"Yeah, but you know how it goes. No DNA, no proof. Too bad he won't do a test."

The Interview

All her research had told Jane that sexual gratification was a common part of serial killings. But hearing it firsthand, from an actual serial killer, was different. It took all the willpower she could summon to maintain her composure, to not just get up and walk away from him. She sat quietly, forcing her face to remain neutral.

Finally, after a couple of long, slow, calming breaths, she asked, "What do you know about the young woman you killed at the golf course in Washington?"

"Nothing. I never knew her name. When I thought about her, she was just 'The Golf Cart Girl'."

"Sophie Jones. That was her name. She was your sixth victim. Why did you kill her?"

"Her looks… Her demeanor… She reminded me of my aunt. Like all the women, to some extent. Anyway, I'd been behind the world's slowest foursome and was running late. Charlotte and I had plans for the evening. And then I noticed that my car tire was low, and I knew I'd have to stop for air or get it changed. That was going to make me even later. I was very irritated at life and people in general that day."

"And?"

"While I was loading my clubs into the trunk, she came up to me. 'Excuse me,' she said. My aunt used to say that to us when she was angry. Anyway, I was in a hurry," he went on, "and didn't turn around. She was abrupt, almost rude, I thought, when she said, 'Excuse me,' again and tapped me on the shoulder. My aunt used to shake me when she said that." He closed his eyes for a moment. "It put me over the edge. I snapped, and I killed her."

"Just like that? You knew nothing about her?"

"No, nothing."

"Again, her name was Sophie, Sophie Jones," she said in a quiet, even tone. "March 2011. It's been more than four years since you killed her. I spent a good while with her parents and boyfriend. She was working at the golf course to pay her way through school at the local community college. She was majoring in sports medicine."

Jane noticed a peculiar look cross Tracey's face. When she asked him what he was feeling, he told her that suddenly he felt sad for the family, for what he'd done to their daughter – and to them.

"They tried to find a way to honor her life," said Jane, "by doing something that would have made her happy. They're preparing to announce the recipient of the first Sophie Jones Science Scholarship for young women at the community college. It's a few thousand dollars each year, paid out of the insurance policy they received from her death. It's given her parents some comfort."

"I wish it were appropriate for me to give a donation to her scholarship fund – to make amends."

"Perhaps the best way to make amends would be to go back and accept the consequences."

Tracey looked over Jane's shoulder at the window behind her and rubbed his face. "I'm sorry I was in such a bad mood that day. I'm sorry that I killed her. And, in hindsight, I'm even more sorry that I enjoyed it."

"Tell me, what drove you to all of this?"

Chapter Twenty-One

MEMORANDUM FOR THE RECORD

TO: Lieutenant Bobby Figg, Major Crimes Unit, Raleigh PD

CC: Tibor Papp, President, Security Consulting International Ltd.
            Edgar Spring, Investigative Journalist

FROM: Penelope Huber, Consultant to Raleigh PD

DATE: May 16, 2014

SUBJECT: Parking Lot Strangler Investigation – Memo #8

This memo covers the week of May 10–16.

The manifest for Oliver's cruise in Ukraine has been received, and the data is being entered into IDAS.

Another guest book from MJW Expressions was provided by Michael (Mikey) Wilson. The names have now been entered into IDAS.

European Developments

Papp is reaching out to all cruise lines to collect manifests for those boats that stopped in Zaporizhzhya, Strasbourg, Budapest and St. Petersburg during the time period we agreed upon. He doesn't anticipate any pushback considering the high profile of the PLS case.

Next Steps

Papp will continue to work with the St. Petersburg police department to get the sex worker's DNA results. There seems to be some unknown delay.

Continued collection, processing and analysis of data as it comes in, to be overseen by Huber.

Page 1 of 1

Chapter Twenty-Two

Tracey came skidding through the front door. As he toed off his hiking boots, he heard Charlotte on a Skype call in his office with Fong and Remy. Sarah chimed in from time to time in her entrancing baby babble.

Still out of breath from his mad dash from the car, he pulled a chair over and sat down, "I'm so sorry, I was hiking with my cousin, and we lost track of time."

Charlotte placed Sarah in his arms. He set her on his knee and pulled her back against his torso, jiggling his leg and supporting her with an arm around her chest. She gurgled and cooed, reaching out to bat at the screen. "She always upstages us," said Charlotte with her familiar chortle.

Tracey continued to bounce Sarah on his knee, blowing gently on the back of her neck. She giggled and gave little screeches of joy. Beaming, he said, "I have big news, unless Charlotte's already shared it." He glanced at Charlotte and caught her, red-faced, making a shushing gesture to Remy and Fong. "I see she's told you already." He turned to Charlotte, "Really?"

"I'm sorry, my love, it just slipped out. I was so excited for you."

"Oh, tell us anyhow, Tracey. I can see how much you want to. I'm sure you'll have things to add that Charlotte didn't share," said Remy.

"I finally met my sister, Sarah. She goes by Penelope – Penelope Huber. My cousin, Mikey, found her through MyDNA."

Remy said, "Penelope, that's a pretty name. What's she like?"

As Tracey described his sister, intense, beautiful, a former police officer, a marathoner getting ready to do her first triathlon, Sarah babbled and blew bubbles. He smiled dotingly at her.

Charlotte scooted closer to him as he continued, "I never thought I'd find her. And then it wasn't even me, it was my cousin who did. Anyhow, we're planning to get together at her house for a birthday celebration on July 4th. Can you imagine, our first joint birthday celebration in forty years!"

"That's very exciting," Fong said. He smiled at the babbling baby, "Sarah, I think you have one happy daddy!"

"Oh yes, she does. I can't remember when I've been so happy… except maybe the day I married Charlotte and the day this little one was born." Tracey winked at Charlotte before lifting Sarah up and turning her to face him, "Pretty soon, you'll get to spend some time with your new auntie, little one. You'll love her so much!"

Remy said with a giggle, "Our guys are as adorable as Sarah, aren't they?"

Charlotte nodded, "Yeah, but this one over here is awfully sweaty. Good thing you're thousands of miles away, and you can't smell things over the computer. He'll need a good long shower before I allow him in my bed," she said emphatically.

"Speaking of smells," said Tracey. He picked Sarah up under her arms and wrinkled his nose at her. "Phew. Oh my, what did you do, Sarah?"

Charlotte took the baby from him, "I've already had time with Fong and Remy. I'll change and feed her and then put her down for her nap while you all catch up. Then," she grinned, "I'll make it up to you for letting your secret out of the bag." Tracey gave her a quick swat on her bottom as she headed out.

Catching the motion, Remy laughed, "Tracey, congratulations on being reunited with your sister. Family is so important. I'm glad you've found her – and your cousin."

"Thanks. It's a pretty wonderful feeling. So, how are you doing?"

"The memory thing, ahhh, not so good. I still have the before time and the after time around the night I went overboard. But otherwise, I'm doing quite well."

It's all going to be fine, Tracey reassured himself.

"The doctor has cleared her to travel," said Fong. "We haven't set a date yet, but we're going to California to visit her aunt and uncle."

"Why don't you go next month and stop here for," Tracey looked around to make sure Charlotte wasn't within hearing distance before continuing in a low voice, "shhh… for Charlotte's surprise fiftieth birthday party."

Remy said, "Oh, wonderful! And we can meet the newest members of your family, Tracey!"

"The last time I was at a surprise party was for Sasha's fiftieth… that was a few years back," said Fong. "Turning fifty is a superb reason to surprise someone. Let us know if we can do anything from here."

"Whoops, I'll fill you in on the details later." He waved a teddy bear at the screen, "I hear Charlotte coming back for this."

Chapter Twenty-Three

Penelope handed Bobby that week's memo, "Hey, if there's nothing more to cover, I have a favor to ask."

"So, ask."

"Tracey is having this big, surprise birthday party for Charlotte, and I need to go with you."

"Need?"

"Everyone is going to be a couple at this party. Eddie will be there covering it for the paper as a society event, and he's taking Jane. I can't hang out with them because three's a crowd, you know. Hugo and I can't go together because we're keeping our relationship quiet in case it doesn't work out. It's really good at the moment," she glanced at Bobby, "but yes, I'm nervous about it because it was really good the last time too."

"But you and I, we can be seen together in public outside of business? I don't know what you want from me, Penelope. First, we're together, but we can't be together publicly."

"Because I was afraid," she said in a low voice.

"Now, while we're supposedly just having a break to be sure we want to be with each other, you take up with Hugo – but you can't be seen with *him* publicly. And now, you can be seen with me – because it's convenient for you?"

"Not because it's convenient. Because I need you, and we're not together now. That's why we can be seen in public. It's not a date-date. You're my friend. You're just accompanying me… as a friend."

Bobby picked up the check, looked at it and muttered, "So now, I'm just a friend." He pulled out his wallet, "Have you told Hugo that you're going with me so that your relationship with him can stay discreet? How does he feel about us going together?"

"Flitting about with the cream of society certainly isn't being discreet. So yeah, even though he's jealous, he understands."

"Do you get off on making men jealous?"

Chapter Twenty-Four

Charlotte stood in their bedroom with a towel around her while Tracey eyed her from the bed, "You know what I would like for my birthday, Tracey?"

"I can only imagine."

"Yes, but with a twist." She dropped her towel.

"Oh, the birthday suit." He reached up and tried to grab her hand and pull her down to him.

Charlotte took a step back, "Oh, no, no, no, my love." She crawled up onto the bed and sat cross-legged. "Sit like this," she patted the sheets in front of her, "facing me."

Tracey looked puzzled, "Okay?"

"I want to try something different. We'll start by just looking at each other."

He sat up, cross-legged. "Sitting naked cross-legged with all my jewels exposed, looking – isn't it a bit odd? I'm not sure I like this, staring at each other."

She swatted his hand in mock annoyance, "Behave yourself. This is supposed to make us more comfortable with each other, and maybe we'll learn something new about what we like."

He groaned in frustration, "I'm very comfortable with you."

Charlotte placed her hands loosely on her knees, "Do this."

Tracey followed her lead. "Now what?"

"Like I said, now we just look at each other."

He looked down, "Well, the view is truly magnificent. I always like to admire it. It's—"

"Shhh. Just look." She looked at his face, his neck, his shoulders, his arms, quietly noticing the planes of his face, the tendons in his neck, the muscles across his shoulders…

Tracey looked at her, finally understanding what he was supposed to be doing.

After quite a while, Charlotte said, "Now, the foreheads." She leaned forward and motioned for Tracey to do the same. They rested their foreheads together for another few minutes until their breathing slowed and synchronized.

"Now, we can touch, but only with our fingertips. And very

gently. We explore each part of the other's body at the same time." Starting with their faces, they ran their fingers down each other's necks, shoulders, arms, until they reached their toes.

"I like this."

"Shhh. No words."

They repeated the exercise again, touching with their hands.

Their breaths slowed even more until it felt as though they were meditating.

"Now, we'll deviate from the regular routine." When Charlotte reached between his legs and caressed him, Tracey's breath caught. An incredible thrill of pleasure ran through him.

His hands moved lower, touching her thighs, the dark hair between her legs, stroking her gently, "I think you're ready for your birthday present."

Charlotte sighed, "Mmmm. Yes, I believe I am."

He slid his hands around her and pulled her down onto the sheets, covering her body with his.

*

"Friday, the thirteenth. What a bold day to hold a special birthday bash," said Remy as she leaned in to air kiss Charlotte on her right and then her left cheek. "Sorry we were late. Fong and I," she blushed, "got a little distracted. He does that to me."

"Tracey does that to me too," Charlotte said, struggling to keep a straight face. For some reason, it seemed incredibly funny.

Remy glanced at her, uncertain, until she saw a tiny twitch at the corner of Charlotte's mouth.

And then, they were in each other's arms, laughing until tears ran down their faces.

"Oh, my makeup," Charlotte finally gasped. She grabbed Remy by the hand and pulled her into the nearby ladies room.

"Eyedrops?" asked Charlotte, peering into the mirror at her red eyes.

Remy gave a nod and handed her a small bottle. "You know, I don't think I've laughed like that since before Lee left." A sad smile flitted across her lips.

Charlotte scooted closer to lean a shoulder against Remy's.

"It's nice, isn't it, to have a girlfriend to laugh with? I'm so glad you don't feel you need to make up silly excuses for being late."

They leaned back against the makeup counter as they began to giggle again. Finally, wiping her eyes carefully, Charlotte said in a mock stern voice, "Enough of this. I have guests," which sent them into another bout of laughter.

Once they had finally composed themselves and touched up their makeup, Remy stepped back to look closely at Charlotte's dress. "Is that the dress Lydia made for the gala? That color is perfect with your hair. She had such an eye for color." She nodded slowly as she continued, "I must say, I was wondering what seafoam blue actually would be." Stroking the tiny silver beads that shimmered under the light from the small Chihuly chandelier that complemented the ones in the great hall, she shook her head in awe. "That is truly stunning."

Charlotte laughed with delight, raised her arms and pirouetted slowly. The very straight lines of the delicately beaded overdress sewn from effervescent aqua chiffon with sharp green undertones dropped from a choker of the same chiffon embroidered in an intricate pattern of silver beads. It scooped beneath her arms where it joined the strapless underlayer, a lightly fitted shadow that showed off her curves. The back of the dress was boldly cut, skimming beneath her shoulder blades and falling in a straight line to her heels. Lydia had designed a clever slit along the left side of the skirt, ending a precise nine inches above her knee and overlapping just enough to make it invisible. She'd asked Lydia about the height of the slit. Her response had been, "High enough to tease without giving anything away."

She repeated Lydia's description to Remy and stretched her foot into a tango position to demonstrate.

"She's right, you know." Remy looked at Charlotte's foot, "I see you are wearing your dancing shoes," she pointed to her 1920s-style closed-toe silk shoes dyed to match the underdress.

"I lived in absolute fear that it would rain today and stain these shoes. If it had, I was prepared to wear a pair of old flats and change when I got inside the restaurant I thought we were going to. Oh, that would have destroyed the grand entrance to the great hall that Tracey had planned." She giggled, "It's too bad you were late. He'd found a scarf that almost matched my dress and blindfolded me with it. Imagine my surprise when he uncovered my eyes and this wonderful group of family and friends all dressed in art deco style clothing greeted us," she smiled. "I'm sure that some of the women's dresses are actual vintage pieces. But the best was that he dug out his top hat and wore it. At a very rakish angle, mind you."

"Oh, I'm so sorry to have missed that," laughed Remy, smoothing her hands down the sides of her red silk, dropped-waist flapper dress.

"Yours?" asked Charlotte. "It's vintage, yes, not a copy? And look at those shoes. They're wonderful."

Remy nodded happily. She'd looked so hard for precisely the right dress, and then it had been Fong who'd discovered it hanging on a rack of beautiful vintage clothing during a weekend in Milan. It had required extensive cleaning and altering to bring it to perfection. The matching shoes they'd found in the same shop had been easy in comparison – after some minor repairs, her favorite Milan cobbler had given them a careful cleaning and then dyed them to coordinate with her dress but in a slightly deeper red.

"Come on, my friend, enough of our private fashion show. Time to get back to the party." As they left the ladies room, she tucked her arm through Remy's, and arms linked, they strolled along, admiring the lovely interior of the Lauch Art Museum's great hall, pausing from time to time to say hello to guests.

"Madam Mayor, this is my dearest friend, Remy Martin. Her husband, Fong, is making the rounds with Tracey. They own a small vineyard in Slovenia. Remy, this is Mayor Erkes."

They exchanged a few words about the vineyard before the two women moved on to look at the paintings by local artists that had been hung in the great reception hall.

"How do you know all these people?"

"Through Tracey, for the most part. But you know me. Making friends is easy for me, so I met a few of them at the tennis club and through the library at the university."

"I really like Mikey and Penelope. But, hey," Remy moved

closer to Charlotte and dropped her voice, "is there something between Penelope and Bobby?"

"Penelope is very discreet about her relationships, so I don't know. I understand they are working together on a project for the police department related to," she whispered, "a serial killer."

Remy stopped and looked at Charlotte.

"I'll tell you all about that later," Charlotte chuckled and continued strolling, her eyes sliding from time to time toward Penelope and Bobby. "But you're right, lots of little touches going on when they think no one's looking. Just watch how they brush up against each other's arms. And when they talk, they lean into each other." She grinned, "It's fun to watch."

"Fong and I struggled with that when we didn't belong to each other. There were looks, but mostly painful ones. There was no touching. Except for that one time... in Berlin."

"You did a better job than these two. I never noticed," Charlotte said. "Anyway, back to your question, the rest of these are people I connected with during previous visits with Tracey."

Charlotte did a little jig of pleasure, "Oh, Remy, isn't it amazing how Tracey pulled this off?"

"How ever did he keep it a secret?"

"Beats me. Maybe because as a lawyer and a judge, it was his business to keep secrets, and I suppose he's never gotten out of the habit. Thank goodness, we have no secrets of any consequence between us."

"It's the same with me and Fong. We're like this," said Remy, holding up two touching fingers. "So, what was his cover story for tonight, then – how did he get you dolled up and out of the house?"

"I thought we were going somewhere posh for dinner. You know, he hired a town car, complete with a driver in a cap."

"Oh, like Sal at the Solstice Party?" They both laughed, remembering that evening.

"Exactly."

Charlotte told Remy about the gift Tracey had given her in the car. Tickets to Casablanca for the following February, complete with a two-week stay in a villa before they would go off touring other cities in North Africa. Charlotte had mentioned that she'd been there before with her ex-husband on their honeymoon, and she'd always wanted to go back.

"What an incredible gift. And even better since it doesn't seem to bother him that you were there on your previous honeymoon."

Charlotte sighed, "Yes, he is wonderful. Then, as we got close to town, he put the blindfold over my eyes and gave me the longest, most lovely, romantic kiss, and he whispered in my ear that there would never be anyone else for him but me. Then he kissed me again. Have you ever kissed someone blindfolded?"

"I can't say that I have. Despite all the men I've been with, that's not something we ever did."

"I highly recommend it. He spoke to me in French the whole time, it was very sexy. Imagine how surprised I was when he took off the blindfold at the foot of that beautiful staircase." Charlotte pointed across the room.

"I still can't believe you and Fong are here." Charlotte gave her a long embrace and pressed her cheek to Remy's before grabbing her hand, "Come along. I need to show you where the tree stands during the holidays. It's truly a thing of wonder." They stopped at the foot of the stairs, and Charlotte described how the twenty-foot-high Christmas tree would stand nestled in the curve of the elaborate staircase, covered with glass balls that had been purchased specially to complement the enormous Chihuly chandeliers hanging from the tall ceiling.

"The tree will still be up for the New Year's Eve fundraising gala. The only downside is that I had planned to wear this dress for the gala, but Tracey convinced me to wear it tonight. He said that my fiftieth birthday was a far more important occasion than a gala that happens every year." She ran her hands gently over her hips, "Not to brag, but imagine how thrilled I was when I discovered that I'm already back to my pre-baby size, and this fits as though Lydia had just made it for me."

"You look fabulous. But didn't Lydia make you two dresses? Have you ever worn the cocktail dress that she made?"

"I'll have lots of opportunities to wear that one," said

Chapter Twenty-Four

Charlotte. "You have an amazing memory."

"Other than my memory of that dreadful night last December."

"I don't think I would want to remember the accident or being in a cold river in the middle of the night. I've been so worried about you. Every time we Skype with you and Fong, Tracey comments about how dreadful it must be to be missing such a significant piece out of your life. He worries that you'll never get it back."

"I do too, but I'm learning to live without it. Fong has been so supportive, and as he's pointed out, it's only one night in decades."

*

That evening, in front of the fireplace in their bedroom, Charlotte and Tracey cuddled together in their light summer robes, kissing in what would surely end up as a bout of lovely, post-party sex.

"You know how to throw one fine party, my love. Thank you so much," She rested her head on his shoulder. "And to get Remy and Fong here! That was masterful."

"We'll get to masterful in a minute," he leered at her and waggled his eyebrows.

Charlotte snickered, took a tiny sip from his glass and handed it back to him with a final swallow left in the bottom.

"Remy looked remarkable tonight, didn't she?" Tracey drank the last of the whisky, "Has she begun to remember that night?"

Chapter Twenty-Five

MEMORANDUM FOR THE RECORD

TO: Lieutenant Bobby Figg, Major Crimes Unit, Raleigh PD

CC: Tibor Papp, President, Security Consulting International Ltd.
           Edgar Spring, Investigative Journalist

FROM: Penelope Huber, Consultant to Raleigh PD

DATE: June 27, 2014

SUBJECT: Parking Lot Strangler Investigation – Memo #14

This memo covers the week of June 21–27.

European Developments

Papp has reported that the lab has found a match from DNA gathered at the crime scene of the St. Petersburg victim to that found at the two U.S. scenes and in Budapest.

As was discussed by phone earlier this week, Tracey Lauch is on our existing lists and was also on the Zaporizhzhya cruise manifest. This is in relation to the Oliver strangling. In addition, he boarded a river cruise in St. Petersburg two days after the sex worker was killed, and he was in Raleigh at the time of those murders. We have requested that the FBI obtain the Seattle airplane passenger lists around the time of Jones's murder in Trigg Pass.

The manifests have finally begun to arrive from the non-Spectrum river cruise lines with stops in St. Petersburg, Budapest, Strasbourg and Zaporizhzhya for the time periods requested.

Next Steps

The team recommends the Raleigh PD draft a warrant for MyDNA to search for a match with the crime scene DNA.

Continued processing and analysis of data as it comes in, to be overseen by Huber.

Page 1 of 1

Chapter Twenty-Six

Raleigh, Late June 2014

Bobby and Tracey sat in comfortable plantation chairs on the terrace at Tracey's golf club. With glasses of whisky in their hands, they gazed out across the first hole and proceeded to dissect their game shot by shot. Ultimately, Tracey told Bobby to remind him never to get into a situation where they were playing against one another. With a little more time on this course, he was convinced Bobby would not only win but beat the pants off him.

For some reason, perhaps the long hours playing in extremely hot, humid June weather coupled with an unaccustomed second glass of Scotch, Bobby broke out into laughter, "Beat the pants off you? Now there's an image I don't care to contemplate." He continued to laugh, and Tracey joined in.

Finally, gasping for breath, Bobby said, "Besides, there's not much chance that I'll spend enough time playing here to be any real threat to you – or your pants," he chuckled. "The club fees here are far too rich for me. I'm a public golf course kinda guy."

As Tracey's buddies wandered past on the way to their carts, they stopped to say hello. "This is Bobby Figg. Bobby, this is Jim, Cal and Sam," he pointed to each in turn as he said their names. "We've played this course for more years than I care to remember."

Bobby looked out across the rolling green vista, "This has to be the most pristine course in Raleigh. You must have a top-notch maintenance crew to keep it in such good shape. And because of the heat we've had, the greens were fast today. Very challenging."

"Watch out. This guy," Tracey said to his friends, nodding his head toward Bobby, "can out-drive any one of you, and he's a pro at reading the greens. He's never played here before, but he still beat me by two strokes."

"Ah," Bobby waved his hand, "it was beginner's luck."

"No, I watched you the whole time," said Tracey. "You're a very good player."

Bobby chuckled, "Maybe if you'd spent less time watching my game and more time…"

"He's got you there, Tracey," said Sam.

"If he's as good as you say, we oughta figure out how we can play in the same group with him at the fundraiser next month," Cal said. "It would be great to finally beat Ken Wayne's group. They've won the last three years in a row. Bring him out, and we'll all play together a few times. We'll see if it was just pure luck."

Sam said quickly, "I've been reluctant to say anything, but my knee has been acting up something fierce. I could step aside and let Bobby replace me. Take one for the team, you know."

"Which fundraiser is that?" Bobby asked.

"Every year, Tracey hosts a fundraiser here for Sarah's House," said Sam. "It pulls in a lot of money. Think about it, young man. If you're as good as Tracey says you are, you should join us next month."

"I think I'd like that."

After the men headed off to their carts, Tracey said, "I told Penelope I was going to see you today, and she asked me to pass on an invitation to a family barbecue at her house on July fourth to celebrate both our birthdays." He chuckled, recalling her story, "No more floating birthdays for her."

"Yeah, she really milked that one. She always enjoyed choosing the day." *What's with this, anyhow? Another Hugo replacement?* "I don't have any plans for the fourth. Count me in – she always does good barbecues."

"So, are you and Penelope an item? Charlotte said she saw something between you two at the party that made her feel like you were more than just friends."

"Unfortunately, right now she works for me and so…"

*

The following Friday, seated in their usual booth at the bar, after reading the memo, Bobby asked Penelope, "I have to ask you again – can you remain objective, with Tracey on the list?"

"We've barely gotten the data in and analyzed it. Quite frankly, I was surprised to see his name. Besides, I can't imagine him with a… sex worker. Almost anybody else. But Tracey?"

Bobby chuckled, "Yeah, I have a hard time seeing Tracey as a serial killer – retired judge, museum board, Sarah's House. On

the other hand, well-to-do, private golf club, tall, left-handed –
those are all part of our killer's profile. But somehow, I still can't
see it being Tracey. Last week, I spent over six hours playing golf
with him, and I've gotta tell you, your brother's pretty straight-
laced. In fact, he can be a little boring, but basically, he's an all-
round good guy. Let's just keep our minds open for now."

She looked at him and raised her eyebrows, "Innocent until
proven guilty – he's my brother, for God's sake. I don't think it's
him."

"Objective, eh?"

Chapter Twenty-Seven

It was a sizzling hot Fourth of July in Raleigh, and so muggy it felt like it should be raining, but it wasn't. According to the weather service, the conditions were the same along much of the eastern seaboard. Charlotte and Penelope wore the lightest weight sundresses possible, one blue and the other red, and sandals, of course. Sarah wore a diaper and a little white sundress with tiny red and blue stars. It had been a gift from her aunt, who found extraordinary pleasure in buying such presents for her. They agreed that they all looked quite festive. The men were dressed in shorts, t-shirts and flip-flops or sandals, clean, casual and definitely picnicky.

Auntie Pens carried Sarah around the grassy area in her backyard, pretending to play cornhole with her, putting the small bags into her hands and "helping" her niece drop them into each hole. Every time she did this, she raised a fist and called out, "Score!" and Sarah clapped her hands.

Tracey, Bobby and Mikey complained that the girls were cheating. Penelope and Charlotte protested, saying that Sarah was a key member of their team, balancing the numbers at three to three, and that was just how she played cornhole. Take it or leave it.

They all laughed.

The girls' team won because, of course, every one of Sarah's tosses had gone into the hole. With fresh cold bottles of beer in hand, and in Charlotte's case, a glass of sparkling lemonade that she and Tracey had made from the lemons growing in their backyard, they all celebrated the win.

When all of a sudden, Sarah began screaming and wailing, thrashing around in Penelope's arms, she took the baby and handed her over to Charlotte, "Wow, this is more than I can handle. How do you manage? It's way beyond my paygrade."

"Moms have no paygrade," Charlotte laughed and took Sarah, blowing gently on her neck. "Oh, my. You are a hot, sweaty little girl. Let's get you a dry diaper, some dinner and a little less stimulation in a cool place."

"Go on upstairs and use my room," said Penelope. "I have a comfy chair in there, and my bathroom counter is large enough to use as a changing table."

Sarah whimpered and nuzzled into her mother's chest as Charlotte whisked her into the cool kitchen and grabbed the diaper bag off a chair in the dining area before heading upstairs. At the top, she saw the open door to the master bedroom.

Twenty minutes later, with a much calmer Sarah in her arms, she whispered to her, "Let's explore before we go back out into that nasty heat. I wonder what's behind this door. Oh, look, a bathroom." She continued, "This is like Goldilocks. That first room was tooo big, and this one is tooo small." She pulled the bathroom door partially closed, "Let's see if the third room is just right."

Charlotte opened the door to Penelope's office and noticed the large window opposite the door looking out into what she presumed was the back yard, "Oh look, Mommy was right, not too big and not too small." As she went over to look out the window, she paused at the worktable in the middle of the room, its surface covered with tidy stacks of files. "Look, Sarah, Auntie Pens works from home. Shall we see what she—"

Printed on paper that had been stuck onto one of the walls, she saw the words, "*Parking Lot Strangler*" in bold letters with notes and photos organized carefully by each murder. Charlotte stared at the wall lined with papers, photos of the victims, crime scenes and evidence, meticulous notes on little stickies and maps with pins poked into them. Her jaw dropped, and she whispered, "Oh, Sarah, don't look." She turned Sarah's face into her neck before stepping closer for a good look herself.

With a quick glance out the window at the backyard to make sure everyone was accounted for, Charlotte saw her family standing around the picnic table, beers in hand, laughing and talking as Mikey tried to fit the oversized Jenga blocks back into their box.

She turned back to look more closely at meticulously curated case details. This was no job, this was a life's work.

"Burgers in five minutes," she heard Penelope yell.

Charlotte couldn't resist, "When am I going to get another chance to witness crime-solving in action?" She juggled Sarah to her other hip and pulled her cell phone from her pocket, quickly snapping photos of the material pinned to the walls.

When she went back downstairs, Penelope was alone in the kitchen. Charlotte said quietly to her, "I'm sorry. I might have accidentally wandered into your office. That's some serious work going on with your serial killer investigation." Charlotte looked around before continuing, "One of the women you have a picture of was the concierge on the cruise we took to Ukraine. You know, Tracey and I wondered what happened when Mari disappeared after that stop. She was lovely. The scary thing is that it could have been me murdered that day."

Shit, I didn't lock my office. But why would she open a closed door? Good thing I put the persons of interest list in a folder in the drawer instead of leaving it where such snoopy old ladies like her could see it. What a Nosy Parker. That was one of Penelope's favorite descriptions for people poking their noses in where they didn't belong, but she'd never in her life had a chance to actually use it herself. Had she not been so angry at Charlotte, she would have gloated.

Instead, she glared at her and snapped, "You never should have gone into my office. I can't discuss the details, Charlotte. *Don't* tell anyone what you saw up there." She turned on her heel and stomped outside to the grill with a large platter of raw burgers in her hands.

On the way out, her phone rang. Shoving the burgers at Tracey, she pulled it out of her back pocket. She recognized the call as the one she'd been waiting for and abruptly said, "I've got to take this. You're in charge of grilling now, bro."

Tracey winced, *Now, there's a nickname I particularly hate.*

Penelope walked across the yard and leaned against the back fence.

Mikey and Bobby were kicked back at the picnic table, talking about the birthday cake Bobby had made. "It's from a box. The frosting – from a cardboard container. The candles – from another box. Those hard sugar roses and letters are ones that you soak off the paper and arrange on the cake."

Mikey laughed, "You went all out, my friend. I saw it in the kitchen. It looks good – except for the missing 'p' in '*Happy*'."

"Yeah, it fell off into the water and kinda dissolved," Bobby grimaced. "I read the instructions afterwards, and it said to put the paper on a very wet cloth until the pieces loosened and could be peeled off." He sighed, "I'm sure Tracey or Penelope could have done better. But I couldn't have the birthday twins making their own cake for this party."

"So, how did you score an invitation to this family affair?"

"When my wife, Hallie, was alive, she and Penelope and I would always celebrate our birthdays together. We were very tight, the three of us. I'm trying to figure out if this is a pity invite or what."

"I doubt it. It's a good party with family here," he clinked the neck of his beer bottle against Bobby's. "It seems like you're pretty close to being family for Penelope."

Meanwhile, Charlotte, feeling a bit embarrassed, had gone to stand next to Tracey at the grill. She bounced Sarah on her hip.

Penelope came back, put her hand on the back of Bobby's neck, bent over and whispered into his ear, "That was my contact in the judge's office in Indianapolis. The warrant to MyDNA finally arrived there for approval." Bobby grinned and gave her a thumbs-up.

Overhearing her, Mikey said excitedly, "A warrant for DNA, that's so cool."

Tracey's stomach plummeted.

After looking at Penelope for a moment, gauging her reaction, Bobby stood up and said to the group, "You all know, we're working on the Parking Lot Strangler case. But what I'm about to tell you stays here."

Penelope looked at him, her face twisting into a what-the-fuck look. *You're sharing this when my brother's on our list?*

Bobby reached over and caressed her shoulder, "It's okay. I'm just going to give some context to what Mikey said." He gave the group a stern look as he continued, "We're trying to match some DNA from the crime scenes."

With everyone fully focused on what Bobby was sharing,

Chapter Twenty-Seven

Tracey felt his face flush, and he broke into a sweat.

Bobby went on, choosing his words carefully, "We're grasping at straws here because judges generally don't approve these types of warrants. But we feel like we finally have a strong enough justification."

Penelope added, "So, fingers crossed."

Oh fuck!! Tracey felt rivulets of sweat run down his back.

Penelope moved over to stand next to Charlotte and said quietly, "Sorry, I didn't mean to snap at you."

Charlotte said, "I understand. I'm sorry. I shouldn't have snooped." She put a hand on Penelope's arm.

After leaning over to give Sarah a quick peck on her nose, Penelope turned to Tracey, "You've been grilling too long in this brutal heat, birthday boy. Your face is all red. Let me take over for you. Go put an ice cube on the back of your neck or get something cold to drink. I don't want you stroking out."

The Interview

"So, I'm curious, what drove you to," Jane paused as she repeated the question she'd asked him earlier, "to kill all these women?"

"Anger." Tracey's voice was toneless. "When I murdered my moth – my aunt, I was angry. Very angry. I felt like she had abandoned me – again. I lost control." His eyes slid to his left, and he gazed into the distance over Jane's shoulder, recalling the early murders. He reached over and picked up the toothpick holder they'd moved to the side of the table and shook out a toothpick. "The first four – I was killing my mother every time. Every time. Each one of them had red hair, and each one of them dismissed me."

Jane watched curiously as he repeatedly pressed the sharp point of the toothpick into his right thumb. "Tell me."

After she'd spoken, he continued to look off into the distance, remembering, before finally shifting his eyes back to look at her face. "It all began that night in the parking lot. At the time, I still believed she was my mother. My mother, who my twin sister and I thought had abandoned us when she went out and left us to be taken away by Child Protective Services. My mother, who never came and got us. That night, in the parking lot, even after I'd shown her my birthmark and told her who I was – I had such hopes that I'd finally have my mother back – she wouldn't acknowledge me as her family, she didn't call me 'son', she just said she had to go home to her family. At that time, I believed I was her family too." He cleared his throat, "And then, when she said, 'excuse me' and turned away so dismissively, it was as though she were leaving me all over again. Something inside me just snapped – and I put my hand around her throat and strangled her."

"*Her* name was Maggie Wilson," said Jane.

"Mmmm," he grunted. Absently, he lifted his cup to his lips and took a sip, having forgotten that it had already grown cold. He made a face and set the cup down and went on, "It was only when I found out from Mikey and his dad that she was my aunt that I understood she hadn't been abandoning me… us. Even though she raised me and my sister for a few years, we were never really hers."

"Mmmm," she said, nodding, encouraging him to continue.

"I wish I'd known she wasn't my mother back then." He looked at Jane, his voice a whisper she could scarcely hear, "I killed the wrong woman that night."

"If you'd known she wasn't your mother, would you have killed her?"

"I don't know. Yes – no – oh hell, I don't know. One of her 'friends', her John, sexually abused me. I was only a little boy. I was so confused. She yelled at him, but then she made me feel like I'd done something wrong too. She scolded me, her voice was so loud. She shook me and told me I was a bad boy and could put her job at risk. And she never talked to me about it. She was the adult, and I was only four years old."

"Do you think talking about it would have made a difference?"

"Because we never talked about it, because she didn't explain why she'd been angry at me, I was sure I'd done something wrong, but I didn't understand what. I felt very alone – isolated – I felt like she didn't want me because I was bad."

Jane watched silently as Tracey struggled to contain his emotions. Her professor in film school had told her that when she was interviewing people, remaining silent often would result in them telling her more than if she prompted them with questions. So, she sat, silent, waiting.

"Then she abandoned me and my sister. At the age of four, I was sure it was because I was a bad boy. That feeling has affected me my entire life."

"Did you and Sarah talk about how you felt?"

"No, just about how we missed her and about what we'd all do together when she came and found us. But she didn't come, and my sister was adopted first. She left me too. A few months later, my parents adopted me."

Jane sat, and as she listened, she wondered how anyone could survive feeling rejected so many times.

"Killing her, killing the other three women in Raleigh. I lost control of myself, of that part of my life. But when the newspaper reporter called me a serial killer, the Parking Lot Strangler, I knew I had to get away, to try to get myself under control and stop killing."

"You didn't stop. What happened?"

"Even though the other women reminded me of my… aunt, I wasn't killing her any longer. I was killing because I liked it. You know, I met my wife on the same cruise when I killed for the fifth time, in Zaporizhzhya."

"Did meeting Charlotte help you control your urge to kill?"

"I suppose…" He scratched his chin thoughtfully, "The young skateboarder in Budapest? She was the last time I killed for pleasure."

He glanced at Jane, "I think I had become a bit of a fuddy-duddy before I met her. My life was work, my golf buddies and only brief romantic interludes. But she made me laugh. With her, I felt relaxed and less concerned about what other people thought. And then we met our wonderful group of friends on our honeymoon cruise."

Jane waited.

"To answer your question, when I first met Charlotte, we became very close very quickly. But I was always afraid she might leave me too. It was only after we were married that I didn't feel such a compulsion to kill." He scrubbed his face with his hands, "Now, I've lost my wife and my child. That wasn't supposed to happen. No one was supposed to find out. So many things weren't supposed to happen."

"Weren't supposed to happen?" she repeated, watching as he struggled with his feelings.

"Yes," he said, an edge to his voice, "…so many things weren't supposed to happen… You know, twice, I've killed the wrong woman."

"Twice?"

"In Strasbourg, I'd planned to kill Mimi. We took a walking tour together, and she would never stop her incessant chatter. I wanted to strangle her, just to make her shut up. It wasn't until her body went limp and her hood came off as I was strangling her that I realized the woman in my hands was the wrong one. But it was too late then." He shook his head sadly.

"Her name was Isabelle. But tell me, what happened to Mimi?"

He raised a shoulder slightly, tilting his palms upward, "She's the one who got away."

"I'm having problems figuring you out, Tracey. Sometimes, you're completely dispassionate when you describe your murders, as though they were committed by someone else. And then, other times, you look, you sound as though you regret it all."

"In hindsight," he glanced upward, "I suppose I do regret it."

Chapter Twenty-Eight

MEMORANDUM FOR THE RECORD

TO: Lieutenant Bobby Figg, Major Crimes Unit, Raleigh PD

CC: Tibor Papp, President, Security Consulting International Ltd.
Edgar Spring, Investigative Journalist

FROM: Penelope Huber, Consultant to Raleigh PD

DATE: August 1, 2014

SUBJECT: Parking Lot Strangler Investigation – Memo #19

This memo covers the week of July 26 – August 1.

The judge in Indianapolis denied the MyDNA warrant, calling it a fishing exercise. Nonetheless, the team has compiled a list of persons of interest from the river cruise manifests.

The data from Spectrum yielded six passengers who were in St. Petersburg, Budapest, Strasbourg and Zaporizhzhya on the dates of the murders or within four days before or after. Based on further analysis, the team eliminated three of the six passengers. The following remain as persons of interest:

- Arthur Elliott, a British citizen, traveled regularly to New York City from London and therefore, could have driven to Raleigh and Trigg Pass to commit those murders.
- Jason Zapori and Connor Newsome, both American citizens, were in all the cities at the time of the murders. They are a couple from Wilton Manors, Florida, and could have driven to Raleigh to commit those murders. They also have family in Seattle, WA, which is near Trigg Pass. One or both of them could have committed that murder.

The data received from the five non-Spectrum cruise lines yielded twenty-five passengers who were in St. Petersburg, Budapest, Strasbourg and Zaporizhzhya during the time frames in question. The team eliminated seventeen non-Americans and seven Americans. The following passenger is a person of interest:

- Harold Davis, an American citizen, lives in Philadelphia. He was in the States during the time of the Raleigh and Trigg Pass murders.

The following person previously surfaced as a person of interest:

- Tracey Lauch was identified in every location except Trigg Pass and Budapest. While we haven't found him on any airline passenger lists for Seattle, we know he was still living in the U.S. when the Trigg Pass murder took place and was living in Sicily at the time of the Budapest killing. So, he could have easily reached both locations by car.

With the identification of these five individuals, we've ceased collecting license plate information from the private golf clubs. Lauch showed up at the club where he is a member. Zapori and Newsome are both golfers and showed up at another private golf club as guests of a member. That puts the three of them highest on our list of persons of interest.

Additionally, since these individuals have been identified, Spring will discontinue his research.

Next Steps

It's recommended that the Raleigh PD interview the above-named persons and request a warrant to obtain their credit card information to help determine their locations at the times of the murders.

Now that the suspect list has been narrowed down to five individuals, the team will contact hotels in the cities where the murders occurred and ask them to review their registration records to determine if these individuals were guests during the timeframe of the murders.

Chapter Twenty-Nine

Tracey and Charlotte sat at the kitchen counter after they'd put Sarah to bed and caught the evening news. She watched Tracey as he washed a small pile of lemons and carefully peeled their zest to make homemade limoncello for themselves and as gifts for the family. As he finished with each lemon, he passed it over to her to cut and juice for the pitcher of lemonade she was preparing.

Tracey had consulted extensively with Fong's investment advisor and had just finished moving his money. They'd had fruitful discussions about what to do with the proceeds once he sold the house and the best way to avoid excessive taxes on it. He told Charlotte that, based on the decisions he and the advisor had made, he was comfortable that his investments were in good hands. In addition, Tracey had received a cash offer on his house, although it was significantly lower than the realtor had told him to expect.

"I'm glad we've gotten our finances in order," said Charlotte. "But I'm not sure you should accept this offer on the house, you can get much more for it. I just don't understand the rush. We plan to be here until February. Why not hold off a bit longer?"

"It's been on the market for four months, Charlotte," Tracey replied in an exasperated voice, "It's *my* house, and I just want to get this done and move on with things. I'm accepting the offer. There will be no more discussion of this." He picked up the next lemon and began to remove the zest with deft fingers.

When he called her by name during a tense discussion, she knew it was time to change the subject – after one last word, "Don't talk down to me, Tracey. There's no need. I want the best for all of us, just as you do. But you're right, it's your house and you should do what you feel is best."

"Sorry, my love. You're right, that was uncalled for. I guess I just got up on the wrong side of bed this morning. I've been grumpy all day." He put down the lemon and peeler and walked around the counter to give her a kiss.

Tracey's rare contrition surprised Charlotte. "Apology accepted," she returned his kiss with vigor. "We can continue this later. Let's finish up here and then maybe we can have an early night." She grinned at him and gave him a final peck on the lips.

"Back to work, wench," he said with a chuckle and a swat on her bottom.

"I talked with Remy this morning. She was quite chipper since Fong has finally agreed to do the addition she wants. She nattered away for a good while about the work they've already begun on the little cottage."

"Fong mentioned that to me too," said Tracey. "He didn't sound opposed to it now that they have actual drawings and have begun work. He said he's running around trying to source old stone to match the existing exterior so it will look like it's always been there. I think it's a good idea to add on. They were tripping over each other when we were there for Sarah's baptism."

"My goodness, they were. That one-bedroom, one-bath cottage is definitely too small for two people." Charlotte put the pitcher of lemon juice in the refrigerator, covering it with a silicon lid. "There, that's ready to finish up tomorrow." She came over to stand beside him.

"I'm glad to hear that she's doing so well. Does it seem like her memory is returning?"

"No, it's still that one night that's missing. She said the doctors continue to tell her that the longer it goes on, the less chance there is that it will come back. I feel so sorry for her."

Tracey placed all the lemon zest in a gallon jar and poured a liter of one-hundred-proof vodka over it before sealing the top tightly. He set it on a shelf in the pantry and draped a towel over it. Charlotte looked at him, puzzled. "It has to be kept in absolute darkness for a couple of weeks, even when I come in to shake it every day," he replied to her unspoken question.

He opened the door to the wine fridge and took out a bottle of his favorite French rosé. With a quick twist of his wrist, he removed the screw cap and poured himself a healthy glass. "Sparkling water?"

"Yes, please, a very large glass. With lemon and lots of ice."

Tracey handed her the glass, and they carried their drinks into the sitting room at the back of the house to relax.

"Oh, Remy also said that Sasha will be calling you in a day or so to talk about the harvest. Since we're accepting this offer on the house, do you think we'll actually have time to make a quick trip over there to help out?"

"I doubt it. We're going to be pretty busy disposing of the contents of this house and arranging to ship those few things we've decided to keep. Is that list—"

"In the little bright red notebook on your desk labeled '*House Sale*'."

"Now that we've decided to accept the offer, this house is taken care of," Tracey said, making a checkmark on his mental list with a smile of relief.

"I've been giving some considerable thought to what to do about the museum and Sarah's House. Tell me what you think. I'd like to ask Penelope to take care of Sarah's House until our little Sarah is old enough to take over. The well-being of those kids is so important to me. And she's told me several times how impressed she is at the concept and the impeccable running of the home. That will tie in nicely with her desire to be an advocate for women and children in need, you know."

"I think you should ask her about taking that on, not me."

"While we were out playing golf the other day, I asked Bobby about his intentions toward Penelope."

"You didn't! You're her brother, not her father, Tracey. How could you?"

"I'm her older brother, and since we don't have a father, that responsibility falls to me," said Tracey solemnly.

"Yeah, a whopping five minutes older. I hope Bobby doesn't tell her about your conversation. How humiliating!"

"He took it as intended. He said he's deeply in love with her, but she's with someone else. He has to respect that. Besides, while she's on this project, she works for him, so they can't have a relationship anyway. It has a little over six months to run. Who knows if they'll ever solve the case. Regardless, then he can step back in and give this guy a run for his money."

"Mmmm, that's interesting. I got a much more positive vibe about the case when they talked about it at the birthday party."

She turned and looked at Tracey, "It sounds like they've made a lot of progress."

Bile rose in Tracey's throat at her comment. He swallowed hard before continuing, "Well, Bobby's a good friend and an avid golfer, a damned good one, to boot. Since they were both at the annual Sarah's House fundraiser last month, they saw how it's run. I hope he'll be willing to give her a hand managing the event. I'd also like to gift my golf club membership to Penelope, keep it in the family, you know, but for Bobby to use. And of course, that means I'll be able to be her guest when we do come back to visit."

Charlotte bit her tongue and shook her head.

Tracey took a sip of his wine, "As far as the museum goes, I'd like Mikey to take over my position on the board of directors. He's young and enthusiastic about life, and a lot of members of his family are artists, his mom, his stepmom, his brother."

"Again, that's for him to answer, not me. But since you asked for my thoughts, he's very young to take on such a responsibility."

"About the same age I was when Granddad appointed me to the board."

"But you'd been cultivated for it long before you joined. What if they don't want to take over for you, Tracey? What if they have other plans?"

"That's nonsense," said Tracey. "Of course they'll jump at the opportunity. Why in the world wouldn't they?"

"I'm just surprised at how fast everything is happening. All of a sudden, you sound surprisingly anxious to wrap everything up and get back to Sicily."

"That's our home now, Charlotte. I'm on the final stretch to turning fifty, and I want to devote my time to my family. This constant travel back and forth between Europe and the U.S., managing all these things here at such a distance, it's beginning to wear on me."

"You just turned forty-four, my love," Charlotte snickered. "You're just entering middle age, the prime of your life."

"These decisions actually aren't all that sudden, Charlotte, at least not to me. I think about things, you know, I mull them over for a long time. Sometimes I need to talk about them and sometimes I just think about them. From the outside, it may look like it's very sudden. Like when I decided to retire after my parents died, when I suddenly left to travel in Europe, when I bought the house in Sicily for you, and now selling the house and giving up my responsibilities here in Raleigh. This might seem impulsive to you, but believe me, I thought it all through long before I first mentioned it. Anyway, it's time to pass the torch to the younger generation."

Charlotte laughed, "Penelope's the same age as you."

"But she seems much younger, or maybe I just feel so much older. I'm going to invite them both to dinner tomorrow night to discuss my proposal. What do you think?"

"What if they don't want to do it?"

*

Bobby had warned Penelope that she might be uncomfortable accepting Tracey and Charlotte's invitation to dinner. Charlotte and Tracey had removed all the leaves from the table, creating an intimate square. Penelope and Charlotte sat on opposite sides at the immaculately set table with Mike and Tracey across from each other. Penelope thought about how right Figg had been, how awkward it was to be at dinner with one of the five suspects on her list. Quite frankly, she'd been able to avoid spending time with Tracey because she'd been very busy with the case and her stepped-up triathlon training. In fact, thinking about it, she realized they hadn't gotten together as a family since the birthday barbecue.

"Why would you want to leave this?" Penelope gestured around the beautifully appointed room and then around the table at the family sitting together. "Tracey, you've just spent all this time talking about how important family is, but now that you've found us, you're leaving and moving permanently halfway around the world."

She paused to take a gulp of her wine. "You're abandoning all the things you love here as well – your involvement with Sarah's House, your seat on the museum board and – and giving them to us," she pointed to Mikey and herself, "essentially a couple of strangers."

"But Penelope, we're family," Mikey said.

Tracey smiled at him, "Exactly, the two of you are family *and* well suited to the responsibilities. Believe me, I'm a good judge of character." He nodded toward Mikey, "And it's good to get young blood involved in the arts. Someday, Mikey, you will be Raleigh's chief medical examiner and…"

Mikey smiled, tipping his head to the side, shrugging with one shoulder.

"And perhaps someday, you'll even hold that job at the state level. The board position will prepare you for those leadership roles. And it will be a wonderful addition to your portfolio."

He turned and smiled at his sister, "Penelope, ever since we met, you've talked about getting involved with children after your gig with the PD is up. I think responsibility for Sarah's House is a perfect fit and the stipend is pretty good." He looked between the two of them, "The two of you are naturals for these positions."

Penelope picked up her linen napkin to wipe her mouth, and behind it, she muttered to herself, "I certainly would never go around arranging other people's lives for them without consulting them first."

Charlotte overheard Penelope and reached over to place her hand on Tracey's, "I know this all sounds very overwhelming. This is Tracey's way of consulting with you, this is his way of honoring you." She looked at him and shook her head, "He's just trying to look out for the things that have mattered to him for so long. Yes, it may seem like he's steamrolling you to do this. He's trying to be generous but also make sure that people he feels are absolutely qualified take over the positions. Take some time to think about it." She looked at Mikey and then at Penelope. Her eyes were soft and understanding, "Tracey's been thinking about this for quite a while, so it seems obvious to him. Truly, you don't need to respond tonight – just give it some thought."

Tracey said with a grateful smile at his wife, "Just don't take too long, please."

Relieved that the conversation hadn't gone as badly as it might have, Charlotte asked, "Penelope, what happened to the

DNA warrant?"

"I'm not comfortable discussing the case… other than to say it was denied."

"That's unfortunate," said Tracey with a silent sigh of relief.

Penelope saw the tension in his shoulders relax ever so slightly. *I hadn't noticed how tense he was until he did that. I guess it's understandable, selling his beautiful house and giving up his life in Raleigh, passing all this on to me and Mikey. I might be a little tense myself under the circumstances.*

*

After their guests had departed and the residue from dinner cleared away, Charlotte and Tracey sat out on the patio. They heard the grandfather clock strike eleven through the windows, "At least I'm not going to need to spend a fortune replacing those old windows." He took a sip of his cognac, holding it on his tongue and savoring the flavor.

Charlotte looked at his drink enviously, "These are the evenings that I think I'm about done with breastfeeding. I would quite like to have a glass of wine or more than a sip or two of any adult beverage for that matter."

"It's your body. I'll support whatever you choose. According to the doctors, eight months is a healthy amount of time to breastfeed."

"I've read about these women who are still breastfeeding after five years. Oh, no, no. I would never do that." She took a sip of her sparkling water with thin slices of their beloved Meyer lemons. "Penelope seemed a bit – mmmm – out of sorts tonight."

"It's unfortunate she couldn't tell us more about the case."

"I think it's absolutely fascinating." She leaned forward, "Imagine, she's been hunting this murderer for so long. Do you think she'll finally find him?"

"I don't know. After all this time…"

"I saw walls filled with information at her house when we were there for your birthdays."

"Honestly, I don't understand your fascination with this, Charlotte." Tracey took a quick, nervous sip of his cognac.

Clearing his throat, he suddenly said, "With the house sold, I think we should give serious thought to moving our trip to Casablanca up to November. We can spend the holidays there."

Charlotte slumped back in her chair, "That means we'll miss your final time hosting the gala. And just when I've found a spectacular new gown for it."

"We'll find some fantastic place in Casablanca where you can wear your spectacular dress for New Year's Eve. It'll be new, different, fun."

"Oh, I don't know, Tracey, I just don't know. I've been looking at some very nice places here that we can rent until February."

*

As Mikey drove Penelope home, she said, "So, that was one of the oddest evenings I've spent in a while. What do you think of Tracey's proposals?"

"He's like an uncle to me," Mikey said. "He's so much older, and he is so wise, so I'll probably accept."

"Hey, watch it there with the 'so much older' stuff. I'm the same age he is."

"But you're so much more youthful and athletic. Anyhow, I'm scared about taking on this big board position, but he's right, it could advance my career. I need to think ahead and plan, even though thinking that far ahead makes me pretty nervous. Sheesh, I haven't even graduated from college yet."

"I agree with Tracey. Dream big, cuz. Dream big."

"What do you think about running Sarah's House? You sounded kinda cranky at dinner."

"It's intriguing. I love working with kids. I just don't like someone else planning my life. It was the way he asked, like he expected us to say, 'Yes, please!' Like it was a grandiose gesture that we were expected to grovel around and thank him for. It annoyed me. I feel like he's overstepped. But I could see the board would be a good opportunity for you. And Sarah's House…"

"Thanks… You know, I really like you, Pens. I'm so glad I found you."

"Awww, I really like you too, Mikey."

She waved to him as he carefully pulled away. After stomping across her small porch, she shoved open the front door to her townhouse and slammed it behind her. Bobby was sitting on the couch, a beer in front of him on the coffee table.

"Goddamn it, who does he think he is anyway?"

"Huh? I hope you don't mean me for walking in and helping myself to your beer," Bobby said with a wary look.

"Not as long as you saved one for me," she replied, stalking into the kitchen. "Man, am I glad to see you." She returned with a beer in her hand. "Hang on, what are you doing here, anyhow?" she said as she flopped down on the couch next to him and took a long pull from her bottle. "Where's Hugo?"

"I finally gave in and was gonna hang out with him. But I was saved by the bell. Just when we'd cracked open a couple of beers, his pager went off, and he had to go into work because the emergency room got slammed. Some big accident, I think." Bobby took a swig. "Hugo said I should stick around and finish both of our beers," he gestured with his bottle at the empty one in front of him. "Hey, free beer, comfy couch, a chance to see you and find out what happened tonight. Why don't you get whatever's eating at you off your chest?"

"Dinner was a production. *His* production."

"Tracey's? He's such a good guy."

"Good – because he already has you running the whole fundraiser for Sarah's House. He has decided – *for* me," she pounded her fingertips against her chest, "that I'll be in charge of Sarah's House, and you'll be running the golf tournament fundraiser. He likes to manage everyone's lives."

"The fundraiser at the club was great. Hey, you and I could rule the world."

"And then, he's decided that Mikey is going to take his board seat at the museum. Mikey's just a kid."

"He's a kid, but he's got potential."

"My brother's on our suspect list, and all of a sudden, here he is, bossing me around, planning my life for me like we've grown up together or something." Surprising herself, Penelope burst into tears and buried her head against Bobby's shoulder.

Her entire life, she'd had an image of meeting her "big brother". Everything would be just like it had been when she was four years old and she'd looked up to him. But it hadn't turned out that way at all.

"Hey, hey. What's going on?" he stroked her hair, holding her and letting her cry herself out.

Her voice was thin and whiny, "I don't know. Ever since Em fired me, I've been uber-emotional. It seems like I cry at the drop of a hat."

"You've had a tough year, kid."

With her face still buried against him, she gave a tiny nod, "He's my brother, and I've wanted my brother back for so long." She sniffled, "And now I've finally found him," she looked up at Bobby, "even though his bossy personality really rubs me the wrong way, I don't want him to be the Parking Lot Strangler. I'm so confused."

He took her by the shoulders, pushed her back and looked her in the eye, "Penelope, it's time. It's time for me to take you off the case. Tibor will take over as the lead investigator."

She stared at him as though she had no clue what he was talking about.

"It's time," Bobby persisted. "Let's be honest. He has no alibi. He's one of the primary suspects, and we'll have to bring him in for an interview. It's too much of a conflict of interest for me to keep you on the case."

Her chin started to quiver, and her face crumpled.

He held his arms out, "Ahhh, kid, come here." He pulled her in close to him and continued to stroke her hair, tightening his arms around her and letting her cry again.

"This feels good," she sniffled and snuggled closer to him.

"I like the way it feels when I hold you too."

"Mmmm," she relaxed into him.

"I've missed you, kid."

"What do you mean? You see me all the time. We work together."

"I mean this kind of us together." He slid his hand under her chin and lifted it. When he kissed her, she kissed him back, a kiss that told him how much she'd missed him as well.

Their kiss grew more passionate, and they both began to breathe harder.

Suddenly, she realized that if it continued, they'd end up in bed and she shoved him away, "What the hell are you doing? Don't." She stood up, her voice rising, "Don't you dare."

"Don't you want this? It sure felt like it. Come on, Pens."

"You're taking advantage of me. I'm upset. My brother is a suspect. You've just taken me off the case. I'm hurting. I don't need complications right now. And I'm seeing Hugo. For cripes sake, he's practically living here these days."

"Damn it, Penelope. I'm tired of waiting for you to decide about Hugo. Don't you understand? I love you!"

"Well don't! I don't need you to love me."

Chapter Thirty

MEMORANDUM FOR THE RECORD

TO: Lieutenant Bobby Figg, Major Crimes Unit, Raleigh PD

CC: Edgar Spring, Investigative Journalist

FROM: Tibor Papp, President, Security Consulting International Ltd.

DATE: 5 September 2014

SUBJECT: Parking Lot Strangler Investigation – Memo No. 24

This memo covers the period from 30 August – 5 September.

To summarize, over the past month, five persons of interest were interviewed, and the investigation team assisted in verifying alibis. Interviews were conducted in London, Philadelphia, Wilton Manors, and Raleigh.

The following three individuals have been removed from the persons of interest list:

- Elliott, a British citizen: Eliminated from the list because he came in on a St. Petersburg Spectrum cruise but flew home to teach a class in Oxford before the murder occurred. Evidence shows he was on the flight to Heathrow and students confirm attending his class.
- Zapori and Newsome, both American citizens: Stated they were traveling in China for a religious conference at the time of the Jones murder in Trigg Pass. Alibi verified with information from the airline and interviews with witnesses who met them at the conference.

Two men remain as persons of interest:

- Davis, an American citizen: Did not provide a solid alibi during the dates and times for the Raleigh and Trigg Pass killings. His location the day before, of or after those murders could not be confirmed because he had no credit card activity on those dates. He refused to provide his DNA and insisted on having a lawyer present at any further meetings.

- Lauch, an American citizen: Was in all six locations at the times of the nine murders; confirmed during the interview. Locations verified through flight records and credit card activity. He refused to provide his DNA.

Cell tower data was not available for either suspect because the data had already been purged, based on the cell providers' retention schedule.

Hotel information continues to dribble in and be added to IDAS upon receipt.

The evidence we have so far is good, but it is circumstantial. Without DNA, there is not sufficient evidence to make any arrests or charges.

Next Step

Recommend that Davis and Lauch be ordered to provide a DNA sample.

Page 2 of 2

260

Chapter Thirty-One

Hot and sweaty from her midday run, Penelope toed off her running shoes and kicked them under the table in the front hall on her way to the kitchen. She held her glass to the water dispenser on the front of her fridge, chugged half a glass without stopping and then filled it with ice and more water. She took a couple of sips, set her glass on the counter and turned on the cold tap at the sink under the window. Cupping her hands, she splashed water on her face and then wiped the back of her neck with her wet hand. A shiver of pleasure raised goosebumps on her arms and shoulders. After another quick splash of water, she grabbed the towel from beside the sink and dried her face and neck.

She leaned against the counter in a modified pushup, gently stretching her hamstrings and calves, gazing out the window, thinking about how much she missed working the case – yes, and she missed Figg, his friendship, the banter, their closeness. She was taken aback at the feelings she still had for him, especially since she'd made the decision to put all her efforts into making things work with Hugo. Those feelings had re-surfaced the night when they'd kissed after she'd fallen apart in his arms, and she hadn't been able to shake them.

Then, there had been Hugo's romantic lovemaking the previous night. They'd made love again early that morning and laughed together at something silly – she couldn't remember quite what – before he headed into work. He'd kissed her goodbye and said, "I'll always love you." It had been the first time he'd told her he loved her since their divorce, even during the months since he'd come back and they'd essentially been living together, he'd never said it. He still had his apartment, but he was always at her house – or at work. She was pretty sure that almost everything he had except his furniture had migrated back to her closets. She thought about him right now, upstairs, sleeping.

"Now… what?" She thought about going upstairs and enticing Hugo into the shower with her as she continued to talk to herself. "I have no job, maybe it's time to take my training to another level or sit and do nothing and read a good book – fat chance there, or maybe drive over to the local community college and pick up a catalog, see what courses I can enroll in for the winter."

She gulped the last of her water, dumped out the ice and put the glass in the dishwasher. "Or maybe it's time to take Tracey up on his offer and go acquaint myself with Sarah's House, start getting involved." These past months, she'd enjoyed being home when Hugo got off work, the free time to train harder and spend precious hours with her little niece as the family prepared for their move back to Sicily. But she also knew that pretty soon she'd be bored stiff.

On her way out of the kitchen, an envelope lying on the counter next to the bowl of fresh fruit caught her eye. It had her name on it in Hugo's handwriting. *Hmmm… he doesn't do notes or cards.* With a sinking feeling, she ripped it open and pulled out the folded paper.

"Pens, this isn't working for me. I need more adventures. I've rejoined Doctors Without Borders."

"He didn't even sign it, that son-of-a-bitch coward," she muttered under her breath. "How dare he? He tells me that he'll always love me, but he can't even tell me face to face that he's leaving. He said it would be different this time. It felt different, like he'd grown up. Like we'd grown up. But he still can't have the hard conversations."

There was something else, something hard in the envelope, and she turned it over, shaking it. The key to her townhouse fell out onto the counter with a very final-sounding clink. And then, the tears came.

She held the cold key tightly in her fist until it grew warm, until its sharp teeth dug into her hand, "Dumped by the same man. A second time. Shit, I wanted to have a do-over where it worked. That's it, you coward," she yelled through her tears, "I won't be taken in by you again." She pounded her fist on the counter and then slid to the floor, pulling her knees tightly against her chest and crying, crying harder than she had since Hallie had died.

When she had no more tears left, Penelope picked herself up and ran upstairs, avoiding the empty side of her closet. She gave her face a thorough wash and put on fresh sunscreen before she changed into her cycling clothes and grabbed her swimsuit. "You've got to stay on track with your training. Don't let that asshole throw you off course," she said aloud, snatching a banana from the fruit bowl to eat during her ride. While she sat on the garage step and tied her biking shoes, she continued to curse Hugo under her breath. Having jammed her swimsuit and goggles willy-nilly into her backpack, she clipped on her helmet and pushed her bicycle out onto the driveway. She'd take the extra-long route to the community pool, she decided.

She'd pushed herself during her swim and achieved a new personal record, following it by a slow double loop on her bike route home. Penelope's legs quivered as she stowed her bike away and hung her swimsuit on the line in her garage. She stood for a long time in a hot shower, letting it beat against her sore muscles before pulling on her favorite comfy jeans and a light t-shirt and shoving her bare feet into a pair of worn Dockers. She braided her hair to keep it from whipping into her eyes, put the rag top down and jumped into her Miata.

She spent hours driving around aimlessly on little back roads with her music blasting, thinking about how their divorce hadn't been the end of her feelings toward Hugo. About how she'd let him back into her life… and her bed… because she thought she still loved him. About how, without missing a beat, she'd jumped right back into their relationship as though it had never ended all those years ago. That morning, when he'd said that he would always love her, she was certain that he thought he was being truthful. But now, she was pretty sure that it wasn't her who he loved, it was the fantasy of something that had never been enduring and never would be. During her drive, she'd realized she'd bought into that. The memories of what they'd had in the early days were so good. She'd wanted that feeling back. The realization that she had just been part of Hugo's fantasy hurt terribly, but it also brought her peace. It wasn't her, it wasn't personal.

*

As the sun was just starting to go down, she parked in Bobby's driveway. She got out of the car and walked up to the porch, then reached out her hand and tentatively rang the doorbell, wondering if coming there had been the right thing. When he answered, Penelope looked down, embarrassed, "Figg, Hugo left. Again."

He pulled Penelope into his arms, "I know. He wanted me to tell you, but I told him he had to man up and do it himself."

"Why couldn't he, Figg? Why? He didn't even tell me to my face, the coward just left me a note."

"The son-of-a-bitch," he muttered under his breath.

"Exactly."

"How are you holding up?"

"After I pitched a fit and called him every name in the book and cried about it, I did an extra hard training session and then went for a drive. When Hugo first came back, I thought I still loved him the way I did when we were first married. In some ways, it was even better this time. The sex was good, we were comfortable with each other, I still found him attractive, and he said he was attracted to me too, I even thought he listened to me." Penelope smiled, "But Figg, the feelings I used to have for Hugo aren't there any longer. Y' know, for a long time, I wondered if it was me, and I thought if I just worked harder, we would be all right, we could make it work. Today, after I calmed down, I realized I was relieved I wouldn't have to be the one to say it, to tell him there was nothing left, that it wasn't working, and I wanted out. I guess that makes me a coward too."

Bobby kissed her forehead, "It wasn't workin' for me either."

They both laughed in relief.

"Why don't we go around back and have a beer."

Sitting on colorful Adirondack chairs, looking out across the adjacent farmland, Bobby asked, "So, you're okay?"

"I think so. Maybe food will help me decide. I need to get something to eat. I'm starving, I haven't had anything but a banana since breakfast. Can I raid your kitchen?"

"I've got some steaks marinating in the fridge, potatoes we

can bake and salad fixings."

She laughed, "Steaks? As in more than one? Are you expecting company? Am I…?"

"I'd hoped you might come by."

They stood next to the grill, shoulders touching, the silence comfortable. Suddenly, Penelope broke it, "Wow, the last time we grilled together was at my birthday party."

"A lot's happened this summer." He remarked that she'd been under an unbelievable amount of stress for several months. "You're holding up well, all things considered," he said, looking her up and down appreciatively. "You were just jilted – again – by your ex-husband. We still have our unresolved relationship to figure out. And you found your brother, and then you discovered that he's a suspect in a case you've been working forever, a case I'm convinced we're going to solve pretty soon." He put his arm around her in a friendly hug.

They carried the steaks into the kitchen. While Bobby took the salad from the refrigerator and set the table, Penelope pulled the potatoes out of the oven, tossing them from one hand to the other, "Yow, they're hot." She dropped one onto each plate.

Bobby laughed, "You always do that. Why you don't use a hot pad or a towel is beyond me." He handed her a beer, "Here, hold this. It'll cool your hands off."

She rolled the bottle between her hands and then after a couple of swigs, she looked at him questioningly, "So what's going on here? Steak dinner? You doing the grilling?"

Bobby sliced into his steak and took a bite, "We need to talk."

He never says that when he wants to talk about work. He just jumps in. Penelope got a little flutter in her stomach that she tried to drown with a swallow of beer. *I thought I'd pushed him away permanently when I told him I didn't need him to love me.*

Her voice was unsteady as she said, "Oh? We already broke up, so it can't be that."

"But we didn't break up."

"You're right, Figg… we're just taking a break." They both laughed before she went on, "You're right. We do need to talk."

"You did a lot of fantastic work, Pens. I hope you realize, it wasn't personal, my taking you off the case."

"I know," she poked at her potato several times, uneasy at how the conversation might go.

"Quite frankly, when you came back to work on the case in March, I didn't think you would find anything more than you already had. I thought it was just a CYA exercise by the department. But in just six months, we found a whole group of suspects. You should be damned proud of yourself."

"Thanks. But it was teamwork."

"Now, with some hard work and shrewd analysis, your team has whittled that list down to two suspects who have both refused to give us their DNA… and our request to make them comply was just denied."

"So, that sucks. What did you want to talk about then?"

"We made the conscious decision not to try to collect DNA from the suspects' trash or stage a scenario to get a sample from a glass or something like that. We want there to be no question that the DNA was collected by the book, particularly in light of the fact that one of the suspects is a well-respected member of the Raleigh community."

"Your point…?"

"It's personal." Bobby leaned over and put his hand on her arm.

Where is this going?

He flipped her hand over and ran his finger down the inside of her forearm, stopping at her wrist.

Penelope felt her heart beat faster.

He traced the vein on her wrist with his finger.

Oh, God, don't stop.

"You know, your DNA is a very close match to one of those guys."

Penelope's eyes widened, and she jerked her arm back, staring at him, "I don't know. I just don't know if I can do that, Figg. He's my flesh and blood. He's my brother."

"But it could eliminate him, kid."

"Or it could confirm that it's him. And it would be me pointing the finger."

"Couldn't you live with that? You've been looking for this murderer – for how long?"

In a small, uncertain voice, she said, "It seems like all my adult life, Figg."

He reached up and took her face in his hands and scrutinized it for a long time. He sat back in his chair, "What does your gut tell you?"

Being asked about her gut feelings while eating, after the day she'd just had, the week, month, hell, who knows how long, something snapped in Penelope.

"*FUCK!*" With an abrupt swoop of her hand, her plate, and all its contents, went flying off the table and crashed into the wall. The plate shattered, and food flew everywhere.

She looked at Bobby, shocked by the violence of her reaction.

"Did that feel good?"

She nodded, "But I'm really hungry."

He pushed his plate between the two of them, and they began to eat.

After a few bites, she laid down her fork and looked at him, "I'll do it."

Chapter Thirty-Two

Their move would officially be complete in a few days. Over the course of the past weeks, they'd made the final, hard decisions about the disposition of the contents of Tracey's house. The furniture and art had all been marked for shipping to Sicily, to Sarah's House or the museum, to stay for the new owners or to be sent off to auction. They'd donated piles of things to charity. Marie and John would stay on to care for the house and gardens until the new owners took possession in a few weeks, and then they'd retire. In addition to their generous retirement funds that Tracey had paid into all along, he planned to give them a very large check as a severance and thank-you for their years of dedicated service.

Charlotte perched on a six-step ladder, carefully removing folded winter clothes from the upper shelves in their capacious dressing room. She had been taking them out and stacking them on the bed. Virtually all of them would be too warm for their vacation in Casablanca and most even too warm for Sicily. Bedding, clothes, coats… When they'd prepared to put the house on the market several months ago, they'd gone through a similar exercise with his summer clothes. That meant they should be able to wrap this up pretty quickly once Tracey returned later that afternoon from a farewell lunch at the club with his golf buddies.

For heaven's sake, Tracey, how many sweaters and long-sleeved polos does one man need? For all of his meticulousness, the man was a packrat when it came to clothes and shoes. They'd been tucked away in chests and closets throughout the house.

Just as she stretched to pick up the next stack from the shelf, her phone rang. Startled, Charlotte frowned. It wasn't any of her special ringtones. Wondering who it was, she struggled to pull her phone from her back pocket while simultaneously descending the ladder, but suddenly, her hip knocked against Tracey's carved wooden box that sat on his chest of drawers. Grabbing for the box, hoping to catch it before it fell onto the hardwood floor while trying to hold onto her phone, she failed at both.

The lid broke off, and its contents spilled out onto the floor. The phone bounced and landed amidst the debris. It rang one last time and was silent.

"Now that's a bloody mess," muttered Charlotte, irritated that she hadn't been more careful.

Dropping to her knees, she began to gather up Tracey's belongings. Cufflinks, watches, collar stays, and… what were these…? Women's earrings?— she ignored her phone as it began to ring again.

One of her favorite chunky Baltic amber earrings from Lydia's shop lay in the mess. She wondered how it had fallen off, since the earrings had those ingenious lever backs that didn't allow them to pull loose, even if they caught in her hair. She reached up, touching her ears to see which one it had come from and frowned. Both of her earrings were still there.

She sat down the rest of the way very slowly and picked up the earring, and it was then that she noticed it wasn't exactly the same as hers. Charlotte recalled the day she'd met Lydia to have her design those beautiful dresses and how she had admired her earrings. In response, Lydia had pressed a similar pair upon her after selling her a necklace that was part of the set.

Flashing back to that night— Lydia lying on her workshop floor, blood beneath her head, Gia kneeling next to her. Lydia— Lydia, with only one earring— in her left ear.

"Lydia?" Charlotte whispered, "How did Lydia's earring get here?"

She picked up the pieces of the elaborately hand-carved box and set it upright. Then she lifted the tray that had fallen out, looking at the specialized compartments for Tracey's watches and other accouterments, wondering if it would still fit into the damaged box. As she started to set it back in place, she noticed that it was designed to sit on top of a bottom layer of small velvet-lined compartments, perfect for – women's earrings?

Charlotte took each earring, slowly lining them up in front of her. There were ten in all. A dangling rhinestone earring, a chain with two small diamonds attached to a larger diamond stud, a gold, teardrop-shaped earring, a bright gold hoop—

She'd seen them before.

Her heart began to pound frenetically. With a shaking hand,

she opened up her photos on her phone, scrolling back to July 4th, to the shots she'd taken at Penelope's house. Of the evidence walls in her office. Of the women. Screen after screen filled with the nine women's faces and the earrings they'd worn. Charlotte zoomed in on each photo of an earring and confirmed that it matched one of those she'd laid out in a careful row on the floor.

It had been so exciting to take the photos, to pore over the evidence that only she knew she had. But now, all she could see were the faces of the murdered women who'd worn the earrings that she'd held in her fingers. Her breath came in short, harsh gasps. Those women were dead because *her husband* had put *his hands* around their throats and strangled the life out of them? She could scarcely breathe.

She looked at the earring she'd picked up again and held tenderly in her hand, the earring that almost matched hers, the one that wasn't in any pictures on the wall. "Lydia?" The realization dawned on her that Tracey must have murdered her friend who'd been his friend too. She shook her head from side to side, "Oh no, no, no…" her voice became more hysterical with each word.

A door slammed, and she heard Tracey's joyful voice call out from downstairs, "My love, I'm home. Where are you?"

Charlotte began to cry in great gulping sobs.

He came to the doorway between the dressing room and their bedroom, "Oh, here you are. Charlotte, what's wrong, are you hurt? Why are you on the floo—" With a sharp intake of breath, he saw the earrings.

Panicked, Tracey's eyes darted from the earrings lined up in a row, each one accusing him of a murder, to Charlotte's bleak face, tears pouring from eyes filled with knowledge and horror at his role in the women's deaths.

Crying uncontrollably, she wailed, "What have you done?" She held out her hand, Lydia's earring lying on her palm, "Oh, what have you done?"

"I'm so sorry. I love you. I never meant – I never intended for you to know. I never meant to hurt you."

She continued to sob.

"I stopped." He stretched out his hands, beseeching her and

took a step forward, "I stopped after Sarah was born." He took another step.

Charlotte raised her arms over her face, defending herself, "Your hands… noooooo… don't touch me," she wailed, scuttling back, frightened by the knowledge that her husband had killed those women, that she had no idea why he'd done it and that he could kill her too.

"Please—" Tracey began, and the despair on Charlotte's face stopped him. He turned deathly pale at having been exposed as a killer by the woman he loved more than anyone in the world. A part of him died at her rejection.

"My love," he said hopelessly before he turned and left her.

She watched him go without a word.

Oh God, if only I hadn't come up here to clear out this closet. She closed her fingers around Lydia's earring, and with it clutched to her chest, she closed her eyes and rocked back and forth, sobbing.

It was dark outside by the time she was finally cried out – for the time being at least. She sat on the floor, staring at her phone and at the earrings, knowing that she needed to call the police. But first, she had to figure out how to breathe again.

Chapter Thirty-Three

That same day, Bobby said, "I'm on my way to pick you up," as soon as Penelope answered his call. "We need to get over to the lab ASAP."

"The results are back?" asked Penelope, her voice so quiet he could scarcely hear it.

Since Penelope had grudgingly agreed to give a sample of her DNA, she had agonized over her decision. How could she not have done everything within her means, including submitting her DNA? If the results today matched the DNA collected from the victims, it would be a huge win for their families and friends – as well as her. And she'd finally be able to stop saying, "The bastard is still out there."

She'd been wracked with guilt ever since she'd gone to the police lab and had swabs taken for comparison. Because if the results matched, she would be responsible for pointing the finger, for her brother ending up in prison, for putting him in the hands of a court that would, without any doubt, hand down the death penalty. He was the one who had looked out for her when they were young children, the one who'd cared so much about her that he'd named the foster home that he'd founded after her, who'd named his daughter after her. It would be all her fault. Oh, what had she done?

She paced back and forth, to the front room window to see if Figg had arrived yet and then all the way back into the kitchen where she gulped down water and set the glass back on the counter, then back to the window. Her stomach was in knots as she walked and waited for what seemed a lifetime.

Finally, it came, a quick tap of his horn. Penelope grabbed her purse and keys, and after a deep breath, she touched the buttons on the alarm to set it and walked out, closing and locking the door behind her. Then, standing beside the passenger door, she hesitated for a final moment before she climbed into Bobby's official vehicle, and they drove off.

"Well?"

"Let's not speculate. The lab tech is waiting for us. As soon as we get there, we'll hear what they have to say. Nothing we do or say now can change the results."

"Aaaagh! You are so frustrating. How can you be so calm?" She pressed her fingertips against her eyelids, "This is tearing me apart, Figg."

"I'm just as torn up inside as you are." He pulled over to the side of the road, put the Escalade in park and took her in his arms. "I'm just better at not showing it."

She sat listening to his racing heart that belied his calm exterior before gently pushing him away, "Then just drive, please."

After checking through the entrance and an interminable elevator ride to the third floor, they stood at the counter in the lab with both sets of DNA results on the large computer screen in front of them. Using his pen as a pointer, the tech pointed out the match between the DNA evidence and Penelope's sample in first the original and then the second round of tests.

Penelope bit down hard on her lip and turned away, trying to steady her breathing and hold back the tears that threatened to come pouring out.

Bobby put a warm hand on the nape of her neck, "It's time to get an arrest warrant."

"This can't be right," Penelope said, shaking her head. "Can't they run the test again?"

"They've run it twice, kid. It's not going to change."

Abruptly, she straightened her shoulders and turned to him. Even though her eyes were still sad, she had resolutely set her jaw. She spoke a little too loudly, her voice hard, like it had been back in the days when she'd had to arrest suspects, "Then we need to find a judge in this city who isn't friends with my brother. If it's him – and this evidence indicates that it is – we need to get the arrest right the first time. Otherwise, he'll get away." She turned to him with anguished eyes, "I can't bear the idea of going through this again."

Chapter Thirty-Four

The little teddy bear lay forgotten near his car's back tire. Lord knows how it got there. Perhaps Sarah had already been asleep when she and Charlotte returned from their playgroup that morning, and it had fallen unnoticed from her hand. Absentmindedly, Tracey tucked it into his jacket pocket as he had done so often before and emerged from the garage, moving slowly, dully, as though he'd aged decades since he'd found Charlotte on the floor of their dressing room just moments ago. He slid a monogrammed leather wallet into his inside breast pocket, the wallet that a few weeks earlier, he'd hidden under the carpet in the trunk to his Mercedes, snug up against the spare tire.

A large black Escalade drove slowly down the street and pulled into the driveway, coming to a halt in front of the steps to the porch. The driver stepped out and opened the back door for Tracey.

Seated in the back of the SUV, with his heart pounding, he took out the slim leather wallet and nervously checked to make sure that everything was there, passports, tickets, credit cards and extra cash, before slipping it back into the inside pocket of his sports coat. He opened his phone and removed the SIM card, tucking that into his pocket as well.

Once at the airport, he bought a roundtrip ticket to New York, knowing the first check would be for one-way tickets going anywhere from Raleigh. After passing easily through security with the help of some breathing techniques to stay calm, ones he'd learned from Lee Fong, *back in the good old days*, he moved on through the terminal. Tracey forced himself to walk nonchalantly until he came to an airport directory. He located a luggage shop where he purchased a small, inexpensive carry-on bag. And in another store, he bought a toothbrush, toothpaste and a few other essentials for the trip as well as a couple of newspapers and a book to read on the flight. In the men's room, he splashed some water on his face and brushed his teeth before tucking his purchases into the carry-on. He knew it was critical not to call any attention to himself at this point when he was so close to escaping. As he passed a crowded bar, he found himself craving a drink to calm his nerves while he waited for the flight to New York but decided to wait until he was on the plane and could relax. He strolled on.

*

In the first-class lounge at JFK, Tracey took a long shower, shaved and changed into the clean clothes he'd purchased at the airport shops there. Feeling refreshed, he tossed the shopping bag holding the clothes he'd worn on his trip from Raleigh into a trash container.

After comfortably making his connection to Marrakesh, he settled back in his seat. The flight attendant approached, "Mr. Jackson?"

"Yes."

"Would you like a drink before dinner?"

"Yes. Scotch, please," he looked up at her with a grateful smile.

"On the rocks or neat?"

"Neat."

"We have a very nice Macallan."

"That would fit the bill."

After she went back to the galley, Tracey pulled the boarding pass out of the book he'd bought earlier and looked at it. "William Jackson," he read to himself, and as he tucked it away in his leather case in front of his passports, he congratulated himself on having had the foresight to use his birth certificate to create a new identity, complete with offshore accounts and two credit cards to accompany it.

Following the multi-course dinner, during which he'd consumed a couple of glasses of Italian red wine, he sipped a cognac, contemplating everything he'd just lost. He'd never laugh or dance or make love again with his wife, he wouldn't get to see his daughter take her first steps or say her first words, much less graduate from high school, and he'd never get to hear her call him "Daddy", he hadn't even been able to kiss them goodbye. He hadn't given his sister or his cousin a final hug. He felt himself growing maudlin and gave himself a mental shake. *You knew this could happen, the need to run at a moment's notice. That's why you redistributed all your money, made this elaborate escape plan... you should feel lucky that it all worked. Did you honestly think you could take your family with you?*

The Interview

August 11, 2015

As the time to end the interview drew closer, Tracey and Jane sat quietly for a few moments. Their table in the small restaurant at the intersection of two narrow alleys near the edge of the Souk Haddadin was tucked off in the corner by a window. This had become his preferred place to sit. The air was filled with the scent of roasting meats and spices and the sound of locals chatting away.

Tracey had explained to his friends, the owners, that he and Jane needed a relatively quiet place to sit for an entire afternoon. He had assured them that she would mention the name of the restaurant in the credits to her film. To accommodate them, the owners had moved the other tables several feet away, and once Jane and Tracey were both seated, they had placed a decorative screen to shield them.

With locals and tourists passing by outside and the walls inside painted in the unique cobalt color known as Majorelle blue with bright yellow trim, he'd thought it would be a picturesque spot for their interview. Suddenly, now, it seemed garish and overly bright, hurting his eyes and making his head pound.

The muted striking of hammers sounded in the background as metal workers in the nearby alleys beat the hot material, forming lanterns of many shapes and sizes, trays, platters and all manner of wares. Instead of his usual pleasure at the music made by the artists' tools as they worked, each clang sent a jolt of pain through his head.

"So, you never answered my first question. How did you find me?"

"It was your sister. You had already planned a trip to Casablanca as a gift for Charlotte. Penelope'd learned that Morocco has no extradition treaty with the U.S. So, she said it was a no-brainer to start there. She looked at flight manifests for the time you disappeared and noticed someone with your birth name was on a flight to Marrakesh. Not a very original choice, was it?"

"I had my birth certificate. It was quick and easy. It was only meant for me to get away."

"So, out of curiosity, should I call you Tracey, or do you go by William these days?"

"What does it matter?"

"Since we're almost out of time, let me ask," Jane pressed on, "during this entire interview, you've not once said the names of your victims or any of your family. Is there a reason you don't name them? Does it somehow give you a buffer between your actions and your emotions? You don't even know what your own name is now. Are you William now because Tracey became a killer, or are you still Tracey because when you kill, you are William, that abandoned child hitting back?"

Tracey squirmed. "I – I don't know. Maybe? But I don't disassociate. I remember every murder clearly. I've never thought about why I don't use their names… or at least, the ones I knew."

"William or Tracey or whoever you are now, you left. You ran away. Why?"

"I couldn't bear to be locked up," he said, his voice so low she had to lean forward to hear him.

"Out of fear – or pride?"

He lifted a shoulder in a brief shrug and tilted his head, "A bit of both, I suppose. And shame that everyone – my family – my golf buddies – the board members – the people who managed Sarah's House – my fellow lawyers and judges – everyone would know what I did."

He looked down and then around the room, pressing his fingers to his throbbing temples.

"Are you okay? You don't look well." She watched his pulse pounding on the side of his neck.

"I want you to stop now. Turn off the camera and the recorder… please?"

With a puzzled look, she reached out to turn them off, "Okay."

He leaned toward Jane. "I need you to promise not to share with anyone what I'm about to tell you." His eyes were glassy and fever bright. "Not a single soul. Ever."

She wondered if he had become ill from the stress of the interview that afternoon but merely raised her eyebrows, not saying anything.

"There's another – an attempted murder – that no one knows about."

"Why are you telling me?"

"Because you're the only one I've been able to talk to about all of this. I've been killing for almost twenty years now. I've never been able to tell anyone about it. No one at all. I've felt so alone." He went on to tell Jane that he'd attempted to murder Remy because he'd believed she'd broken up Lee and Fong's marriage, a marriage everyone had thought was perfect. And all she said was 'excuse me' when she'd turned her back on him after he greeted her on the bow of the boat – turned her back – to take pictures of the fog over the river. When he'd found out that Remy had survived, his first thought had been that he needed to kill her. He talked about his relief when he'd discovered that she hadn't regained her memory of that night.

Jane swallowed, sour liquid rising into her mouth, and then asked him, "How did all that make you feel?"

"Sick. Like I'd made a huge mistake, one I can never undo, one that will haunt me for the rest of my life. Frightened that someday she'll get her memory back and know that it was my hands around her mouth and throat. That she'll hate me even more than I'm sure all the others do."

"Why are you telling me this?"

"It's become too much to carry by myself. I can't do it anymore." He looked at her, shamefaced, "Now, I'm not alone."

"Oh, so now, I have to carry your burden too?"

"I suppose so. I worry that if Remy remembers, she'll tell everyone. Every time she sends me an email with a picture of Sarah, I wonder if she'll tell me she's remembered."

"What am I supposed to do with this information, Tracey?"

"Nothing. I just needed to tell someone." He sighed in relief. "Let's go back to the interview."

"I'm restarting the recording. Okay?"

Tracey nodded.

"You left, so the families have no justice because there can be no arrest and no trial. They won't have the opportunity to confront you, the killer. Did you ever think about the victims' families and what was left behind?"

"No. Other than my aunt, up until today, I knew almost nothing about them." He rubbed his forehead between his brows. "I think I must have compartmentalized it. Maybe that was the only way I was able to live with the knowledge of what I am."

"What about Lydia? You knew her. Wasn't she a friend?"

"She had become part of our group of friends, but I had to do it because she saw me kill the woman in Strasbourg. She told her friend she had to tell the police about me – to turn me in. That would have ruined my wife's life as well as my own. It was self-defense. I got no pleasure from it, then or later."

Jane looked at him, puzzled, "I thought you were answering me honestly, until that comment. Self-defense? Really?"

He thought for a moment, "You're right. It was selfish on my part, it was out of fear. I'm a coward."

"Sometimes, it seems as though you have no emotional response at all to my questions. Why is that?"

"Because sometimes, I just can't deal with the feelings. I have to suppress them."

Watching him closely, she noticed how drained he looked. She was afraid she wouldn't get much more from him. *But I only have this one afternoon,* she reminded herself. *I need to press on a little longer.* "Let's talk about your family, Tracey. Charlotte… Sarah… Penelope… Mikey."

Tracey's pulse jumped, "Have you spoken to my wife?"

"Charlotte?" Jane paused for a moment, choosing her words carefully, "Charlotte refused to be interviewed. She was very clear that she would not discuss," she paused again, "this matter with anyone."

"She refuses to talk to me too," Tracey's voice sharpened slightly. "I called her, and she didn't answer, and then she changed her number."

"Does that surprise you? I did talk with Penelope and Mikey. They're both shattered."

Tracey sighed and nodded his head regretfully.

"Mikey talked with me for a few minutes, off the record. But he wanted me to share this with you. You're his older cousin, and he admired you greatly, and then he found out you killed his mother. He felt that you developed a relationship with him under false pretenses, and in doing so, you utterly betrayed him. He's devastated, confused, hurt – everything you'd expect when you find out a close family member is a murderous monster. So beyond telling me this, all that Mikey would say is that, as far as he's concerned, you don't exist."

Tracey sucked his breath in with a hiss.

"At first, Penelope wanted nothing to do with me." Jane looked at him with a sharp gaze. "Penelope is suffering pretty much the same as Mikey. She's your sister, and even though she scarcely knew you, like Mikey, she feels a deep sense of betrayal. She said you ran off like a coward who was unable – I'm quoting her here – to man up and face the music. She always referred to the Parking Lot Strangler as a bastard, but when she put a real name and face to the killer, who turned out to be her twin brother, well, let's just say she needed a lot of support. And in reality, the thing that eats her up, that she can't get past is that she got so close to putting you away, but you slipped through her fingers and you're here, you're still 'out there' as she puts it, enjoying life, out of reach of the law."

"I wanted to find her for my entire life. I never thought I would – but I did. And I was so happy. And now I have nothing."

"What do you expect, Tracey? Even if you weren't her brother, you're still a serial killer who she tracked for a large portion of her career. And then she found out that it was you – her brother, her flesh and blood – who she'd been searching for all these years, who killed the woman who raised you both and all those other innocent women. How do you expect her to feel?"

In a forlorn voice, Tracey said, "My wife won't return my calls, I'll never see my daughter again, my cousin says I no longer exist to him, and my sister calls me a bastard." He paused to take a shaky breath, "I didn't realize until I lost it, but my family is all I ever wanted. And I only had them for a brief time."

"How does that make you feel?"

"Angry. Ashamed. Heartbroken."

In a gentle voice, she said, "Tracey, do you ever think you'll find peace? Do you think there's someone who will forgive you?"

"I'm relieved it's over. That might be as close to peace as I'll ever feel. Forgiveness? I think that's more than I could hope for."

"You've betrayed every person you were close to. How does it make you feel?"

"Awful. I've even betrayed myself."

"How so?"

"It started in anger at what I perceived as abandonment, as rejection by my mother. And it just got out of control. I founded Sarah's House. I was a lawyer. I was a judge." His voice shook, "I've betrayed all my morals and principles."

"Tracey, now I'm going to ask you a very difficult question. You felt rejected as a child, how do you feel now about running off and leaving *your* family? Your wife and your child, Charlotte and Sarah, but especially Sarah. Do you think it was selfish to run off? Leave them? How do you think Sarah's going to feel twenty years from now?"

Tracey listened to her accusation and replied furiously, "But I keep reaching out. Charlotte has taken Sarah from me."

"Why did you finally say their names?"

"For God's sake, it's my wife and my child I'm talking about."

"So how does it make you feel to have... abandoned them?"

"What do my feelings matter?" Tears welled in his eyes, close to running over.

"I want to understand your feelings. In a way, you're one of the survivors too."

That afternoon, she had succeeded in touching him. She'd seen it all... cocky... angry... haughty... unfeeling... And she'd discovered how very lost he was.

Is he hiding what he feels from himself or is he hiding it from the world? Is it part of the whole normal-person mask he wears? Most of the time, he's this healthy, happy, well-grounded, compassionate person, especially toward children. Even though he doesn't disassociate, he does separate his normal self from the serial killer living inside him. Going way back to when he was a four-year-old, he was damaged. And it's manifested itself in this feeling of abandonment by everybody.

Having come to understand this about Tracey, Jane wasn't surprised at the compassion she felt toward him, despite her intention to remain objective throughout the interview – even after all the dreadful things he'd done and all the lives he'd destroyed.

"To paraphrase what you said when we first talked on the phone, we don't always come to learn the impact of our actions… but now you have. How does that make you feel, Tracey?"

Jane watched his face and his eyes as he sat in silence for several minutes, trying, failing to blink back the tears that threatened to spill over.

"There is no way – I've hurt so many people – I'm devastated – I wish I'd never done any of it – I'm heartbroken – I want Charlotte and Sarah back – I want to have a relationship with Penelope and Mikey." He gasped for breath, "I don't know what the answer to your question is… Just stop. Please… stop." With tears running down his face, he stood abruptly, left the table and walked out through the restaurant.

His breathing was ragged as he entered the souk and pulled out a handkerchief to wipe away his tears. He shoved it back into his pocket. *I wish*—

Through the general chatter and noise, he heard a woman's voice saying in French, "Pardon." He turned to see her use her fingers to comb her red hair back behind one ear.

Chapter Thirty-Five

Slovenia, Twenty Years Later, Mid-June 2035

The overnight train from Lake Balaton had just pulled in and stopped alongside the platform. Remy squeezed Fong's hand tightly as she jiggled from foot to foot in excitement, just like she did every year when Sarah arrived for the summer. A duffle bag came flying out of the door of the train, and Sarah jumped down behind it, her long, curly red ponytail bouncing. She grabbed her bag and ran down the platform, dropping it to throw herself into her Aunt Remy's arms. Remy gave her a long, hard hug. Sarah wrapped her arms around her, "I always look forward to your hugs, AR. They're the best."

Remy chuckled at the nickname that Sarah had given her years ago. She didn't call anyone else by their initials, and Remy treasured it.

"I keep her working hard in the vineyard. That's why she's so strong."

"He's a real slave driver," Remy laughed.

"But what's wrong with my hugs, young lady?"

Sarah turned toward Fong and wrapped her arms around him, loving the way he always smelled of the vineyards and grapes. "Nothing, Fong," she laughed into his shoulder. "But it's different between me and AR..."

Fong picked up her bag and tossed her his car keys. Sarah pointed to herself and raised her eyebrows, "What? You're letting me drive your car?"

"I figure it's about time," Fong called after her as Sarah ran ahead into the parking lot to find the Range Rover.

As they climbed in, Fong in front, to watch over her, and Remy in the back seat, Sarah said, "I love this car. It reminds me of riding around the vineyards in Uncle Sasha's antique Range Rover. It's the same color inside and out. But it isn't all dusty and dented like his was. I'm going to miss him this summer."

Sarah looked out across the countryside toward the Slovenian Alps as she drove along. Slovenia was her other home, and if she were honest with herself, she was more comfortable there than in Washington. She could be completely open with Remy and Fong, ask any questions about almost anything, without having to tiptoe around her mom's feelings.

After Charlotte had found the earrings and the police had confirmed that Tracey was the long-sought serial killer, she'd taken Sarah and moved back to her house on Whidbey Island where she'd been extraordinarily reclusive for months. She'd had all her groceries delivered, spent hours snuggling with little Sarah, reading to her, singing songs, playing games. She'd bought a Saint Bernard dog to keep them company and leaned heavily on Remy and Fong and Penelope and Bobby. After Penelope and Bobby had made that initial difficult call to Slovenia, they had handled straightening out all of Tracey's affairs in the U.S., and Remy and Fong had handled everything to do with the property in Sicily, including Little Phoebe Cat. Charlotte had been adamant that no way was she having "that man's cat" in her house. That was almost the last time she had said anything unkind about Tracey to her friends, except for one long tearful evening she'd spent with Remy when she'd spilled out all her anger and sorrow over too many glasses of local Washington wine. Then she'd closed the door on that part of her life.

Remy had found the orange tabby cat a good home with the buyers of the property. Fong, with some very shrewd legal and financial advice, had eventually managed to put all the money from the sales of both properties into a trust for Sarah until she turned twenty-five. Independently, Tracey had established a second trust from his investments that had begun paying her a stipend at eighteen. She'd put all the money from him in the bank, not sure what to do with it.

That first Thanksgiving, everyone had gathered at Charlotte's house and stayed into the new year. They didn't want Charlotte to be by herself at such a vulnerable time. The house was big enough that she had space to grieve, but she was never completely alone. And after that, Penelope and Remy alternated with regular, long visits. Charlotte refused to ever return to Raleigh. When Sarah was old enough to fly alone, she would visit Penelope. And during those visits, Remy would come to Whidbey Island by herself or with Fong, to be with Charlotte.

Charlotte had always kept her maiden name, and so, to protect Sarah from the press and curious neighbors, she had legally changed Sarah's name to French as well.

When Sarah was just over a year old, Sasha had invited them to the vineyard. The group of friends drew close around Charlotte and Sarah, and everyone participated in raising the toddler. After six months, with most of her time spent out in the fresh air, walking in the countryside, Charlotte was much better, but she never seemed completely herself again. Her laugh was not as spontaneous, and some of the light had left her eyes, her step was just a little heavier. She was always warm and loving, but a piece of her seemed to be missing.

After that trip, Charlotte brought Sarah to the vineyard every year for the summer. At first, they would stop in Hungary for a couple of weeks to visit the Budapest and Balaton cousins, explore the city and go sailing on the lake. Then Sarah and her mother would stay for a month or so at the vineyard before traveling to England to spend a couple of weeks with Charlotte's mother's family on the way home to Washington. Over the years, Sarah had begun to arrive by herself and her mother would join them all at the end of the summer.

That was when the whole family would gather there in Slovenia with Sasha, Remy and Fong – Charlotte, Sarah, Penelope, Bobby and Mikey, though Mikey had stopped coming early on. He said that, while he knew it wasn't intentional, he felt like an outsider when he was with the whole group. He did still spend time with Penelope and Bobby – and Sarah when she visited them in Raleigh. But they hadn't seen him as often lately because he was very focused on his job, his partner and his responsibilities with the museum board.

Sarah hated going to England and then home to Seattle. It wasn't because she didn't like either place, but because each year, it signaled an end to a wonderful summer with everyone at the vineyard. As she got older, her mom would let her spend the whole summer in Slovenia with Sasha, Remy and Fong. Those trips were when they had gradually evolved from being dear friends of her mother's into Sarah's chosen family. With them all together there in the countryside, she felt as though this was her other home.

Sarah was thoroughly indulged there, but by no means pampered. Over those years, she had worked hard and come to understand the winery business, and at a very young age, she had declared she was going to become a "wine grower". While in Slovenia, she even helped with the bookkeeping, a task dealing with numbers that she normally hated. But Fong had stressed the importance of understanding the cost of the business, and so she sat with him each summer right after she arrived and reviewed all the numbers for the past year.

She was studying viticulture and oenology, as well as business, at Washington State University. She'd considered other schools and never told her mom that she'd been accepted to the prestigious program at UC Davis. She chose to go to school in Washington so she could be closer to Charlotte. She still viewed her as somewhat fragile and worried about what would happen once she moved away permanently.

A few weeks into that summer, after first Sarah and then Penelope and Bobby had arrived, everyone sat at the long table on the terrace, enjoying the warm summer evening with the smell of the grapes beginning to ripen in the vineyard. They talked at length about the upcoming harvest. "According to all indications," said Fong, "since it was a good year for the grapes, the wines should be particularly good."

After dinner was finished and the kitchen cleaned up, Penelope reached into her pocket and took out a flash drive that Jane had sent over with her. "Are you ready for this?" she asked. Sarah looked at it in trepidation. "This" was Jane's documentary, the one she'd filmed in 2014 and 2015, the documentary about the survivors that included her interview with Sarah's father.

The previous year, Jane had reached out to Charlotte to let her know that she had finally completed the video and that she planned to release the shorter version that contained the interviews with the family and friends of Tracey's victims. She'd wanted to discuss the timing of the release with her. Jane wanted Charlotte to be comfortable with the shorter video being out on the internet because it would be easy for Sarah to accidentally come across it. She also told Charlotte that she had made a longer version for Sarah that included her interview with Tracey as well as a personal message from her.

Charlotte was adamant that she had no desire to see any version of the video. When Jane asked if she was comfortable with Sarah seeing it, Charlotte had said she wanted to discuss that with their therapist. After a lengthy discussion among Charlotte, Sarah and her therapist, the three of them agreed that Sarah would watch the longer version in Slovenia with AR, Fong, Auntie Pens, and Figg.

With the only light from candles that Remy had placed around the dark living room, the group sat on sofas and chairs staring at the large TV screen. Remy went over and took both of Sarah's hands between hers. "We can stop this at any time if you want. We can watch it in bits and pieces or in one session. It's totally up to you, Sarah."

"Okay," Sarah replied in a small voice.

Remy gave her a warm smile and went to sit in the chair next to Fong's. He reached over to take her hand in his.

*

As the documentary ended, the picture softened to black and then shifted to a room where Jane sat, wearing a loose, white shirt and blue jeans, with her feet bare. Instead of her usual topknot, she wore her long dark hair in a thick braid that hung over one shoulder. She was curled into a comfortable armchair, one foot tucked under her, the toes of her other foot pointed, just touching the floor. Behind her stood a bookcase overflowing with volumes on film, biographies of filmmakers and photographers, large coffee-table-sized books, textbooks and other reference material. The corner of a small table was visible at the edge of the screen with a colorful pot and a vine trailing over the side. It was obvious that the room was not only her workspace but a place she had thoughtfully designed to give her comfort and visual pleasure as well.

Jane reached out and touched a disc on the table next to her, and the light from the reading lamp overhead dimmed until it glowed, a soft spotlight on her, with the rest of the room retreating into shadow. Looking directly at the camera, she spoke.

"Sarah, when I first outlined this documentary, I planned to explore the impact murder had on those left behind."

"After I filmed the interviews, I felt your father's perspective would be critical for all this to make sense because I thought there would be a significant contrast between the survivors' emotions and his reactions. So, I set up an interview with him. As we talked, I realized that not only was he the serial killer, but in a way, he was a survivor as well.

"What I heard from the other survivors had been heart-wrenching for me. More painful than I'd ever expected. But your father—" Her voice cracked, "I wish I'd never interviewed him. Because once I did, I couldn't unhear his words. I couldn't make them go away."

Jane took a deep breath. She reached over to the small table next to her, picked up a pen that lay on top of her notepad. She left the notepad on the table and began twisting the pen between her fingers, clicking the button with her thumb. She looked down at the sound, and with a small smile, she stilled her hands.

She looked at her pen for a moment and then abruptly threw it across the room. "His interview detracted from the rest of the documentary which was supposed to be focusing on the other survivors.

"It took me far too long – decades – to finish this. At first, I was going to prepare a longer version for release that would include your father's interview, but I couldn't. I couldn't find a way to pull it all together and have it make sense. It was too painful, and I'd let it become too personal."

Her voice remained calm as she continued. "So, I made this for you because, as his daughter, you are one of the survivors too." She pushed an errant strand of hair from her face and tucked it firmly into her braid.

"I'm so sorry, for what I'm about to say, Sarah. No one should have to hear this about their parent. I wanted your father to be one-dimensional, a monster, a horrible person, someone I could dislike intensely or maybe even hate. I was very angry at him about so many things – his refusal to acknowledge the women by saying their names, the trauma he had caused so many people, including your family, his arrogance. I realized I had been using that interview to punish him. I was being mean and arrogant myself. That isn't who I am. I was so ashamed of what I had done.

"But listening to him and watching the emotions that surfaced throughout that afternoon also humanized him for me. As you saw, when I spoke with him, he went from apathy to expressions of pleasure to regret. And listening to that, I couldn't bring myself to portray him solely as a monster. I didn't want to make him a total bad guy... or make excuses for him. He's a tormented individual, but even saying that in the documentary would have made me feel like I was letting him off too easily.

"We're all grieving, including your father. I felt it was important for you to hear his words, to decide how you feel about him for yourself. I hope this film helps you understand what a complex person he is and perhaps gain some insight into what drove him to kill."

The screen faded again to black. They sat in the dark. Sarah sat cross-legged on the couch, leaning forward with her face in her hands, tears dripping through her fingers, as silent sobs wracked her body. Penelope sat beside her and gently rubbed the back of her neck.

Fong got up slowly, a bit stiff in his knees, and turned a couple of the table lamps back on. His hair was pulled straight back into a man bun, the lamp light caught and gleamed in its steel grey. The hairstyle was no longer fashionable, though it still had been many years earlier when he'd adopted it. It was apparent that he too had wept during the film. Tracey had been his best friend for a few years and the father of this dear girl whom they'd welcomed into their lives. Fong worried about the impact the film would have on her.

Penelope whispered, "It's okay, Sarah. It's okay to cry."

Through her tears, Sarah said, "That's the first time I've ever heard my dad's voice." She gulped, "All these years, my mom told me the good things about him. What a wonderful, funny, smart, loving man he was. She told me about the look on his face when he first held me in his arms at the hospital the day I was born. She told me that he said it was like a miracle had happened for him. When I was ten, she told me that he was a murderer, but she never used the term serial killer. She never talked about how much it had hurt her. I never realized that she knew some of his victims. She just spent a lot of time reassuring me that, even though he was a murderer, there was a part of him that was good as well."

Fong said, "I think your mom managed very well, balancing what she told you and when. There was no need for you to hear all the bad things. She was a very strong woman to protect you and give you a sense of normalcy in your life."

"We hung pictures of him in the front hallway once I was old enough to choose which ones I wanted. I was maybe seven or eight. That way, he was always there to greet me when I came home. I loved seeing my dad and my family in those pictures. It made me feel so much more normal. But after that, Mom always came in through the side door.

"She told me the stories behind most of the pictures. Later, when Mom told me he was a murderer, she said he had left us so he wouldn't be captured. At ten, I thought that was very romantic. My dad, an escaped murderer, protecting his family from what he'd done. I didn't quite understand what it meant that he'd left us. Later, I was just confused. But I kept it to myself because I didn't want to upset my mom."

Remy went over and sat on the floor in front of her, put her hand on Sarah's knee and looked into her face. "You're old enough now. It was important to see your dad and his pain as well as the hurt he caused all the survivors."

Sarah said, sniffling, "Mom didn't want to watch this. I didn't understand. Now, I do."

"That was hard for me to watch, even after all these years," said Remy. "I can't even imagine how difficult it was for you."

Sarah looked around at everyone, "That film was so upsetting, disturbing, painful, shocking – I don't even know how to describe what I'm feeling after hearing from the families and friends of the victims – and from my dad."

Her voice quavered, "After she viewed the video, my

therapist said I might regret seeing it, that I might hate him. I don't regret seeing it," she said, her anger finally breaking through, "but I do hate him right now – for killing those women, for causing all that pain to my mom, for running away so I never got to know him. Mom worked so hard to only show me the good side of him. But I'm the daughter of a serial killer," she whispered. "There's no changing that. And hearing him talk about those murders from his perspective makes me want to hate him. Is that wrong, for a daughter to *want to hate her father?*"

"Whatever you're feeling is okay," said Fong.

"I'm so conflicted. He was a terrible person," Sarah said. "I want to acknowledge the good things about him too. But I don't want to hide my head in the sand either, never talking about the horrible things he did. I need to balance all of it. I don't want this stuff we heard tonight to be the only way I remember my dad. I don't want him to be a monster in my mind and heart. He's still my dad, and I still want to love him." She looked pleadingly around the room, "I'm glad I decided to do this here with all of you. My therapist told me that if I watched this, I would need lots of support. I do. I need your help. You knew him. Tell me about your memories of him… please?"

"It's like a wake – first you mourn, and then you celebrate the good memories," Bobby said quietly.

She looked at him and nodded, "Exactly. Figg, what do you remember?"

"He was a hell of a golfer. The first time we played golf, he and his buddies conned me into playing in his foursome at the charity event for Sarah's House. And then he talked your Auntie Pens and me into taking over running the tournament for him."

"I was so angry at the time," said Penelope. "I felt like he was manipulating us for his own benefit."

She looked over at Bobby, and they exchanged a smile at the memory of the night she and Mikey and Bobby had all been given their "assignments" before she continued, "But he had this almost uncanny ability to read our characters and our capabilities. Even before we knew it, he recognized how good we would be at taking over for him in Raleigh. Look at us, two decades later, we're still doing those things he asked us to do. And I think I can speak for all three of us, Mikey included, in saying that we actually enjoy it."

Bobby picked up the conversation again, "I learned so much during the few months I got to play golf with him. Not just about golf. During our times on the course, we also had long conversations about," he grinned, "the meaning of life, deep stuff like that. I'm glad I got to see that side of him." He looked at her drawn face and said kindly, "I'd like to believe that he did stop when you were born, Sarah, and that he's not killing anymore."

"Figg, you are such a good person," Sarah said and held out her hand to him. He came over to sit on the other side of her and put an arm around her.

"I'd wanted my brother back for so long," Penelope said. "For years after that final DNA match, I was so angry that he was the serial killer I'd tried to find for so long. I was angry and sad that it was my DNA that confirmed it. I felt like it wasn't fair that it was him, as though he'd done it to me, being the murderer I was trying to find. I took it very personally. He was a serial killer who'd done dreadful, unimaginable things, but at the same time, he was a philanthropist, his family used their money to do a lot of good things for Raleigh, and he continued that work. Some of it, like Sarah's House, was truly a passion for him. I'll never be able to reconcile those two sides of my brother. But finally, I did manage to get beyond the anger. He'll always be my brother."

"Used to be angry? How did you get over it?" asked Sarah.

"You know, we were all angry as kids – me, Mikey, your dad. We talked about it when we first met. We had all felt as though we had been abandoned in one fashion or another. Now he's abandoned me and you too. We all developed anger issues as a result of that. Mikey still grapples with his to this day – he won't even talk about Tracey. Your dad, I don't mean to be flippant when I say this, but he channeled his anger into killing women. And me?" She gave a short bark of laughter, "I did triathlons. The training exhausted me, and the endorphin high made me feel better. And I worked hard to consciously overcome it. I got some counseling, and one of the things my shrink said was that it takes a lot of energy to carry around all that anger. I didn't want to spend my energy on that."

"Is that why you told me I should get into sports?" Sarah asked Penelope who nodded at her. "I tried soccer, but I ended up taking it out on my opponents and sometimes, my teammates. When I got into distance running, it helped me a lot."

"Ahhh," said Penelope, "That's why you changed."

Sarah looked over at Fong who was leaning forward, his arms on his knees, "Did Sasha like Tracey? He knew him, right?"

"Yes," he said thoughtfully, "Sasha had become very fond of your father, especially during the times he came to visit me here after Lee and I separated. In his journals, Sasha wrote extensively about himself and all of us, as friends. Sarah, he did mention how finding out about your dad's murders hurt him deeply. Someday, if you want, you can read what he wrote."

"I – I don't know. Not right now."

Sarah thought about how sad she had been when Sasha had died peacefully at the house late the previous year. At least Fong and Remy had been there with him. They'd been his family, and he'd left all his property to them. He was buried at the top of the hill near the oak tree and the bench he'd put there to admire the view. She looked around and thought about how comfortable it was at the farmhouse and the vineyard. "I wonder if my dad found it as peaceful here as I do."

Fong smiled at her gently, "I'm sure he did, Sarah."

"Do any of you remember a little bear?" Sarah showed them the size with her hands. "There're a couple of baby pictures of me with it. I keep one on my dresser. And then the bear's not in any more pictures. That's one of the things I don't ask Mom about, her eyes get so sad."

"I remember that bear," said Penelope. "Your dad bought it for you before you were even born. Your mom said he moved it around the nursery as though he was trying to find the best spot for it to welcome you home. You slept with it all the time. You'd pitch a fit if you didn't have it."

"Actually," said Remy, "your dad sent me an email with a picture of the bear. I sent him pictures while you were growing up. I saved them in an album so, when you are ready, I can share them with you as well. He sent me a few of him, like the one of him with your little bear. Fong wasn't a fan of me interacting with Tracey, but now—"

"—Now, I understand how important it was. Now, I'm okay with it," he said.

She continued, "Your dad said he accidentally took the bear when he left."

"I'm not surprised. He was always sticking it in his pocket when you dropped it," Penelope leaned back, chuckling as she shared her memory of the impeccably dressed man with a pants or jacket pocket bulging from the bear he'd stuck inside it.

"Do you have other pictures, AR? Other pictures of my dad?"

"Yes, I took a lot of photos of our group of friends during that time. We can look at them all summer long if you want."

"That would be great." She turned toward Penelope, "Auntie Pens, there's a photo at my house of you and Dad high-fiving. I was wearing a little dress with stars on it. You're holding me on one hip. Do you remember what that was all about?"

"I bought you that dress to wear that day. You were only, what, six months old, maybe? It was at your dad's and my forty-fourth birthday party, and we had just beaten the men's team playing corn hole. You were on the women's team with me and your mom. You'd scream with delight and clap your hands every time I'd throw a bag into the cornhole. That was a fun day."

"Your dad has a wonderful voice." Fong told her about his road trips with Tracey, how they would drive fast, far too fast if the truth be told, in his dark green Alfa Romeo two-seater with the top down, singing at the top of their lungs.

"Do you still have the Alfa?" Sarah asked.

"It's in the barn, along with other good memories," he winked at Remy. "It's stored safely under a tarp. I still take it out sometimes, for old times' sake."

"Ooooh, can I drive it?"

"Mmmm, perhaps," he said with a smile. "But I think we'll have to go a little slower than I used to."

Remy talked about the cruise when they'd met Tracey and

Charlotte on the river boat, and how at dinner that first night, they'd figured out that they were all artists in one way or another. They'd immediately formed an incredible bond of friendship. "Your dad and mom were newlyweds and were truly in love. Fong was there with his ex-wife, Lee – we all thought they looked like movie stars—" she smiled at her husband, "and I was traveling with my cousin, Frannie."

Sarah said sadly, "I think my mom is still in love with him. She just can't forgive him. She's locked that love away inside like he did with the murders."

Penelope moved to sit on the other side of Sarah, close to Bobby, and whispered in his ear, "And the bastard is *still* out there." To Sarah, she said, "The first time I met you and your dad, he took you in his arms and waved your hand at me. It was very sweet. He loved you so much."

"Do you think he would have chosen this for me, Auntie Pens?" Sarah asked. "This is where I'm happiest. Working in the vineyard with Fong and AR, growing grapes and making wine."

"I think he would have told you to follow your dreams, to do what makes you happiest."

"So, you've finally decided what you'll do after you graduate?" Bobby asked.

Sarah looked at Remy and Fong, and the three of them smiled. "I'm going to buy AR and Fong's little vineyard with the distribution from the trust my dad set up for me. After I finish my degrees next year, I'm coming back to start a formal apprenticeship with them. The cottage will be my new home."

"I think that's a wonderful decision," Penelope said.

Sarah grinned at her in thanks, "I want you and Figg to continue to run Sarah's House. To go on living in the caretaker's house on the grounds, if you want."

Penelope looked at Bobby who smiled and nodded. "We would love to," she said. "There are so many things that we'd like to do. We'd planned to talk with you about them at the end of the summer when you stop in Raleigh on your way home. A while ago, we were cleaning out the little building that Tracey had converted into a kind of office at Sarah's House and found some notes that he had made years ago, plans to expand by building a second house and a proper clinic to support—"

"I want to meet him," Sarah said abruptly.

"Are you sure?" Fong asked, looking at her with worried eyes.

Sarah nodded slowly, her voice low and thoughtful, "My mom taught me to love him, she never said a single harsh thing about him even when she told me he was a murderer. But now I know, after watching *that*," she pointed at the TV with a shaking finger, "that he killed ten women... and it gave him pleasure. But he also told Jane that he regrets it."

She rubbed her face and shook her head. "I'm so confused. Can't I just continue to adore him? Or should I detest him now that I know what he's done? Is he a monster or just a very sick man?"

Her voice grew stronger, "I need to hear his voice when he answers all *my* questions. I need to decide for myself, after looking him in the eyes, if I can still love him... after all that.

"Auntie Pens, Figg," she looked at first one and then the other, "I want you to come with me."

Chapter Thirty-Six

The old dusty car slammed to a halt in front of a pair of gates set into tall stone walls. The three passengers climbed out and stood catching their breath. Bobby counted out enough dirham to cover the fare and a small amount for a tip. He was pretty sure no tip was necessary, but… He turned back, noting the two women's pale faces and gave them a grin. "Well, I must say, that was quite the ride."

Penelope gave an unsteady laugh, "I wonder what Tracey was thinking, recommending that we come here by taxi instead of driving ourselves. There were a few close calls where I wasn't sure we would survive."

Sarah nodded distractedly in agreement, gripping her hands together to control their shaking while she stared through the gates that led to cool, shady grounds that invited visitors to come in and linger. A long, straight gravel walkway led back toward an imposing church and its monastery. And branching off from it, neatly raked pathways wound among the trees and greenery. Stone benches stood along the paths beside olive trees, pomegranate shrubs and other plants obviously chosen to grow in Marrakesh's climate, while a fountain splashed and burbled in the background. Somewhere in there, in that peaceful place, she would find her father.

Bobby put his arm around her and rested a hand reassuringly on her upper arm. Gratefully, Sarah leaned her right side against him, clasping Penelope's hand in hers. "Are you okay, Auntie Pens?" she whispered.

Penelope looked at her, and suddenly she shook her head, "No. No, I'm not. I can't do this." Her voice caught in her throat, and she swallowed convulsively, "I thought I could look him in the eyes and it would be okay. But I just can't." She continued shaking her head, "I'm not angry with him anymore. But he's a monster, Sarah. I was supposed to catch him and put him away forever. I failed. I can't do this." She tugged her hand from Sarah's. "I'll find a bench over here and wait for you. Come find me when you're ready."

She gave Sarah a quick kiss, and when she came around to kiss Bobby, he stroked the backs of his fingers over her cheek. "It's okay, kid. I'll take Sarah to her dad," he said before Penelope bolted off to the left.

They stood watching Penelope until she'd disappeared behind a group of bushes. Then, with his arm around her shoulders, Bobby said, "Okay, Sarah, let's go find him." Gravel crunched under their feet as they walked down the long path to the magnificent church. He felt Sarah's body trembling violently and pulled her tightly against him. "You don't have to do this, you know. We can stop right now and go back, get Auntie Pens and go home."

An old man with a stoop to his shoulders sat on a bench, his head bent, his lips moving softly as his fingers caressed the beads in his hands. Sarah turned to Bobby, "I have to do this, Figg. He's my dad, and I need to meet him and look him in the face and ask him – I need to ask him why. I know Jane asked him that, but I need to have him tell me himself. I need to decide if I can love him or not." She drew a breath, "Go. Wait with Auntie Pens. She needs you right now." She pulled away and walked on by herself.

Tracey's face lit up as he looked at the slim young woman who stopped in front of him. She was the spitting image of her grandmother and her great aunt, the same green eyes and curly red hair, the same fresh skin, with Anna's tiny mole above her eyebrow. He drew his breath in with a quiet hiss and closed his eyes momentarily.

"Tracey? Are you Tracey Lauch?"

He opened his eyes with a small hopeful nod.

"I'm Sarah French."

"Remy told me your mom had changed your last name."

Sarah stiffened, "She did it to protect me."

"It's okay, Sarah. I probably would have done the same in her shoes. Please," he gestured for her to sit down. "What do you call me?"

She sat, keeping some distance between them and tilted her head, not understanding his question.

"I'm curious, do you ever talk about me? What do you call

me?"

"Oh. Uhhh, I – I say 'my dad', and when I ask Mom about you, I say 'Dad'."

"Do you suppose you could call me Dad? I'd like that."

Sarah looked at her father, tears welling in her eyes, "I'm sorry," she whispered, slowly shaking her head, "I don't think I can do that. You haven't been a father to me since you left me and Mom that – that day." She noticed how different he looked compared to the pictures that had welcomed her home. His face was tanned dark brown, deep lines creased his cheeks and ran in furrows across his forehead, and his scalp showed through silver hair that he wore cut short. His clothes were clean, though old and worn, a chambray shirt with the sleeves turned up tucked neatly into blue jeans that were nearly white at the knees. On his feet, he wore a pair of scuffed work boots. His hands were calloused, but they were clean, and his fingernails were trimmed short. A pair of work gloves lay on the bench beside him.

Tracey reached over, his hand gently comforting her, "I'm sorry too. But I understand." He sat quietly for a moment, thinking. "What would you like to call me," he finally asked.

She looked at him, startled. "Nothing. I don't want to call you anything right now."

"Sarah, why are you here? Why did you come all this way? What is it that you want?" He fingered the beads in his hands.

She reached out a tentative hand and took the rosary from him. "I have one almost like this." She stroked the small tassel at the bottom of the little wooden cross. "But mine doesn't have this."

"Yes," he said with a brief smile. "I remember. The priest at the church where you were baptized gave it to your mother for you. He said that it was the custom of his parishioners to give a new rosary to each person baptized in their church. He said it meant that person would always have a tie back to them." His smile was warm as he went on, "I chose these because they reminded me of yours. It was a way to maintain a sense of connection to you."

"Oh, Mom just said he gave it to me at my baptism. That's a

nice tradition. You know, I still go to church there during the summers I spend at the vineyard. It's just AR – Aunt Remy and Fong now." She gave him a long look and then said sadly, "Sasha is dead, you know."

"I know. Remy sent me an email. I was sorry I couldn't say goodbye and thank him for all he did for you and your mom. He was a good friend."

"What you did hurt Sasha. It hurt everyone. But especially, it hurt my mom," she lashed out, suddenly angry with him. "Why did you have to do that? Why did you have to kill all those women? Why did you have to ruin our lives?"

"I don't know anymore, Sarah. You saw Jane's documentary. She sent me a copy too. I made excuses about abandonment and anger... and pleasure. I thought I—"

"You cried at the end. All those tears? What was that about? Who were you crying for anyway?" Her voice hardened at the edges, "For the women you killed? For everyone else it affected? Who? Who?" She realized how strident her voice had become and stopped abruptly.

"For me, Sarah. I was crying for myself. Jane had taken me to task. And for the first time, I was confronted by someone else about what I'd done. Before that, my actions, the murders, almost didn't seem real, like something *I'd* done. I'd done horrible things, and nothing I could do would ever make it right. And my actions had made me lose everyone I loved. I was angry and ashamed and desolate. So, like a spoiled little child, I cried." He turned toward her, and she saw how anguished his face had grown during that confession.

"I'm sorry. I didn't mean to hurt you – no, that isn't true," she shook her head. "I wanted to hurt you like you hurt us. But I am sorry. It wasn't kind of me." She twisted his rosary, winding it between her fingers.

"Careful, they're old and might break."

"I broke mine one day when I was angry with Mom. I feel like she's so fragile that I can't say anything. I was twisting them between my fingers just like this, and I pulled too hard, and they broke."

Tracey reached out and gently unwound the beads from her hands and closed his fingers around them, running his thumb over the smooth surfaces.

"I'm sorry. I'm sorry," she said again.

"Sarah, this is hard for both of us. You mustn't apologize to me."

"I'm sor—" She stopped and gave him a twisted, half-grin.

"Would you like a tour? Would you like to see where I live and work – and attempt to pray?" He stood without waiting for an answer.

She got to her feet, "I'm kinda surprised you asked me to meet you here. And to find you praying with that," she gestured at his hand where he continued to caress the rosary beads. "Mom always said that both of you were spiritual but not religious. Have you, I'm not sure how to say it, have you converted to Catholicism?"

"I'm trying, but I still have a very hard time with organized religion. Despite my struggles, the clergy and the monks here have welcomed me into their family." He looked down at the rosary. "I use this to try to focus my thoughts. Not quite traditional, but I do try out a 'Hail Mary' or an 'Our Father' now and again."

He held out his hand in a gesture to join him. They began to walk slowly, so engrossed in their conversation that Sarah was oblivious to the serene beauty of the grounds and the cool breeze that blew her hair across her face.

"How did you end up here?"

"It's an odd story. When I left the interview with Jane, a woman passed me in the market. She was lovely, with red hair that she tucked behind her ear. I was distraught from the end of the interview and fell into my old habit. I turned and followed her."

Sarah gasped, "Did you—?"

"I planned to. I was feeling hopeless. I had done horrible, unforgivable things. I'd lost everything. 'Why not?' I thought. So, I followed her from the souk, and she came to this place. She went into the church, lit a candle and knelt down. I slipped into the gift shop near the entrance to wait for her. I began to browse, and a small selection of icons caught my attention. They were attractive, but I knew I could make better ones."

"What happened to the woman?"

"While I stood there, looking at the icons, a young priest came in. We struck up a conversation. Out of the corner of my eye, I saw the woman leave."

Sarah realized she had been holding her breath. She gradually released it as Tracey continued.

"He said I seemed troubled and asked if he could hear my confession. I told him I wasn't Catholic, and besides, I had no idea how it worked. It didn't matter, he told me. I was afraid, Sarah. He was inviting me to talk about what I had done, about what I'd just planned to do. I didn't know if I could. I didn't know how to do it."

"Bless me, Father, for I have sinned," whispered Sarah to herself.

Tracey smiled at her and nodded, "He said it didn't matter. We could use the confessional – sometimes it's easier if you can't see the person you're talking to – or we could just sit in his office and talk. He told me God would hear me either way."

"Which did you choose?"

"The confessional. I was afraid to see the loathing on his face if we just sat face-to-face and talked," he said with a glance upward. "So, he heard my confession and gave me absolution. My penance, he said, wouldn't be a few 'Our Fathers' and 'Hail Marys' since I wasn't much of a believer. Instead, I was to come back to the monastery with him to share their evening meal. The clergy and the monks eat together there."

"And…?"

"And we talked until very late that night. At some point, our conversation came back to the icons I'd been looking at earlier. I said that I had some experience painting icons. He acknowledged that the ones in the gift shop weren't very good, but tourists seemed to buy them. I offered to paint one for the monastery, and well, one thing led to another."

She looked at him, waiting for him to go on.

"You asked why I asked you to meet me here? I live here in a little room, a shed really, that we made habitable. I help care for the grounds, and I teach isography. I also paint a few icons myself for the shop."

"Isography? What's the difference between that and iconography?" asked Sarah.

"Iconography is a branch of art history. The study of icons as an art form," he smiled at her curiosity. "That's where it started for me. Isography is painting icons. Replacing sacred words with visual images. Even though I'm still not very religious, I try to follow tradition and include a prayer with each brushstroke. I'm no expert, but I enjoy the focus it forces me to bring to my work."

"Oh, I didn't realize it was so complicated. I would have just called it icon painting."

"That certainly would be easier to understand," Tracey said, looking at her with a twinkle in his eye.

They walked on through the grounds to the gift shop, the church, the vegetable gardens and fruit orchards, and finally, to his small room, as he'd described, scarcely more than a shed with a window and door, and a cot, a small table with a lamp and a pitcher of water, and a straight-backed chair. In the lamplight, a single icon glowed on the wall. On the chair sat a tiny, well-loved bear.

"My bear," said Sarah. She picked him up and cradled him in her hands. "He's so tiny."

"Yes, that's why he always ended up in my pocket. Do you mind if I keep him? He's all I have of you, him and the pictures and emails Remy sends."

She touched the button in the bear's ear and then kissed it on the nose. "Of course you can have him." She set it down on the chair, looking around, trying to imagine living in such a tiny, cramped room. She compared what she saw with images of the spacious house on Whidbey Island where she lived with her mother and of the pretty, renovated cottage in the Slovenian vineyard that she would move to the following year.

With a brief shake of her head, she walked outside before turning to ask, "How do you manage to live like this? I couldn't."

"I don't want anything more. This is all I need."

"But you're incredibly wealthy. Why do you do it?"

He led her to a wooden bench outside his door. "Sarah, listen to me. After that first night here, I asked to stay for a while – at first, as a kind of retreat. I was afraid to go back to life outside, afraid I'd give in to the temptation to kill again. I was like an addict. The hotel was so kind as to pack up my belongings and have them delivered here. After I set up your trust fund, I gave the rest of my money to charity, a large portion to this church. Now, I help out however I can in exchange for room and board – and a new set of clothes now and then," he said with a smile.

She looked at him in shock. "Everything? That was very – brave of you, I guess."

"While I'm in a kind of recovery, I don't trust myself. I'm still afraid. I've never left here since I came to that realization."

She took both of his hands in hers and said compassionately, "I'm sorry for you because, I suppose that means you haven't healed."

"No, but I've found a way to live with myself, a kind of peace, Sarah."

"I'm happy, then – I guess – that you seem to have found that here. I think Mom would be happy for you too."

"How is your mother?"

"She isn't doing as well as you are. Emotionally, she's stuck back at the time you left. She still loves you deeply, but she's locked it all down inside. She just goes through the motions of life. When she's with Remy and Fong, she seems to be almost happy. But we can see how sad she is underneath, even though she tries to hide it from all of us."

Tracey leaned back against the wall of his shed and closed his eyes. "Oh, that makes me sad as well. I think in most relationships there is an imbalance. I loved her deeply, but I know that she loved me far more. I'm so happy she has you and her friends."

"Can I ask you something?"

"Of course."

"Have you ever written to the survivors, as Jane calls them? To say you're sorry? To make amends?"

"No," he said firmly. "The only way to truly make amends would be to go back."

"You can't do that," said Sarah.

Chapter Thirty-Six

"I can't do that," Tracey echoed. "There's a death penalty in North Carolina."

"If they put you to death, that would kill Mom. You can't do it," she said, panic filling her at the thought.

"I'm afraid to die that way, Sarah. So, I'm stuck here, in this beautiful place, behind these high, stone walls. Not to sound trite, but while it's a prison, at least it's one of my choosing, one I could leave if I wanted to." He looked around and said again, "I've found a peace of sorts here."

"But not forgiveness," she responded.

"No, I can't imagine anyone being able to forgive me. The church has granted me absolution… but forgiveness?" He shook his head.

"I'm sure Remy told you that Mom sent me to Catholic school. Part of the curriculum was world religions. She wanted me to have the knowledge to make my own choices and not be influenced by her beliefs. One of the things I learned is that forgiveness is looking beyond the injury to the person in need of mercy and healing."

Tracey looked at her with a smile. "You're very wise, my daughter." They stood. "Shall I walk you back to your Auntie Pens and Bobby?"

"No, this was our time. I don't want to share."

"Can I write to you?"

Sarah paused and then gave a quick nod of her head, "Just emails. Because of Mom." Suddenly, she stepped forward and put her arms around him.

Surprised, he hesitated for a moment before returning her tight embrace.

"There is someone, you know, who understands," she whispered, "*I* forgive you… Dad."

The Killings Begin

In a new twist on traditional murder mysteries, *The Killings Begin* introduces the killer in the first chapter and a river cruise leads a young woman to her death.

After escaping her father's threat of an arranged marriage and settling in Madrid, Spain, Gia Delgado enters into an unconventional contract with three men she meets in a bar.

In exchange for a life of luxury, she'll act as their no-strings wife, whether they want to display her in public or lead her to the bedroom.

But there are vital rules: they are all bound to secrecy. And no one is allowed to fall in love.

In Raleigh, North Carolina, Tracey Lauch, an eminent judge, is harboring his own secret. Haunted by his past, he kills, and after that first murder, he finds himself driven to do it again – and the Parking Lot Strangler is born. Desperate to break the cycle, he retires and flees to Europe, hoping a change of place will control his desire to kill.

Gia and her friends bond as fate draws them closer to Tracey. They meet on the same river cruise through Ukraine, where this tranquil voyage delivers one unwitting victim to their death… giving rise to a new, international serial killer.

***The Killings Begin* intertwines gripping contemporary romance with a dark, psychological twist that will leave you reaching for the next book in the series.**

Death in a Dark Alley

A lifelong friendship, a daring criminal alliance, and a killer who hides in plain sight make *Death in a Dark Alley* an innovative take on conventional murder mysteries.

For Frank Tomas, life's too short for hard work and monogamy, it's all about instant gratification, even if that means breaking a few rules here and there.

Isabelle Ronaldo thinks otherwise and has worked hard all her life to achieve success.

But despite their differences, the pair are the best of friends.

That is until they learn of each other's secrets.

As they navigate through their own complex lives, Frank and Isabelle are unwittingly drawn closer to a deadly threat. The Parking Lot Strangler is still on the loose, despite the efforts of the U.S. investigators, and is at large again in Europe on another Spectrum river cruise.

When their lives finally collide in the city of Strasbourg, France, one person will die, and one person will get away.

A heart-stopping ride with near-unbearable suspense, *Death in a Dark Alley* is the second book in the SPECTRUM SERIES.

A Body Washes Ashore

In this suspenseful third volume of the series, our serial killer becomes careless... his killings are now personal and for the first time, his family and close friends feel the impact of his murders.

Tracey Lauch's new social life seems perfect.

For as long as he can remember, he's felt like an outsider, struggling to make connections. And living as an unknown serial killer certainly hasn't helped.

But now, he and his new wife have developed a circle of friends that fulfill his need for close relationships. He's one step closer to living a "normal" life, despite the persistent cold-case investigators who refuse to give up their pursuit.

Remy Martin, a renowned professor of art history and one of Tracey's new friends, bears emotional scars of her own and has developed an unusual set of rules to protect herself from further heartbreak.

However, the stakes rise when she breaks her biggest rule and takes things too far. But how can she resist? She never meant to fall in love – she never meant to hurt anyone.

Like Tracey, Remy can't erase her past. She must deal with the consequences of her affair, whatever the cost.

A Body Washes Ashore will captivate you as it sweeps you into the heart of mortal danger.

Acknowledgments

We began the Spectrum Series with a bunch of crazy ideas for a story – a series about a Turkish rug dealer who was a serial killer – and no idea where it would go and what it would take to make it a reality. It's taken years of fun and good laughs and some hefty bouts of frustration. We've had the good fortune to work with a lot of extraordinarily talented people. They've provided us with feedback, motivation and support.

To our Beta Readers – the hundreds of comments you provided after reading our drafts helped us define our characters and shape each novel. You told us what you thought there should be more (and less) of. Your ideas were great. This story evolved as we listened to what you had to say. We are indebted to you: Dale Burke, Jennifer Cranston, Rae Ann Dilks, Jan Erkes, Mallory Paxton and Sandy Wilson.

To our copy editor extraordinaire, Miranda Summers-Pritchard – you live thousands of miles from us, but somehow, you always manage to read our minds. In some cases, you recommended stronger language or a more detailed or more intense reaction by a character, particularly in response to traumatic or life-altering events. And what an added bonus – your enthusiasm for true crime that definitely helped enrich our storytelling. You created the Investigative Data Analysis System (IDAS); what a brilliant idea that was! Thank you from the bottom of our hearts for your recommendations and painstaking editing.

To our cover designer, Karina Granda – we truly appreciate you because the cover to this book wasn't easy to conceptualize. It took *so* many iterations to find the right image and then to make this cover tie together with the first three, but we finally got there. Thank you for hanging in there with us as we chased perfection. Simply put, you did a spectacular job, thank you.

To our Proof Readers – we love your sharp attention to detail. Even though we read our manuscript countless times, we welcomed your fresh set of eyes and applauded your ability to find what needed to be fixed before publication. Thank you for being so meticulous: Grace Huppert and Gavin Pay.

To our Advance Readers – your commitment to reading the book and posting an early review is invaluable. Thank you for your honest reviews: Julia Barugel, Denise Beyer, Vicki Costello, Jennifer Cranston, Diane French, Ramona Garcia, Mary Gilbert, Gina Manola, Jessica McCaleb, Mallory Paxton, Joan Perry, Ken Pitz, Fred Riedel and Melissa Watson.

A massive thanks goes out to our family and friends. Over the years, we have spent hours and hours working on these manuscripts. You stood back, provided support and encouragement when we needed it and graciously accepted our excuse, "I'm writing at that time and can't make it." And you were our biggest cheerleaders, bragging about our accomplishments. We are forever grateful. Our series wouldn't have become a reality without you.

About the Authors

Robin Bradley grew up in California. Her family had no TV until she was sixteen – it wasn't high on their list of needs – so everyone read voraciously and played with words. She often says things like, "Speaking is one-way; talking is two-way, a conversation." or "Passive voice? Really?" and eschews (her word) jargon for the most part because it grates on her ears. She loves a good story, whether reading, hearing or telling it. She comes from a family of writers – her mother was an English teacher and published poet, her uncle was a reporter for the San Jose Mercury who wrote short stories on the side, and her siblings write as well. Robin also writes poetry, although she hasn't published any yet.

Additionally, Robin finds great pleasure in good wine, cooking, and reading – you'll notice lots of the first two in our books.

Robin's writing partner, Jody Leber-Pay finds writing fulfilling and challenging because she gets to be a collaborator, an inventor, a researcher, a storyteller, a problem solver, an editor, a marketer, and a techie. She finds the process of going from an idea to a published book fascinating, and that's what keeps her motivated. Before writing fiction, Jody authored technical documents for work and published a technical book.

When she's not writing, Jody enjoys Pilates, walking, golfing and lingering on her back patio in the Arizona desert.

Robin and Jody met in 2016 on a European riverboat cruise from Budapest to Nuremberg. As a way to pass the time one afternoon as they traveled through the series of locks from the Danube to the Main River, Robin, Jody and a handful of friends sat around drinking Chianti, laughing and making up silly romantic stories, stories that started with a comment by Jody when she looked over at the prow of the boat lashed to theirs and said to Robin, "What if that man over there," she pointed to a tall man stretched out in a deck chair, his hat pulled low over his eyes, "what if he walked to the railing and looked into your eyes and you fell madly, passionately in love?"

The development of those stories into the Spectrum Series began a couple of months later with an email from Jody to Robin: "By the way – you still interested in the Lock Series? … it will be fun." That was the beginning of an unusual, long-distance friendship and their collaboration on novels about a serial killer, the women he targets and the women he kills.

Working as Bradley Pay, they found that their unique backgrounds and interests were complementary, but it was their enjoyment in creating stories that kept them going. Writing the first book and outlining the remainder of the series was fun but far more hard work than they had imagined at the outset.

Some original characters from the Chianti days remain, albeit much evolved, and many new characters have appeared. These are no longer the early bosom-heaving romances. Instead, although the love stories remain, they are now haunted by an international serial killer who changes the course of the characters' lives.